Joe Manning
Lived Here

Ted Miller

Order this book online at www.trafford.com
or email orders@trafford.com

Most Trafford titles are also available at major online book retailers.

© Copyright 2012 Ted Miller.
All rights reserved. No part of this publication may be reproduced, stored in a retrieval
system, or transmitted, in any form or by any means, electronic, mechanical, photocopying,
recording, or otherwise, without the written prior permission of the author.

Printed in the United States of America.

ISBN: 978-1-4669-5375-8 (sc)
ISBN: 978-1-4669-5374-1 (hc)
ISBN: 978-1-4669-5373-4 (e)

Library of Congress Control Number: 2012917082

Trafford rev. 09/20/2012

 www.trafford.com

North America & international
toll-free: 1 888 232 4444 (USA & Canada)
phone: 250 383 6864 ♦ fax: 812 355 4082

JOE MANNING

Joe was a man who had values—honesty, kindness, and love for every person. Joe lived in the Shenandoah Valley in Virginia. He came back from the civil war and bought some land and water rights in this valley. Joe built his home, married, and had a daughter. When she was a child, four men came upon Joe plowing in the field unarmed and shot Joe twice in the back and shot his daughter and his wife. They burnt the house down and left. Joe survived being paralyzed from his waist down, almost mentally destroyed.

Joe, a Christian man, did not believe in violence; but these men had to be stopped before they kill any more people who were his friends. Joe set out to find the guilty people who had done these things and more. He intended to stop them and take them to the law and let the law mete out justice. Joe fought overwhelming odds and kept his faith in God, although he wavered like any other mortal man. But he held on to his values and was victorious. God gave Joe another chance at life and a much better happy prosperous one. Joe tried to keep his humor; at times, it came to him as a result of the heartache of life. At others, he could only find tears. He showed his men and partners what a Christian can do during a crisis. Life can be cruel, but we do not have to be cruel to ourselves.

CHAPTER 1

It was early morning on a Tuesday, like any other day. Joseph Manning woke up to the sound of the early-morning wind coming down off the high mountain that Joe loved to hear. As the sun was coming up on the back side of the mountain, the warm air started pulling the air from the cooler valley up the mountain. It had a sound like no other wind. The air moved slowly but steadily, and this was the awakening of the day. This was the greatest time of the day. It was just before dawn, and Joe got dressed in his daily work clothes of faded blue jeans, a blue plaid shirt, his slip-on work boots, and a red bandana that sometimes he wore around his neck. And Joe went to the table and grabbed a biscuit that was left over from the meal the night before. He spread butter on the biscuit and started out the door, and then he thought of the honey that he had found in an old tree a couple of weeks ago. Joe was an honest man, but he robbed the bee tree of the riches of their work. He was cutting some fence posts on the hillside back of the barn; he saw a bee flying past him. He did not think much of that, but a moment later, another bee went by in the same direction; he followed the bees with his eyes, and they were headed for a little sunken place in the hillside. They flew so fast that he could not tell what kind of bees they were. Unless they were honeybees, he was not interested in them. But he had a craving for some honey. He walked down the valley in the same direction that the bees had been flying, and he saw another one. These were bees that were working a hive of some sort. He kept following the bees with his axe in his hand. He watched them again, and they were coming toward him. Again he saw them flying in the other direction; he knew that bees flew in a straight line. There was a water seep low down on the hill, and it pooled up. When there was calm water, the bees could land at the edge of it to gather water and carry it to the hive. Therefore, the hive must be behind him. He turned around and started walking back away from the water. He went slowly this time as he was watching this line of sight that they were flying; he saw more bees, and this time, he saw where they went. They went into a tree that had a hollow place in it. He came close, and he could hear them working in the tree; he went back home and brought back two buckets, a large oil cloth, some dry wood, and some smartweed that was green. He took his axe and knocked a chunk of wood out of the side of the tree to make the hole larger. This got the bees stirred up. But with the larger hole, he could reach down in the tree. He started a small fire by banding the wood together with a leather strap like a torch, and he put the weeds on the fire, which made a horrible smoke. This he held close to the hole. The bees left the hole because they were afraid of the smoke. He wrapped the oil cloth around his arm and reached down in the hole and took out honey with his hand until he filled both buckets with honey, and then he moved away from the tree and let the bees go back into their hive. It was springtime, and the honey had lasted the bees through the winter; and now that it was spring, they had no more need of it. Joe left them enough honey to last the hive until the blossoms and flowers bloomed out in a few weeks, allowing them to start making more honey. Of the two buckets of honey he took, one was for family use, and the other one was to be taken to Sam's mercantile to trade for what they needed. He spread the honey on the biscuit. Biscuit, butter, and honey are food for a king. Joe was thinking about his life on the ranch, and he came to the conclusion that he had a wonderful life. He really lacked for nothing. His wife and his daughter completed his life here on the ranch, which he loved dearly. God had been so good to him. He stepped through the door, down off the porch, and stopped with a smile on his face, looking at the light that was coming over the mountain behind him. He could see on the top of the mountain range far away in front of him where the light was working its way down the mountain and onto the huge valley floor, and he could see all that God had given to him, but the vast green valley between the ranges of the mountains was still bathed in darkness. He stood there and watched as the sun coming over the mountains was forcing the darkness down the mountains to the west of him. He looked around him up on one of the limbs of the oak tree close to him. He could see a couple of mockingbirds. They were just waking up and shaking themselves to arrange their feathers and singing like they had to make music for the whole world to hear. Joe watched the small animals moving out of their place of protection from the predators of the night. The night is when the predators of the world do their work; now that daylight was coming, the predators would go back to their place of hiding, waiting for the next night to hunt again. Joe watched the world come alive—a beautiful world, a world full of many things for every person to enjoy, to fear, to love, to hate; but whatever this day brought to him, Joe felt that he could handle it. Joe was a hunter too; he was a man who at one time was hunting his own place in this world. He hunted for a place to live, a place to work, and most of all, he was hunting somebody to love and to share this world with him. He thought that he had found all of these things once before, but along came a war, which took everything from him.

Joe fought in the war. He was a good soldier; he had to kill good men. He hated the killing and the maiming of good men, but he had a job to do, and he did the best that he could do. He felt maybe it would help to end the war.

After the war, Joe started over again and moved into this country. He came into this valley for a new start in life. He still had his hopes of one day finding a good woman to work with him and give him a family. Joe had plans for his wife and family to prosper on this land that God had given him to use the rest of his life. Or however long that God would allow him to use this land as his own. After he found this land and settled down on the land, he found his wife and had a daughter. Finding a wife and having a daughter completed his wonderful world. Life was good. Maggie, his wife, and Jennie, his beautiful daughter whom he loves dearly, are in the house behind him sleeping and soon rise and join him in this new day. Joe had bought this track of land in the beautiful country of the Shenandoah Valley in Virginia. He had worked hard to clear a place on top of a knoll. He cut down the trees to build his log cabin and other buildings and made a homestead on a high place that overlooked the very large valley that lay before it. Joe Manning had bought some of a new breed of cattle called white-faced Herefords. They were a tough, strong breed of beef cattle. These cattle were brought onto Joe's place and were growing fat on the sweet grass that was everywhere in this beautiful valley. Joe thought about the very large valley. He looked almost as far as his eyes could see. The grass was tall, about up to the belly of the cattle grazing on it in one of the fields. Joe did not leave his cattle or his horses in the field long enough to eat all the grass down close to the ground. He moved his herds over to another field and let them graze there.

Joe worked hard to build himself a small but beautiful log house on top of that knoll; he made it a one-bedroom house. He cut the logs and hauled them down off the mountain. And he cut some logs out of the valley so more grass would grow, and he used these logs to make the outside walls of the house. He sawed lumber out of some of these logs and made the inside walls out of the sawed lumber. Using the sawed wood inside the house was something that was unheard of in this country, but Joe did not care. He wanted a house that his wife would feel proud to live in. And it would be warmer in the winter and would cut the wind off also. The wind in the winter can find cracks in the logs and chill a person to the bone, but Joe's house is tight and snug. He also used this lumber to make the outside door, and he made furniture out of the sawed lumber. The house was not large, but it was spacious with a large kitchen that any woman could feel good about. He made a sink out of White Oak lumber to wash dishes so they could wash up without going out to the creek or the spring. He built the dining room and living room together, making a large dining table and four chairs. He made some stools for different things; there were wooden pegs to hang clothing and other pegs to hang kitchen utensils, pots, and pans. There was a large fireplace that took up most of the wall of the living room but would still warm you real good if you were sitting at the table eating the wonderful food that the wife cooked on the wood-burning stove in the kitchen. He was glad that he had found the right woman to share all of this with him. The last thing that he did in his new house was to pipe the water from the big spring of water that was in a little cove at the base of the mountain behind the house. He took stone and mortar and built up around the spring to keep the animals out of it and keep a nice reservoir of water against a dry season if they would ever have one. Joe piped the water to a hand pump that he mounted on the edge of the kitchen sink. Now Joe knew that very few houses had such a thing; he had to order the pump from the merchant in town. Who thought that it was a total waste of money to spend on a pump? What could Joe be thinking of was he and his wife were too good to go to the spring and carry the water back to the house, like all of the wives did. I have never heard of such a thing. Before long, all of the wives will want the water piped to their kitchen sinks. Joe might be starting trouble for all the men. The storekeeper liked Joe a lot; he was probably the best man in the country. He is the first man to arrive when someone is in trouble or needs help. Joe had helped about everyone in the area at one time or another.

It had been many years since the war ended, and the nation was supposed to be one nation again, but there were still people who would not let the country have peace. There were people who had turned to killing, robbing for their own profit, and for their own pleasure; there was a group of men that came through the country many years ago. They had robbed people and killed those that resisted them. But the people who had set down roots in this area of the country had fought Indians; most had come through the war, and they did not give up lightly, and some of the people of the area stood up against them. Some were killed, and some were injured when they were attacked, and most of them were driven off. And one day as they came into the area, they were about to strike the town. It was the wrong day because Joe and a few more of the men who lived in the area were in town. Someone riding into town gave the warning that there was a group of armed men approaching. The town rallied most of the men; they stayed out of sight and let the armed men ride into town peaceably. Some of the raiders stopped at the stable. There were men hiding in the hayloft; others were in the blacksmith shop. Others were in Sam's mercantile waiting for them. Some were in the saloon across the way. The men covered their faces and pulled their guns and started into the different stores all at the same time. Sam yelled at them to give up; across the street, Joe called to them to give up because they were surrounded, and they would shoot them down if they resisted, but they did not give up. They figured that if they were caught, they would be hung. This was a group of outlaws that carried one or two pistols on their hips. They were quick to draw their guns, and they were accurate when they shot at someone. They would kill anyone who got in their way. They knew that they were better shooters than these townsfolk who spent their lives behind a counter or however they spent their lives; they were sure that these men were afraid of them. So they drew their guns, and they started shooting at the windows and the doors, anywhere a person could shoot back from; they did not know that they were shooting at seasoned men who came through the war and those who had fought Indians. Bullets were flying like hailstones in a winter storm. The townspeople opened fire just after the first shot from the outlaws, and the townspeople are men who were used to fighting in the civil war and fighting Indians. These men who had to hunt game when they needed food opened fire on them; it was a short battle. The men from the town were behind walls where they had placed sacks of feed and other items that would stop the bullets from coming through the walls. The outlaws were standing out in the street to start with; they were bold. They thought that the town was going to bend to their wishes and surrender. They stood there with their feet spread apart and their pistols in their hands, brave. But when the bullets started taking them down, the fear turned them into what they were really. They tried to hide behind their horses, behind the water trough, or any place that they could get behind something. There were town men on both sides of the street, and the outlaws did not have a chance. Most of the outlaws were killed, as one by one they exposed themselves and tried to shoot at the stores, and some of the outlaws were wounded. The town people think that two of the men who were at either end of the street rode away when the shooting started, and they could not find them. It took a while to look after the people of the town, to make sure that nobody had taken a bullet and that the houses were safe. After that, they did what they could for the wounded outlaws, binding up the bullet holes and even removing some of the bullets where they could. The men and women did the best that they could because there was no doctor in town or anywhere close to them. They tied up the others and put them in a safe place because at that time there was no jailhouse in town, but they all agreed that would or should be the next building to put up. And they did what was necessary to do in town, and the rest of the outlaws gave up. All of them were wanted men, and among those who were arrested, none of the outlaws would admit to there being anyone else with them. They were tried in a court of law when the judge came to town, and they were sent to the state prison. There was nothing heard of them after they were put into prison. Life went on after this incident, and mostly it was forgotten.

A few years later, Joe was out in the field plowing. He was turning the sod under with his team of horses, getting ready to plant his house garden to supply the needs of his family. The field was just in front of his house so they would have easy access to the garden. He saw four men coming down the road; he took notice that they were wearing guns in holsters on their hips, and one man held a rifle in his hand. Joe stopped the horses that he was plowing with and turned toward the house were his wife and young daughter were. His wife was unaware that there was anyone coming in their direction, and Joe wanted to get to the house and be there when they arrived; he did not know them. They were still a ways off; Joe did not know who they were or what they wanted. He lived off the main road and normal traffic; if there was any traffic, it would be on the road that led to town—this road ended at his house. Joe did not want to seem excited, but he wanted to get to the house before they did. The man with the rifle turned his horse toward the plowed field and put the horse into a gallop. Joe started running toward the house. Joe hollered at his wife to get the gun and come to him. Maggie and Ginny, his daughter, were singing as they often did and could not hear his warning. The other men also put their horses at a gallop toward the house. Joe was in the yard close to the house; he thought that he might make it inside the house where his rifle was and where his family was; he just might make it. When he felt something hit him in the back, it felt like a sledge hammer blow; there was a burning pain in his back and legs. Vaguely he heard the report of the rifle; he could not make his legs move; he tried to keep going, but he fell on the grass. He started to rise and felt another bullet hit him again in the back. He was lying on the ground, almost unconscious; he heard the horses come to a stop at the house. He could not see anything; it was like there was darkness all over him, but he reasoned that it was near midday. He heard Ginny screaming, then came a sudden silence; he heard shots he did not know how many. He heard boots scuffing along the ground. His mind was trying to find out what was going on. He knew that he would not live through this, and he also knew that Maggie and Ginny were in a lot of trouble. In this day and time, men did not bother decent women and especially children. There were not men low enough who would harm them; they might tie them up and leave them for something else to harm them such as a wild beast. But unless they were animals, they would not harm them; if any man did something like that, they would be hunted down and hung like a mad dog. He knew that these men would kill; they had proven this by shooting him in the back. What was going on in the house? What were these men looking for, why did they come to his place? He had a nice herd of cattle; they could have the cattle, and he had no money for them to rob him of. The sounds of feet were coming to him; he felt a toe kick him in the ribs; he was rolled over, and this person yelled, "This one is done for Mr. Cole. Should I put another bullet between his eyes?"

Another man said, "No, let him bleed to death. We want this to look like a simple robbery."

Joe received another vicious kick, this time on the side of his leg; he felt no pain and did not cry out; the man walked away. It seemed that he went toward the barn; he heard more sounds at the house but could not tell what was going on. He heard another voice talking; this man sounded like an Indian. The man who kicked him had a very deep voice, kind of raspy and slow of speech. He heard another voice giving out orders to others; he could not make out what was being said, but he listened to every sound, hoping that he could hear something from Maggie or Ginny; but he heard nothing. He said to himself that if he could just have a gun, he would take these men and protect his family, but he also knew that this was too late. He had been a fool and moved his family way out here in this country and away from any help, away from any neighbors. There wasn't any law nor anybody here to help in case of trouble; he wanted to be out of town, yet close enough so someone could help his family. There was a fair doctor in town and a sheriff in town, but way out here, there was nobody. There was a voice coming from somewhere close by, calling for Denver; the voice from the house asked, "What was the matter?"

The voice called back, "I see some dust coming miles down the road. They will be here."

Amos turned to Joe, and when he came closer, he found that Joe was still alive; he could just tell that Joe was breathing, and he bent closer to Joe and could feel a good heartbeat. He was excited and yelled at a young man whose name was Thad Kinsley who was looking around the barn which had not been burnt. Thad was not looking for anything special; he was just avoiding the awful sight that Amos was looking at. Thad ran to Amos as fast as he could; he heard the excitement in his voice, and he saw that Joe was breathing. They turned Joe over and was checking him; they had seen the two bullet holes in his back, but no holes in his chest or stomach. He was pale, and his eyes were closed; he was not moving so they could not tell how bad he was hurt. There was blood on his shirt in the back but not a lot of blood. They knew nothing about medicine, but Joe should have been awake, or moving, or something. Amos told Thad to bring the wagon over and they would lift Joe into the wagon and take him back to town.

Thad said, "Won't the ride kill him?"

Amos agreed; he said, "Let us put him into the wagon and pull the wagon over here under the big shade tree, and you grab Joe's best horse and race to town for the doctor."

Thad said, "The doctor is over at the Lincoln ranch tending a broken arm of one of the hands. I can have him over here in a few minutes."

Amos said, "Then hurry, boy. Joe may live long enough to tell us who did this awful thing, but I will stay with him and do what I can which is not much."

Thad went into the barn and took the first horse that he came to put a bridle and saddle on him and took out for the Lincoln ranch at a hard gallop, where he was supposed to find the doctor. Thad knew the way across the country; he was not paying much attention to the surroundings. He was just watching ahead for holes that his horse might step into or something that would harm the horse that he was riding; he knew all of this country very well. He sometimes works for Joe; he loves to come to Joe's ranch to work, and Maggie makes the best meals in the country. Besides that, she always treated him like he was someone special; of course Maggie treated everyone special—that was the way that Maggie was. Thad noticed horse tracks traveling the same way that he is going; these are not horses that are turned loose and wander around while they are traveling, but horses that are being ridden like he is now. Thad judged that they came through here only minutes ahead of him by looking at the tracks. Thad stopped his horse and looked around; he is not looking at the countryside as beautiful as it is—he is looking for something that is out of the ordinary. He looked at the great flat fields of grass that Joe has to graze his cattle herd on over to his left. He looked straight ahead almost two miles and at the rolling land of grass; now those men could be down in one of the low areas and could come out on the other side soon and see him behind them. This frightened Thad now; he was not afraid, but he was the only one who could help Joe right now and find the doctor, so he had to get through because there is some indication that there is other men close by. Because someone just shot Joe and burnt up his family, along with his house, and they might know where the Lincoln ranch is located. Could they be headed there also? He sure would not want to run into them; there is only one of him and four of them, and they are proven killers. There is no dust cloud; there is no dust in the air, so they must be traveling at a walk, or there would be a cloud of dust in this area, because there is not much grass here, and he looked behind him and saw dust where his horse had run. Where are they? Could they be waiting on him and shoot him as he rode by? Or they just might wait along the road for the doctor. Thad became worried; he knew that he had to cross this small hill and go down the valley on the other side. If they are headed for the Lincoln ranch, maybe Thad can take a shortcut over an old trail that is really bad. It has not been used for a long time, and he is not certain that he can get across the hill that way, but it will get him to the ranch a lot sooner. Thad turned right and headed south and looked for the little valley that will lead him to the path over the ridge. This country right here is one range of hills after another and another kind of like the ribs of a person. They lay alongside each other with a valley in between each one of the hills, and they had little small gullies going from the valley up the side of the hill, where water had run off the hill and eat away the dirt and rock and left ridges at different places, and animals used these gullies to cross over these hills. This country was so beautiful the valleys mostly had a stream of water coming down through them somewhere and watered the valley; this valley of Joe's had more than one stream, which watered the valley and made it one of the richest, grass-growing valleys in the whole area. The ranch that Thad was headed for over the hill was another valley that was very rich in water, and it had a lot of grass and great stands of timber, some of these valleys you could ride almost all day and not reach from one end of it unto the other end. They were so long, and in places they were miles wide between the mountains or hills as some people called them. But Thad was not thinking about this beauty as he did when he rode sometimes for Joe; today Thad was thinking about Joe—what a good man Joe was and what a great ranch he had; he was managing the place, and one day he would have the best herd of cattle in the whole state. He had been thinking that Joe might give him a job so he would have a place to live.

Thad had just been moved wherever the wind blew him, wherever he could get a meal and a place to sleep. He had slept out under the stars enough times to last him for a long time since his dad and mom had been taken with the plague. He was too young to get out and work and make their farm pay, and the bank took everything away—everything but his paint horse that he had kept hidden in a box canyon about a mile away from the house. He had found the paint when it was just a colt; it was sick with something. They did not know what the sickness was, but his dad told him he could not bring the paint horse to the barn until they knew what was wrong with him. He might infect the other livestock, and they could not afford to have any of their livestock come down sick. So Thad kept his paint horse in the box canyon at the base of the hill where there was some water and a little grassy place, which was big enough to keep the horse from going hungry. Thad would bring the horse some corn when he could get by with it, and the horse grew stronger and better; he would sit on a rock and watch his horse eat grass and the corn when he could get it. He would talk to his horse especially since he did not have anyone his own age to talk to. When the horse was old enough, Thad started working with him, training him to lead on a rope. Then one day, he carried an old saddle that was lying in the back of the barn; his dad said he could have it, but he could not rely on it because it was too rotten to support the weight of a man. Maybe a boy could train his horse to ride with it; Thad put the old saddle on his horse and would pet him and rub him down until the horse did not mind having the saddle on him. Thad would lie across the saddle and talk to his horse and ride him around the open grass; finally, he took some old pieces of leather and made a bridle, and he tried the bit in the horse's mouth. By this time, the horse trusted Thad and would allow him to do anything to him. He carried a currycomb and a brush over and curried his horse, and man, did the horse like that! When Thad stopped, the horse wanted more, but that was the only comb and brush that his dad owned, and he had to take it back home. Thad would ride the horse back in the mountains to give him exercise; he would stop every time that he came to some good grass and let his horse eat. While the horse was eating, Thad would rub him down and pet him; they became real friends. Nobody knew about his paint horse because he never rode the horse anywhere he could be seen by anyone. When the bank came and put Thad off the property, he was told that he could take his personal things and nothing else. So one morning, he put his few clothes in a canvas bag and left; he took a coffeepot, a couple of pans to cook in, his blankets, and what little food that he could find and walked away while they stood on the porch and watched him leave. As soon as the bank told him he would have to move away and before they came to the farm and went through his dad's things, Thad took his dad's good saddle, blanket, and bridle away from the farm and hid them in some rocks. So when he was forced off the property, they did not realize that he had taken anything away. He brought the old saddle and bridle that he had made to the farm and put them in the barn. Nobody cared where he went, just as long as he cleared out away from the property that the bank owned now. And Thad and his horse wandered over the country until now; when Thad came to this town, the people seemed to really care for him, especially Joe and Maggie who gave him work when they could. Other people also gave him some work, and he could at least eat. And sometimes he would clean the stables, and the owner would let him sleep in the hay, especially in the winter.

He became aware that the tracks had turned aside, and he was sure that he was alone in this part of the country; he put the spurs to the horse and entered the small canyon that led to the shortcut. Thad was glad that he had a horse that was used to the mountains, because this was a steep trail that went almost straight up the side of the hill. It was a slippery narrow path across the mountain. Sometimes around the edges of the cliff, no wider than what a man or a horse could walk on, he could look down a hundred or more feet. When Thad looked down from this kind of height, his stomach would really knot up, and he would feel kind of sick. But he did not have a choice but to go on; he did not forget for a moment why he was going over this dangerous trail—to find the doctor and to warn the rancher that strange riders were coming this way. Thad was coming to one of the bad places where it was very narrow, and today there was water seeping out from under the rocks on the upper side of the trail. Thad stopped and looked around; there was no way around this. He had to go on or turn back, and he could not do that; it would take too long. He urged the horse on, but the horse did not want to go; horses have enough sense to know when a place is dangerous. Thad had to take the chance; Joe was depending on him, even though Joe did not know that he was putting Thad in any danger, because Joe would not ever put him in any danger. Thad touched his spurs to the flank of the horse, and the horse started on. He was walking as if he was walking on eggs, and any misstep would break all the eggs, but indeed they would wind up on the rocks about a hundred feet below. Thad kept his eyes straight ahead and let the horse pick his own steps, and they went through. A few yards farther on along the trail, there were a lot of boulders that had fallen down from a rotten ledge high above him, and they had fallen in the path; the horse did not want to go back, so he picked his way through them so they could go on. While he was doing this, Thad wondered if Joe was still alive, just how bad he was hurt. All of that did not matter right now; he had to get through. This was a lot to ask of a boy of fifteen years old, but Thad had done a lot of things since he had lost his family and been on his own. Coming down off the mountain, he could see the ranch house about a mile away; this ranch was a pretty place—the big two-story wooden structure was painted white, with the black roof really stood out with all the green grass. And the big green trees around it, the barn, bunkhouse, and the other outbuildings were white washed and really looked good, but not as bright white as the house was. He was looking for dust, horses, and riders, any horses at the ranch yard; but he could not see anyone else around. This meant that he had probably beaten the strange riders to the ranch. He rode in pretty close to the ranch house and hollered to the house. Mrs. Lincoln came to the porch and said, "What is the matter with you, Thad? You are no stranger to this house. Come on in and quit sitting out there, hollering."

He came close, dismounted, and asked if the doctor was there.

Mrs. Lincoln said that he was, and they were sitting down to eat. "Come on in and join them at the table." Thad hurried in the house and was telling the men what had happened to Joe, and he tracked four men, strangers to him; and they were coming this way.

The doctor said, "Just give me a minute to get my bag. I am finished here, and we will go over there and check on Joe. With two bullets in his back, I doubt if there is anything that I can do for him. You know that I am just an old-fashioned country doctor."

Mr. Lincoln said, "Abb, you are anything but old-fashioned, and to us you are the best doctor that this country has ever seen or ever will see."

Abb, short for Abernathy, said, "I wish that was true, but every time I have to treat something like these gunshot wounds in the back, I wish that I had a lot better training." Thad had saddled Abb's horse and a fresh horse for himself and was waiting at the porch. Mr. Lincoln said, "Aren't we forgetting about those four men that you tracked on the trail here?"

Thad said, "You reckon that we could beat them to the turn off across the mountain."

One of the ranch hands who had been working on a fence line above the ranch house came into the yard and said, "You folks get ready for company. I just saw some dust coming this way and thought you might want to put some coffee on."

Mr. Lincoln told the rider what had been happening and said, "Get to the barn and get the blacksmith and your rifles and stand out of sight, and we will see who is coming. If it is someone that we know, then go on about your business and keep a watchful eye on the ranch until we seen what will happen about this problem. If these folks are people we know, then get over to the north range and send two men here to look after things and send that young fellow that works for me to town for the sheriff and some men to track these people down and get rid of them. I need to go with the doctor and Thad over to Joe's place and take care of things there as soon as we can get some men over there. We will need to take care of Joe and his family and do a proper burying for them."

The rider took his horse and moved over to the barn. Thad moved the horses around the back of the house and tied them to a small tree and came back to the front porch. Thad was handed a rifle and told to get inside and open a window and stay out of sight. The riders came into sight and stopped; they are too far away for Mr. Lincoln who is sitting on the porch to tell who they are, and while he is supposed to be sitting in the shade and reading a book, hidden in his lap behind the book was his pistol. One of the riders broke away from the others and came on alone. When Mr. Lincoln laid the book in his lap, he covered the gun and laid his right hand innocently in his lap inches from the pistol. When one of the riders came closer to the house, he looked everything over as he came to the house; the other riders sat on their horses far enough away to be out of pistol range. As that one man came close enough to talk to Mr. Lincoln, he walked his horse to the side so that Mr. Lincoln is not looking at the other men. And when he turned his attention to the one rider, there is another rider who is carrying his rifle in his hand who moved to the other side and started coming closer; if Mr. Lincoln was not wary of these men, he would not have noticed this movement, but his eyes missed nothing. He got right to the point and said, "What do you want here? This place is off the beaten path, and we get very few visitors here."

The man on the horse pressed his knee to his horse's side, and the horse is nervously moving around and as the rider wants him to do. He now was turned slightly to the side and his handgun could not been seen; he is innocent enough at first glance. He is dressed in range wear. He had blue jeans on tucked down in the tops of his cowboy boots; he has a wool shirt on a faded blue, a red bandana around his neck. But he had on a very expensive Stetson hat which most cowboys could not afford to buy; Mr. Lincoln noticed his gun and holster when he rode up, and it was one of the best that could be bought; his saddle also was a very good one. It looked very worn, but it was a very good one. He said, "We are looking for work. And if you would not mind, we would like to water our horses at your trough over there."

Mr. Lincoln said, "I have never refused any man water or a meal. Bring your horses in to water, and when my men come in off the range we will eat lunch, you can rest under the trees over there. By the way, from the direction you came from, did you come by a small ranch over on the other side of the hill?" The man said, "We have not seen any ranch for days."

Mr. Lincoln said, "Did you not see that smoke from over there across the hill to your left, a few hours ago?"

The man said that they had not.

Mr. Lincoln said, "You are lying to me. You could not have missed that smoke when you burnt down Joe's house."

The man started to draw his pistol, and Mr. Lincoln shot him through the heart. As soon as he shot the man in the yard, he rolled out of the chair and a bullet hit the wall behind where he had been sitting. The other three men started running their horses toward the house and the men at the barn. And the ranch house opened fire on them, they did not inflict any damage to the riders because the riders turned their horses and rode away. Fearing that other men might hear the firing and come in from behind them and cut off their escape, they looked at the fallen man in the yard, but there was no need because he was dead. Mr. Lincoln gave orders to his men to take the body into town to the sheriff; and he, the doctor, and Thad started back to the ranch to check on Joe and the merchant who stayed with him.

CHAPTER 2

Joe was lying in the shade of the big oak tree on some saddle blankets and saddle for a pillow; he had not moved. He was still breathing, but otherwise, there was no sign of life. Joe's mind was working; in his mind he was looking toward the house, and he saw his daughter, Ginny, who was now six years old coming out of the house and running toward him with a big smile on her slightly freckled face with her long black pigtail hair bobbing up and down as she ran. She came to him, and there was a sparkle in her eyes that he had seen a hundred times; she ran up to him and threw her arms around his waist, which she could just reach around him and gave him a great big hug. He in return picked her up in his arms and carried her along with him. He would sit her on his shoulder, and she would wrap her arm around his head after taking his hat off and placing it on her own head. Every time that Maggie saw this picture, she said, "I wish that I could draw, because this is a picture that I would draw and hang in the kitchen so that I could always look at you two when I am working in the kitchen."

Ginny was the delight of his life; it seems that she is what makes life worthwhile, except for his beautiful wife who he also cherished.

They met one day about eight years ago, as he was coming out of the feed store. Joe was carrying a 100# sack of feed on his shoulder; he did not see her coming; the sun was shining in his eyes. She was walking down the sidewalk, and he ran right into her as he came through the door. She fell down flat on her behind; Joe dropped the sack of feed that he was carrying and looked down at a gorgeous black-haired beauty, and without thinking, he bent down to help her to her feet. He forgot that his hands were covered with the dust off the feed, and he left two large handprints on the sleeves of her dress. She was quite disarrayed and somewhat angry, not to say she was hurting in a place that she could not rub in public. Besides her pride was badly bruised also, this big oaf, whoever he was that knocked her down then with dirty hands, ruined her dress by physically picking her up; she was so embarrassed that she had not even look up. Then this voice said, "I am so sorry that I am so clumsy. I did not see you coming. I would never have done anything like this to someone as beautiful as you, and can you ever forgive me?"

Now this got her attention, and she raised her eyes with the full intention of really telling this person just what she thought about his actions; but when she looked into those steel gray eyes, and that kind, very pleasant face, she could not say that he was handsome, but he had a face that was pleasing to look at. And the strength of his body, so strong when he picked her up; it was as though she were a small child. There seemed to be no effort at all. She forgot all the things that she had in mind telling him, and instead she said, "That is all right. I should have been watching where I was going."

Joe said, "I do not believe that I have ever seen you before. I thought that I knew everyone around here, and I am sure that I would not have forgotten you if we had ever met."

Joe stood a good six feet two inches tall, broad of shoulder, and slim of hip; he looked down at a beautiful oval face with large dark brown eyes, a perky nose, a slightly larger than normal mouth and beautiful lips, all of this was topped off with long black or very dark brown wavy hair. She had a figure that was full in all the right places and Joe was so sorry that he had dust on his hands from the feed that he had been carrying to his wagon and when he had lifted her from the side walk he covered part of her dress with the dust. He was so struck with her beauty that he had forgotten to ask her if she had been hurt. He asked her if she was hurt and was there anything that he could do.

She said, "No, there is nothing that you can do. And if you will excuse me, I have to go and get cleaned up."

She started to walk away and Joe said, "Wait a moment please; I do not even know your name." She looked at Joe for a long time and finally smiled and said, "My name is Maggie Butcher. And I just came to town to teach school in this town. If you have any children, bring them into town, and we will get them started."

Joe smiled as he said, "No wife and no kids, but I would like to have a wife that could teach my children though." Smiling at her, he asked, "Are you married, Ms. Maggie? If you are, I bet he is a proud man."

Maggie blushed slightly and admitted that she was not married either.

Joe said, "I have a small ranch a few miles outside of town, and I am planning to have one of the largest ranches in this part of the country. I have enough water to take care of a lot more cattle than I now had."

He said that he had a nice house though, not big enough for a good-sized family; at this, Maggie blushed thoroughly and excused herself and walked on down the sidewalk. Joe felt that he had talked very trashy to Maggie, but when he looked into those beautiful eyes he just could not help himself. He just wanted her to know that he thought that she was the most beautiful woman that he had ever seen. When Joe went back into the feed store, he found out that Maggie was staying at the rooming house. Joe had always heard that the food there was good, but he had always ate at the diner, but Joe started eating supper every now and then at the rooming house where Maggie stayed. And it was Joe's turn to blush when one of the men who also started eating at the rooming house when Maggie moved in said, "Joe, what is the matter? You can't seem to cook much at your house anymore, have you run out of wood to burn, or is the food here all of a sudden much better?"

Joe just smiled and said, "I have plenty of wood, but the scenery is much better here. Is that why you started eating here?"

Widow Jenkins said, "I do not care what the reason. It is good to have a good-looking man like Joe wanting to eat here, and it is good to have Maggie eating here. It has brought me a lot of customers, and I like it. If I could keep the two of them here, I would own the bank before long."

Joe looked at Maggie who was looking down at her plate, but Joe thought that he saw a little smile on her face. He knew that he felt like smiling a lot, but he kept his face straight. One evening, he asked Maggie to go for a drive in his buggy; it was not his buggy, and he borrowed the buggy from the livery stable. In order to make the trade, he had to shoe two of the livery stable horses for the use of the buggy. Maggie accepted his offer, and she packed a lunch, and they went out in the country for a picnic, but Joe took her out to his ranch—to one of his favorite places at the ranch. It was a plateau that overlooked the ranch house and looking at some of Joe's cattle; it was a beautiful place indeed. They were sitting under a big shade tree close to a stream of water; with a slight breeze blowing, the day was perfect. The place was perfect. Maggie spread a blanket out on the grass and opened the basket of food, and Joe said, "Before we eat, let me ask you a question."

Maggie looked at Joe, and a look came over her; she was sort of smiling, but a pleased look kind of took over the smile. Joe saw that look, and Joe's face turned red, and he cleared his throat a couple of times and said, "Maggie, I have been thinking that maybe . . ." And as hard as he wanted to ask her to marry him, he could not get the words out, and he felt sick.

She said, "Joe, I would love to marry you if that is what you are finally getting around to asking me."

Joe was smiling and felt such relief; he had faced down an old mountain lion one time, with less fear than he had when he was facing Maggie with a question like this. Now that he had his answer, he felt like shouting to the whole world that he loved this woman more than anything in the world. He got up and went around the picnic basket which was between them and took her by the hands, and she was coming up off the blanket to meet him; he took her in his arms and looking down into those beautiful eyes for a few seconds, he said, "I will devote my life to making you happy, and my desire that after fifty years of marriage we are as happy as we are right at this moment."

Tears came to her eyes and he kissed her, then she kissed him and a few more. They went on to Joe's house, and he showed her around; he also said, "Is there anything that you would like for me to change on this house, or in it before we are married and you move in?"

She looked the house over and said, "Only one thing and it can be done years from now. But I would like to have an outside door that leads off from the kitchen."

Joe said, "I thought that I might want to put another bedroom on that part of the house for a child's room."

This time, it was her turn to blush, and he laughed heartily at this, and soon she was laughing also. It took a couple of week for the ladies of the town to get ready for the wedding, but they were married in the local church; the wedding was a celebration for the whole town. Everybody in town seemed to want to have a part in the wedding. The local sheriff was Joe's best man, Mr. Lincoln who owned a large ranch close to Joe's place gave Maggie away, because she did not have anybody else. Maggie wore a beautiful long white gown that she had brought with her to town; very few women in this area had ever seen such a beautiful dress. There was a ringlet type of hat or halo with a lace veil that covered most of her face, and a train that came almost to the floor. Joe went to the mercantile store and bought a black broadcloth suit; most of the men just wore the best that they had. There were tables set under the big oak trees behind the church and the reception and dinner on the lawn so to speak, and the whole town brought the food, dishes, and flatware and everything. There was enough food there to feed an army. That was the way that things were done at the church where Joe was a member and had been for years, and Maggie had joined a few weeks ago. They moved Maggie's things in the ranch house, but Maggie kept teaching school and still stayed some at the boarding house. Especially when the weather was bad, otherwise she rode one of Joe's best horses, back and forth to and from school; she rode side saddle because it was not fitting for a lady to ride straddle a horse. As soon as they could find a new teacher for the school, Maggie became a full-time wife; their life on the ranch was wonderful, and a couple of years later Ginny Lee came along. Maggie started showing, and Joe noticed, and he said, "Maggie, I had better get started on another bed room for this house, don't you think?"

He was sitting at the breakfast table and smiling at Maggie; she returned his look and said, "Joe, I am afraid."

She came to Joe, and he took her in his arms and said, "Maggie, what is the matter? Aren't you happy that you are expecting?"

She said, "Yes, I am happy, but all of the women in my family have lost their first child and could not carry the first baby, and I am frightened that this is going to happen to us. I am almost afraid to tell someone that we are going to have a baby."

Joe held Maggie and said, "Don't you realize that God gives life? And God takes life away, so let us pray to God that he will give us a healthy baby."

And while standing together they prayed to God that his will be done. She carried the child perfectly; she was so beautiful when she was so big. There were times that Joe would put his arms around her and put his ear to her stomach and would talk to their child. Maggie would put her hands on Joe's head, and big tears would come to her eyes; she loved this man so much, and life was perfect. The cattle herd was getting larger, and Joe sold off some of the stock along and supplied them with about everything that they needed. All of these things went through Joe's mind; he felt that is was real, but sadly it was not.

Joe was lying under the shade tree; his eyes were closed. He could not seem to open them; he could not feel any pain; he could not feel anything, but he could see Ginny coming to him, and behind Ginny he could see Maggie looking more beautiful than he had ever seen her before. He felt happy to see her and Ginny, but at the same time he felt so sad for some reason. He did not understand his feelings; he did not know what was happening to him. He knew that he had been shot, but he must be alive just as Maggie and Ginny are alive because he can see them, but why can't he move? He is trying to move, but he cannot. He can hear something, but he does not know what. He cannot understand what is happening to him. Abernathy, Mr. Lincoln, and Thad arrived at the ranch, and the merchant ran out to meet them. He said, "Doc, I believe he is dead, but I do not know for sure."

Abb went to the shade tree and checked Joe, he said, "Joe is not dead, but he is very close to it. The bleeding has stopped, but we have to try and get the bullets out of him, or he will die for sure."

The doctor took his bag and pulled the probes, scalpel, and necessary things out of his bag along with some bandages and told the men to hold him down. Abb said, "I do not have anything to give him to take away the pain." He sliced the place where each bullet entered the body so he could get the probes in and probed for the bullets and found one lying against the bone of the spine. He said, "I am afraid to touch this bullet because one little movement and Joe will be paralyzed in both legs. But if I don't take it out, he will surely die, and the other bullet just missed the lung."

The doctor removed both of the bullets and sewed up the torn flesh. Joe did not move or even flinch when the doctor was probing for the bullets, and he did not move when the doctor sewed up the flesh. He put a bandage on both of the places and put Joe's shirt back on and covered him up with a blanket and said, "This is all that I can do for him." They decided to take Joe over to Mr. Lincoln's ranch so the womenfolk could take care of him. They made a stretcher type of thing out of stuff they found in the barn and blacksmith shop; the stretcher was put over the side boards of the wagon and stretched tight, and Joe was laid on it, and he was suspended in air over the bed of the wagon. This would take some of the shock off Joe when the metal wheels of the wagon would ride over the hard rocks and holes that were on the ground. There was no road the way that they were going, and the bouncing of the wagon was hard enough on a healthy person, but on Joe it would have tore him to pieces and started back to the ranch with him. The doctor went on down the road toward town, stating that this is an awful thing that happened, and he would tell the people of the town about it. And he would be out to see Joe in a few days; he also said, "But if you need me, send someone after me. I don't know what I can do, but I will do whatever I can for my friend Joe."

It was still unknown if Joe would make it or not, but they had the bullets out of him; and if the surgery in these bad conditions did not give him blood poison or a dozen other things did not occur, then Joe might make it. It was still unknown how much damage the bullet did to the spine; it may be that Joe would never walk again, or who knows what may be the results of all the things that have happened to him here today. Even if Joe comes out of this and lives, just remember he has lost his wife and child, to someone who he does not know, or does he know? They finally arrived at the ranch, and Joe does not seem to be any worse off than when they started. Mrs. Lincoln came to the wagon and looked at Joe; she called for Maria, the housekeeper, to get people out here to carry Joe to the guest room and to make all the things ready for him. By the time they carried Joe up to the guest room, Maria's people have all the preparations made for his comfort. They bathed Joe and cleaned Joe up and got him to bed, and she assigned one of the ladies to care for Joe and see that all of his needs are tended to. Joe is still in a coma and knows nothing of this; Joe is still dreaming of his family, and he does not realize that he is clinging to life. He has memories of when he met Maggie and how beautiful she was, their courting days, their marriage, their home that Joe took her to, the birth of their wonderful daughter, and how he loved her and all the fun things that they had done. Of the day that he bought the first bunch of cattle and brought them to the ranch; Joe's mind would not think of anything but the beautiful things that his life had brought him; Joe's mind would not think of what had happened today and how close he was to the door of death that Joe was seemingly unaware of.

Weeks later, Joe started to come out of the coma; he is now showing signs that he is returning to reality; he moved his upper body and groans. Maria is in the room at the time; she sends the girl that is tending to Joe to bring Mrs. Lincoln, and the girl ran to Mrs. Lincoln to inform her of the change in Joe. Mrs. Lincoln hurried to Joe; when she arrived at Joe's bed, she spoke to Joe and tried to revive him by gently shaking his shoulder; she was hoping to wake Joe out of his sleep, or at least to find out what kind of condition that he is in. After a short period of time, Joe stirred and opened his eyes and looked around; he blinked his eyes as though he cannot see; he looked at Mrs. Lincoln and fixed his eyes on her. After a moment, he opened his mouth and having trouble he asked, "Where am I? What is going on?"

Mrs. Lincoln has tried to prepare herself for these questions; she knew that if Joe pulled through that these questions would be coming. "Joe, you have been shot, and you are at our ranch. We have been caring for you." Joe has a puzzled look on his face, and he looked around the room, then he looked at Mrs. Lincoln and asked, "Where is Maggie? Where is Ginny?"

Maria is standing across the room with her back to them; she is silently crying for the sadness that Joe would be feeling when he heard about his family, and for Mrs. Lincoln who had to tell Joe the terrible news. She told Joe everything that happened that his family had died in their house, and then the house had been burnt down, and some of the townspeople came, and they have been buried on the back of the knoll; temporary markers have been put up at the grave site. Thad had volunteered to stay on the ranch in a tent that Samuel Edwards of the mercantile has loaned you until you can get things fixed, or whatever you want to do. "Do you remember any of this?" Joe looked at her for a long time and shook his head that he did not remember. Joe tried to move his arms and legs; he began to move his arms and after a few days slowly came to where he could hold a fork or spoon but had trouble eating; he did not want to eat for a while, but in a short time he began to feed himself. Maria shaved him, and he washed himself off; this was very painful and took a while to get finished. He kept trying his legs, but to no avail; he just could not get them to move. Joe knew that he could not live here any longer and impose on these people any longer; this is not the way that Joe does things; he needed to get back to his own place and live over there.

Thad came to see him regularly and report to him what was happening—the condition of the cattle and how things were going; Thad came and told him that a rancher from over the east of them came over and offered to buy out his ranch and his cattle. Joe said, "There is no rancher east of us. That land is so dry that it cannot support cattle. I could not run cattle over there for more than two or three months out of a year. Thad, go over to the ranch and get the wagon and bring it over and take me home. I have been here far too long. I need to be there so I can look after my own ranch. If you would like, I want you to stay on and help me. Somehow I will get back in the saddle and take care of the cattle." Joe was not nearly as brave as he let on to everyone around him; actually he was terrified as to how he was going to live without any legs. But he was a proud man who had always done his own work and took care of himself for many a year. And he was not going to lie here in another man's house and another man's bed and be a burden to them; he knew that they would let him stay here for as long as he wanted to stay, but he could not do that. While Joe was waiting for Thad to come back with the wagon, he heard another rig pull up to the ranch. He was informed that a niece of Mrs. Lincoln had come for a visit and was asked if he would like to meet her before she left. Joe said that he would be honored to meet any relative of Mrs. Lincoln's.

He was not ready for the person who came into the room; she was a strikingly beautiful young woman with honey blonde hair and the deepest blue eyes, a quick smile, and a perfect figure. She came over to Joe and looked him over with a small frown on her face, and she looked at him like she was appraising him or something. Mrs. Lincoln made the introductions; she introduced Joe as one of the best men in the country, kind, gentle, and honest and a great friend of the family. "Joe, this is my niece, Beverly Waters, from New York who recently lost her mother. Her dad was killed in the war. She just graduated from nursing school and decided to move out here and work with our doctor in town." Joe said sincerely, "I am glad to meet you, hope to see you around."

Beverly stepped back and with a puzzled look on her face said, "Where are you going?" Joe said, "I have put these good people out long enough; I believe it is time to go home." Beverly said, "Do you have someone to look after you?" Joe said, "Yes, Thad can do quite well for me. He can cook, or I can cook for myself." "You cannot even stand, can you?" Beverly asked. Joe said, "No, I cannot stand." Beverly said, "Then how can you reach a stove to cook." Joe said, "We don't have a stove. We will be living in the tent at least for a time, but as soon as I am up and about, I will make some changes around there."

Beverly glanced at Mrs. Lincoln who was standing out of the line of Joe's vision, and she shook her head from side to side. Beverly held her peace. They told Joe that she would look in on him before he left for his own ranch and left the room. After they left the room, Mrs. Lincoln told Beverly what had happened to Joe. About his wife and daughter, how the raiders had burnt the house and left Joe for dead. That man has the constitution of an elephant, to have lived through all of that. Beverly just nodded her head in agreement. "Why can't he walk?" Beverly asked.

Mrs. Lincoln said, "Because of the bullet that lodged against his spine at least that's what Dr. Abernathy thinks."

Later Beverly goes back to Joe's room and asked him if she could look at his wounds before he leaves. Joe said that he did not need another woman to look him over; he had too many the way that it was.

Beverly explained that she was a nurse, and if Abb comes to check him, she will be the one to look at him any way. Joe surrendered and rolled over; she checked the bullet wounds and asked about some other scars that were on his back and neck. He told her about the war. The horse that threw him and the bull that put a horn in him; Beverly was amazed at the stories. Back in New York, she had never heard of things like this, and she told him so. Joe said, "Well, we do not live in New York, and things are a lot different here." Beverly just nodded her head. "Well," said Joe.

"Well what?" asked Beverly.

Joe said, "The bullet holes, wasn't that what you were looking at?" Beverly said,

"The bullet holes are almost healed, and they look good. It is what happened inside that I am worried about."

Joe asked, "What do you mean? I thought that the bullet holes were all that I had to worry about?" "That is not the whole story," said Beverly. "There is some reason that you cannot move your legs, and you are having some trouble with your arms also."

Joe said, "What do I do about my legs, how do I get everything to work the way that it used to work?"

Beverly said, "We will have to talk to the doctor and let him figure out what would be the best thing for you to do."

Joe said that he had to get home first and see to things there; he had a ranch to run; there were so many things that needed to be done. The cattle had to be tended and plans to be made for the winter feed, fencing to be done, water dams to be tended, spreader dams to be finished up to irrigate the grass lands; the land was coming along fine very soon. He could support three times the number of cattle than he is running now.

Beverly said, "I do not understand what you mean. If you have the land, why don't you just move in the rest of the cattle that you want to run?"

Joe said, "Having the land is only part of the picture; you have to have the water to grow the grass so the cattle will have something to eat. The reason that some ranchers get into trouble is that they overgraze the land and the cattle eat the grass too close to the roots and kills it out and then the land turns to dust and is not any good for years. I will not let that happen to my land I have the water, the best water in this whole country, but I have to control what water that I have. And irrigate the land so that I can get the most benefit out of the water that I have. If I do not lose any of the water or let it run off and sink into the ground somewhere, then I can turn more land into good grazing land, and slowly recover some of the land that was at one time good grazing land, but now is not good for anything. That is what makes the difference."

Beverly was amazed that there was so much to herding cattle; she had thought that all you did was buy some land, buy some cattle, and turn them loose on the land and let them grow. But what Joe is doing is so much better; he is looking forward to the future and not just stripping the land for what he can get out of it. Joe was looking at this woman who he just met, and he could see that she was a beautiful person, and she seemed to care about other people—someone who he would like to call a friend, but that might come later. Right now he could not think of anyone but his late wife; he felt sick in his stomach. Just thinking of the term late wife is a term that he knows is a fact, but a term that he is not ready to even think about, certainly a term that he is not ready to voice. Plus the loss of his precious daughter—he does not want to think about it either. But it keeps coming back in his sleep and every waking moment. Who were the men that came down on them and why did they pick his family? Everyone knew that he did not have anything of value, why would anyone want to rob a small rancher? None of the small ranchers that he knew of would have more than a few dollars at this time of the year. There were a couple of big outfits that might have some money for payroll lying about around the first of the month. But they hit Joe's ranch about the sixteenth and nobody would have any money because all the outlaying people used credit at every place that they dealt with in town. And between them they bartered one with another, which means that if one person wants an item or work done by another person, then that item is traded one thing for another of the same value. Or trade work for an item that they need; an example would be if a merchant wanted a blacksmith to shoe his horse, then he would trade him merchandise for the skill of shoeing the horse. Farmers who had hay that needed to be harvested would hire men to help them put up their hay and give them so much hay for their labor; most people did not have much cash, and they traded with another person, instead of paying money back and forth. The debt was settled with whatever both parties decided what a worthy price was; the contract was settled with a shake of hands—when two men of honor shook hands over a deal, it was a very binding contract. There is nothing more binding between honorable men than their word. A signed paper contract is not as binding as an honest man's word. Joe could not come to a good reason why they would do this unless it was just by chance that they wanted to rob them and shot him to get him out of the way, but why did they kill his wife, and murder his little girl, one who was just starting to live. All they had to do was cover their faces, and Maggie would not know who they were. Joe did not like to hate anyone, but he was feeling something like hate, and he wondered what he would do if and when he came across these men again. Joe could hardly wait until Thad came back with the wagon to get him; he wanted to get to his ranch even if the house was burnt down and all that was left of his family was two graves; it still was his home. It does not matter how long a person lives at a certain place, a house becomes a home when a person starts putting something of their selves into the place. People can live in a house for years and put nothing into the place, and it will not be a home it will only be a house. But if a person moves into the house one day, and the next day this person starts building the house into a better place for the family to live in, then it becomes a home. If the whole family helps in the building of the house, then the house will start becoming a home to the entire family. One reason some people are so unsatisfied in the place that they live is because they have never done anything to add to the betterment of the house or land to make it better. So therefore they will never consider the house as a home; Joe had built this place from nothing to what it is now, and that makes this land his home. The only home that he had known since he had come out of the ending of the war, and he had lived here for nearly fifteen years.

CHAPTER 3

He remembered the first time that he had seen his valley; there was nothing there but a few Indians and plenty of wild animals. The tall straight timber that covered the mountains there was oak, hickory, maple, ash, and many other varieties of trees, also some pine, a lot of different varieties, of that wood. Enough that a man could make anything out of wood that he could dream of; the timber came down into the valley. It looked like there were islands of timber down through the valley untouched by the axe, or the saw of the white man. In the valley there, was grass so green and rich that it looked like a great ocean of green that waved in the wind like billows of the ocean waves, flowers in patches of all different shapes. Different sizes and different colors of the flowers like they were placed there by God to accent the beauty of all of his handiwork. All in all the most beautiful place in the world. He went down in the valley and wandered back and forth looking the valley over for hours. In his mind, he saw his house on top of this knoll, over to the left was going to be the barn, over a little closer to that would be the tack room. Behind the tack room would be a huge root cellar where his wife would store the potatoes, apples from their orchards years from now, the canned vegetables, which would be put up in jars. The garden would be over on the other side of the barn down off the knoll where it could be watered by the stream when the weather was dry. The corrals a couple would be close to the barn where they would keep the saddle stock, handy to the bunkhouse which would be between the house and the barn. Now that Joe had the ranch headquarters laid out, he was looking farther out through the valley and could see where the stream would be dammed up. To make a lake in that large valley as the water came down off the mountain, he could store enough water to irrigate the whole valley for a full dry year if needed. This valley could support thousands of head of cattle. He searched out all of the water in the area clear up the mountain so he was entitled to all of the water. He contacted a lawyer he knew in Washington DC, and after buying the land, he received a clear deed to all of it. Then as he could he purchased tracks of land that covered the whole valley; there was a trading post miles away from his valley, and he figured that one day there would be a town that would grow up in this area, and he figured that being ten miles away from that place was about the right distance away. Farther away over to the east from the valley the land was not so good because the stream that came down through miles of the valley was mostly used up, and in the hot summer there was very little water in that area. But there was another source of water that was close to it, and if someone wanted to work that land, it could be pretty good but not as good as the valley that now belonged to Joe.

Thad finally came with the wagon, and Thad put hay in the wagon and covered the hay with blankets, and Joe was placed in the wagon freshly bathed again, and hopefully the final bandages put in place on Joe's back. His clothes were patched and washed and ironed, and Joe was looking pretty good for a man that came to this ranch weeks ago almost dead. Joe could hardly wait for Thad to get him over to the valley ranch. When they came home, it was in the late morning, Joe glanced at the house, barn, and he just shut everything out and did not look at anything. Thad pulled right up to the tent door, and Joe kept trying to help Thad get him out of the wagon and placed him under the tent. He was worn-out; he could not believe that he was so weak. But he stretched out and went to sleep for a while; he woke up and felt ashamed that he had slept in the middle of the day like a child. Thad pretended that he did not know that Joe had slept; he made noise before he came to the tent door and announced that the evening meal was ready, and he would be serving in a few moments. Thad had some news for Joe, and he could hardly wait for Joe to eat in order to tell him. After Joe had eaten, he asked Thad to help him outside so that he could look around before dark.

Thad said, "Be better if I could show you, or demonstrate it to you. Rather than tell you what it is." Thad asked, "Joe, how strong are you in your arms?"

Joe said, "I am as strong in my upper body as I have ever been. Why are you asking, boy?"

Thad said, "I have made something that I believe that you will like, but you have to come and see."

Joe scooted to the tent door and Thad handed him a rope and said, "Pull on the rope, pull as hard as you can."

Joe pulled on the rope, and he was pulling himself out of the tent door; he was intrigued, so he kept pulling. He was now standing up by holding on to the rope. Joe was looking around, and Thad had installed ropes just a little ways apart, that were supported by the large tree. And where the tree would not reach, he had cut long poles and put them in the ground. Joe could with his arms pulling himself along in different directions standing with his feet dragging along behind him; he knew that this did not look very pretty, but with his legs paralyzed, he did not have much of a choice. He could go to the fire and sit down on a stump seat that Thad had made for him; he could even reach to his left side and get some wood that Thad had cut and stacked there for him so he could feed the fire. He could also with the aid of the ropes swing himself over to the outside bathroom. This would not be as embarrassing to Joe as it would be if Thad had to carry him over to the toilet and help him inside and have to wait on him to finish and then carry him back to where he wanted to go. Joe could go to the corral, the blacksmith shop; Thad even fixed ropes to carry Joe over to the burnt-out house. Joe kept looking over at the house, but he was not ready to go over there yet. Since the tent was beside the barn, it would be easy to come out of the tent and go into the barn; he could feed the horses. But he could not get to the hayloft; he asked Thad to fix ropes so he could put hay down and take some of the work off Thad, but Thad just never did find time to put those ropes up. He was afraid that Joe would fall if he tried to climb up high, and Thad did not mind getting the hay down for the animals.

A few days later, the doctor and the nurse came around to see about Joe. He knew their names, but that was the way that he wanted to think of them at least for the time being. They were not ones, it seemed, that was bringing him any good news. It did not seem that everyone believes that Joe will never walk again, nor have any use of his lower body, but Joe is not ready to accept this kind of news. He believes that God will give him back his body the way that it used to be; he refused to accept the fact that he will be a cripple the rest of his life. If this is true, then he figured that he just does not have a life. Every day Joe is up before Thad is, and he climbs out of the tent with the rope and swings from rope to rope until he gets to the fire, and he builds up the fire. Then he goes to the toilet and takes care of personal business; he is always searching the hills and the shadows along every crag and every point; by now he has memorized all of the places that a man could hide or shoot from. He still has not come up with a reason why someone would gun him down and leave him for dead; he still has not come up with a reason why someone would kill his wife and daughter. The sheriff has not been able to follow the track of the killers; their tracks vanished in the rocks southeast of here, and according to reports nobody have seen or heard from these men in any of the towns, according to the reports that the sheriff has received back.

Every morning Joe travels from one place to another on the ropes; his arms keep getting stronger; he feels that his whole body is getting stronger. If he is going to spend the rest of his life without his legs, then he will find some other way of traveling beside horseback. Maybe he could travel in a wagon on the seat. He brought this up to Thad, and he said, "Only if someone is riding right beside you, we might work something out." Joe said, "Why would I need someone beside me?"

Thad said, "What if you lost a wagon wheel? What if you had to get out of the wagon? How would you ever get back in?"

Joe did not know how to answer that question. So he dropped the thought for now. Every evening before Thad came back to the ranch work, Joe would make the same trip to all of the places swinging on the ropes, and he again would stop and look all around. There were times that he thought that he could see a brush move or something, or someone move far back in the timber high up on the mountain. It could have been an animal; it was too far for anyone to try a shot at Joe or anyone in the valley, so he thought he was wasting his time looking, but he kept at it every day. One day, he asked Thad if he would make a large circle around the camp and see if there are any fresh tracks.

He did not tell Thad that he thought he had seen someone. But he did tell Thad to be extremely careful. Thad left before daylight the next morning and started on the east side so that he would have the sun at his back, and this would make it easier for him to see anyone who might be close to the camp. He took a mirror with him so that if he did come across anything that Joe might need to know, he would flash Joe with the mirror. They went over the codes so if danger was around, he could flash two times, a pause and two more flashes to Joe; and then he would move on around the hills and continue his circle and use the same method to let Joe know that he found something alarming. If Joe wanted him to come to camp, he would flash his mirror at Thad wherever he thought that Thad would be, and Thad would come to him but use extreme caution unless he used the signal that all was clear; then Thad could use is own reasoning as to what he wanted to do. It was dark when Thad came into the camp; he said that he had come across a place back in one of the canyons that three men had been camping in for quite a while. But today they were not in camp, and the camp was empty. There was a place over on the ridge where one man at a time had stayed there and was watching the camp. It was too far for a shot, but he found a place where someone had laid down a pair of binoculars, so now we know that they are interested in us, or more likely checking on Joe. Joe looked at Thad and said, "I want you to go to town tomorrow and stay there; I do not want you to come back until this thing is over. Thad, I do not want you to get hurt; and I do not want you to kill anyone. If you ever do kill someone, it will haunt you for the rest of your life." Thad argued with Joe, but he would not listen to Thad; so the next morning, Thad packed his things and put them on a horse; he also took a little dried beef and some coffee and an extra coffeepot. Joe did not pay any attention to what Thad had packed. Thad also took one of the rifles and some extra shells. They agreed that Thad would come back with the doctor the next time that he came out and not until. Thad left camp and headed for town; he had a long way to travel before he could turn into a valley he had to go until Joe could not see him anymore, and then he doubled back around the back side of the camp. He went behind a small ridge so as not to be seen by Joe, and he went slowly so there would not be any dust; he did not want Joe or anyone else to see the dust. He went to where the mountain came the closest to Joe's home; there he found a little box canyon, and there he turned his horse loose into the small box canyon and set up a rope gate. A place that if you did not know that it was there, you could walk right by it because of the brush and the lay of the land and never see the valley. He unsaddled his horse and took his bedroll and moved up on the side of the mountain so he could see Joe and guard his horse at the same time. Along about sunset, Thad was watching Joe, and he turned his head to get his canteen; and he saw a flash of sunlight on something bright, maybe a pair of binoculars. Thad could not tell for sure, maybe it was a gun barrel that was worn and bright. But someone was over on the next point about a half mile away, and he or they were also watching the camp. Thad decided that he would leave the horse where he was, and after full dark, he would move closer to the camp where he would be close enough to aid Joe if someone was going to move in on him in the dark. Thad had done a lot of practice on moving around in the dark when he was traveling around the country; he could move up on a person in the dark and never be heard. Joe was sitting next to the campfire in the shade of the tree when he glanced up on the mountain, and he saw a flash of light on a point of the mountain rather close to the camp. If there was no wind and the target was standing still, a rifle shot could score a hit from that distance. Joe knew that he would have to stay awake all night tonight, but what if they come to him during the daylight instead of the night. He should not have sent Thad away; that was just not a sound idea, but Joe thought that he would lie down for a while in the barn where he would be out of sight so they would have to get close before they could shoot him. The horses would let him know if someone came too close; horses will hear a stranger and smell him like a dog would and let his master know, because horses get nervous and move around when strangers come too close. Joe knew that he was weak after the shooting and decided that he would conserve his strength; he spread out a blanket, and he lay down and was immediately asleep. He started to dream, the same dream that he had been having for weeks. He was standing on his porch at the house, Ginny was sitting on the top step of the porch, and Maggie was in the house singing as she was doing her work. She stopped singing, and Joe wondered why she was not singing anymore. He told Ginny that he would be right back. And he stepped through the door to ask Maggie why she stopped singing in the middle of his favorite song, and Maggie was not in the house. Now this was strange because there was only one door in the log house; he was waiting for boards to come from the mill so he could make another door for the back of the house. He had been waiting for a long time for those boards; Maggie had asked him a couple of times to order them, and he had put it off. They really did not need more than one door at this time. He had been planning to add on another room or two, and he would cut the door in the logs at that time. But Maggie was not in the house; he turned around to tell Ginny that her mom had disappeared, but Ginny was not on the step. He stepped back outside and called for Ginny, but she could not be found; he was frightened now, and he kept calling for Ginny as he ran to the barn to see what she had ran off for. He still did not trust Ginny around the horses; he had not trained her to handle the livestock yet. That was another thing that he had not done. Why did he let these important things go? Why did he not put another door in the house? He ran to the barn, and Ginny was not there; he had searched the barn, stable, corral, all of the outbuildings—calling all at the same time. Then he looked back at the house, and the house was burning down. He ran back to the house, and the fire was gone. Maggie was gone. Jennie was gone; he fell down and could not get up. He kept trying to get up, and he kept calling out for someone, but nobody answered. He would wake up, bathed in sweat and trembling. It was the same every time; Joe woke up and found that it was total darkness in the barn and outside; he had slept too long. He grabbed a rope and stated to swing up so he could stand, but that would make noise. His pistol was in a box very close to him; he had not even told Thad that he had a pistol. He rolled over and over and shifted his angle and rolled over again until he was at an old feed box that was buried under some old sacks. He slowly moved the sacks away; he wondered if someone had come close while he was sleeping; maybe nobody was even close by. He opened the box and felt inside for his pistol, belt, and holster, which were rolled up; and a box of shells was in the oil-soaked rag with them so moisture could not get in and ruin the gun. He took the gun out and the shells and started feeding the shells in the gun. He checked everything out in the dark, and all seemed to be in good shape. Ever since Ginny was big enough to reach the gun where it hung in the house, Maggie urged him to get it out of the house. So he, for safety's sake, brought the gun to the barn and put it into the feed box; and it had been here every since. Joe felt a little better now that he had a means to protect himself; he looked out to the fire, and it was burning very low. He would have to get to the fire and put some wood on the fire in order to have a light to shoot by. If someone came, they could get close enough to fire the barn, and he could not stop them. Joe was getting frightened, and he did not like that; this is not any way for a man to act. That reflection that he had seen could just be something that his mind had seen, just like the dream. He might not have his legs, but he still had everything else; he was still a man—he could still see and hear and pull a trigger, and he could still move about. He remembered the war. One time he was caught behind the enemy line, and it was open country; the enemy was under the trees and heavy brush. He could not go through there. He lay in the woods across the valley and was looking the land over, and he could see a low place in the middle of the valley. He waited until dark and moved out into the open; he crossed about a mile of open terrain; one sentry gave a call during the night that he had seen something in the field, maybe a fox. And someone called back and said if it has a blue uniform on it to shoot it; otherwise, let it go on its way. Others chuckled, and that was all they ever heard of his movements on that night. He did not need to walk that night, and he made it safely through. By daylight the next morning, he was back to his own lines; it was really hard for them to believe that he had enough nerve to come back through that open valley, but he had information that he had obtained on his scouting mission that was vital to the Union Army. But that was a long time ago; he was a much younger man then and had his legs that he could use them if need be. Here he did not know who his enemy was or what he looked like—that was the worst part; he had been thinking back to that day when the riders came down upon them. He remembered a name of Denver and of Mr. Cole. Were they the same man? His first name is Denver, last name is Cole. Joe did not know or were there two of the men? He remembered the slow, deep, raspy voice; he thought that he would never forget that voice, and another man, the Indian who was silent. And the man that Mr. Lincoln had shot, they had described him to Joe, and he did not seem to be any of the other men. Joe was still lying in the barn beside one of the big doors. He could look out through the walls through the poles and see if anything moved along the walls. He could not see anything or hear anything; wait there was something—all of a sudden the crickets are quiet; the frogs at the spring are not making a sound. There is something or someone moving around because the insects and frogs can see or hear them. This is behind the barn. Are they working around behind him so the hill behind them will not let them be seen in case the moon comes out. There is very little light tonight, and the sky is dark. Which means that they cannot hear him or see him if he stays quiet and does not move around much, and in the soft dirt here he would not make much noise. What is out there? Think. What would make noise and where would it be? Yes, there is a brush pile behind the barn over on the side away from the house, lying as he was that would be on his right; if someone came from that side, he would probably hear them; it was not much brush, but it was dry and would crank if stepped on. The Indian, he would not step on any twig or branch no matter how little it was. On the other side next to the house, there is the gravel he gathered and put down on the walk from the barn to the house to keep the mud off his feet when he rode in to the barn and walked to the house. The house is burned, but the gravel would still be there. What about the area from the valley side? There was nothing there that would make a noise, only the ropes that Thad had hung up for him; those would move the branches if touched, and that might make a noise. Joe just relaxed and waited; it seemed for a long time, then he heard a grunt, a kind of a thud. He did not know which came first, the thud or the grunt, then silence again. Maybe he just imagined the sound; now he heard some kind of movement but no sound. It was like cloth moving against cloth, not walking, not crawling. He cannot make it out, then it stopped also. Maybe some animal softly chewing or something his mind was racing trying to figure the sounds out. There he heard a sound that was human; someone was moving around the corral; one of his horses snorted—he did not like the smell of someone. They act different when it is a person; his big bay horse does not like strangers and will give a warning when someone is close, but he will not make a sound for a small animal. Joe adjusted his position to look through the spaces in the logs on that side of the barn; they are going to expect him to be in the tent. He just thought of that; they have been watching him, and he always goes into the tent to sleep, and they would expect him to be asleep by now. He saw a very slight movement; the person was crawling up to the tent; he would move then stop, move then stop, move then he stood up. He was under the tree where the tent was, where Joe was supposed to be, just outside the barn door. Joe could not see him from the door; Joe was going to have to move. Could he do it without making a noise? This man was waiting, waiting for what, or for who? Joe held his pistol in his right hand and his gun belt in his left hand, and he knew that he was going to have to roll over one or two times to get far enough away from the door to see the man. He could not groan or breathe hard; he had to do it in one easy smooth motion. He knew as soon as he cleared the door, the man would see his movement and would fire at him. Where were the other men? Maybe they thought one man could handle a cripple, and maybe all of them were out there, and maybe they had brought in more men. Joe did not know. What he did know was that if he was to die tonight, he would not die alone; he would take as many as he could with him. Joe slowly started to roll, and he stopped; right in front of him a man stepped around the other door, so silently that Joe never heard a sound or movement; he knew that this was the Indian—he had to take this man out first. Joe had never killed a man that was not facing him and had taken a shot except in the war; now this was a war of survival. The man started to turn, and as he turned, he looked down. Joe fired as the man was raising his own gun; Joe shot twice and hit the man in the chest and in the face; the man was dead before he hit the ground. Joe rolled over and over; bullets were hitting the ground where he had been. He fired at the muzzle blast of the other gun. Joe shot three times, and the man went down; this was not the man that he had first seen; that man was coming at him. Joe fired his last bullet at this man just as the man fired at him; they both missed, but Joe was out of shells. And the man was circling and was coming at Joe now from his feet. What could he do? Joe saw a knife glisten in the little light that there was in the barn. As the man came close enough, Joe does not know how it happened, but one of his legs came up and caught the man in the stomach; and Joe grabbed the arm that was holding the knife, and Joe vaulted the man over his head. He was surprised that his leg had worked, but he knew that he had to hold on to the arm of this man or he was dead; the man would back off and just shoot him while he lies here helpless. As the man landed on his back and Joe holding to his arm, Joe felt and heard the arm break; the man let out a scream, but Joe twisted his body and grabbed him with his other hand. And with the strength he had in his arms, he quickly overcame the man and knocked him out. He could have easily taken the knife away from the man and killed him, but to Joe all life is precious, and he did not. All was quiet for a moment, and Joe heard another movement; he scrambled for the man's gun, and he heard. "Joe, are you all right?" It was Thad out in the darkness.

Joe said, "There are three of them here. I do not know about any more. Be careful."

Thad came close and checked the other men and said, "They are dead, just like the other two out in the meadow."

Joe said, "Where did you come from?"

Thad did not bother to answer for a moment; he lit a lantern and came close to Joe and said, "Man, am I glad to see you are all right."

They looked at the man that was knocked out, and Thad tied him up and moved him in a place that he could keep him from getting loose. Joe wanted to know who the others were; Thad did not know; one reason because it was dark, and the other he did not know very many people in this area. Thad started the fire up, and with light they looked at the three other men in camp, and only one of them did Joe know—the one that he called the Indian. He was still no closer to who these men were. Joe did not tell Thad about using his leg to kick the one man and throw him to overcome him; there would be time for all of that later. Thad removed the bodies and put them in the barn until morning when he would find their horses and take all of them to the sheriff and let him deal with them.

In the morning, Thad went to where the men had been camping and brought back the horses, guns, and camping equipment so that Joe could see if he could find a name or something that would lead him to the truth about who these men were and who they were working for.

But there was nothing anywhere they checked the men and found three hundred dollars gold in the pockets of each of the men, including the man that was wounded. Joe tried to question the man, but he would not say anything. Thad took the men and horses, gear, and everything that he found to town to Sheriff Toby Griffin; he was the law in this area. After turning all of the men over to the sheriff and telling him the whole story, he went to the of mercantile of Samuel Edwards to pick up supplies. As he was coming out of the store carrying his supplies, he ran into Beverly Waters, and she asked about Joe; she seemed very concerned. Thad told her what had happened the night before, and she was appalled that something like this could happen especially to a man that was crippled and helpless. Thad omitted the fact that Joe had ordered him into town, and he disobeyed his orders and stayed there in a hidden place to help Joe if he needed anything. Thad headed back to Joe with the supplies that Joe had ordered, strange but Joe ordered new clothes and boots for both of them; it did not seem that Joe would want new work clothes, but Thad followed his orders and brought back everything. By the time that he came back to the ranch and rode up to the barn where they were storing their supplies, he did not see Joe. He thought that Joe would be in the tent asleep, but he went to the fire and fixed him a cup of coffee, thinking what he would do today. He heard steps behind him, and he jumped up and turned around; there stood Joe who without holding to anything with his old boots on and work clothes walking a little unsteady, but walking on his own power. Thad let out a yell of glee. He said, "Joe, what happened to your legs?" He was so amazed that Joe could walk.

Joe told him what happened last night in the fight, and Joe said he moved his legs in his bed last night, so this morning by himself he tried his legs and found that they could work. Not fully ready for a day's work, but they were his legs; he was smiling and thanking God for giving him back his legs. Joe wanted to stay in camp for a few days, and he let Thad go about the business of running the place so Joe can get back some of his strength, and he will go ahead and exercise and try to strengthen his body. The unknown people who want him dead are still out there, and Joe wondered from where they will come from the next time. He had done a lot of thinking about this, and the man that he heard spoken of as Denver or as Cole maybe the same man, and he thought that there is someone who has ordered this man Denver to come after him and his family. He told Thad to avoid any place that he could be ambushed from and just watch from certain places and keep track of the cattle and make sure that they are not rustled and moved off the ranch. If someone does go after the cattle, Thad should get back to the ranch as soon as possible or if close enough go for the sheriff, but get word to him as soon as possible.

Above everything else, Joe does not want for Thad to get hurt or killed for helping Joe on his ranch. Joe does not think that anything will happen for a few days, and now that he knows that God is going to give him back his life, there is a whole new possibility to look at. Joe is going to find out who killed his wife and his daughter, and he is going to make them pay for everything. And he does not mean in money; he knows that God does not want him to kill out of revenge, but Joe does know that the sheriff has tried but maybe the sheriff is not looking in the right place or for the right man. Joe will be looking at every man and in every place for the guilty ones to pay for the life of his family. There has to be a reason nobody will do that kind of a thing just for some loose change, maybe revenge, but who would want revenge from Joe? Did Joe do someone wrong and not remember it? What about the war? Was someone holding a grudge against Joe for fighting for the north? Some in this area had fought for the north, and some had fought for the south, and some had not fought for either side. Joe thought about the men that had been killed in town years ago when there was a raid, and some of those men had gone to prison. Could they be out by now? The next time that Thad goes into town, he would have him check with the sheriff about those men who were sent to prison. Joe had not been over to the house that was burnt down around his wife and his daughter. But just as it was getting dark, he walked over to the house and stood and looked at it, then he walked up on the knoll and looked at the two graves; Thad kept finding wild flowers and putting them on the graves, and there was a board that was used as a headstone for each of the graves. It was after dark when Joe came back by his house, and he stopped and looked at the two stones that he had hewn for the two steps that were at the porch; they were rough, but he could finish them up and make two headstones for his two women.

When Thad came riding in, he told Thad to put a rope around each one of the stones and pull them into the barn where he could work on them in the shade, but more importantly he could work on them in the privacy of the barn. Away from eyes that Joe did not want to see him up and walking. Joe went out to the fire and pretended that he still needed the ropes to move around in the camp area; he had a pistol tucked into his belt and well hidden under the tail of his jacket, just in case that he had any company. Joe was also secretly in the barn practicing his draw of the pistol—something that he had not done for many years, at one time Joe was fast, not the fastest but fast enough that he had come out of a fight or two; some considered it lucky, and Joe did not want anyone to think otherwise. He did not want to be known as a fast gun, because someone was always ready to try their luck to make a name for themselves. Joe did not want anything to do with a quick gun reputation, but he did not want to die because someone else was stupid enough to try him. Joe kept working; he could feel his body starting to come back as he did his exercise and his practice; he wanted to be back to the best shape that he had ever been in his life. Joe and Thad had eaten their supper, and Thad said that there had been a couple of horses nosing around the mountain higher up than the men who had come to the camp before. So they knew what had happened here the other night, or they knew what had not happened here the other night. By this time it was all over the country that some men had attacked Joe's place and had died in the process.

Whether or not they knew that one of the men had been taken captive was another thing, but he did not know that Joe could walk; he only knew that Joe had been on the ground and had fought him and took him. Now they were starting all over again; Joe did not want Thad to get hurt, so the next morning he told Thad to stay in the area of the ranch and start cleaning up the area of the house. He used the excuse that he could not look at the burnt-down house any longer; he wanted to move on and start changing things around the immediate area. Joe did not know if he fooled Thad or not, but he did not care. It was still morning when Dr. Abernethy and his nurse, Beverly Waters, came up the road in the doctor's buggy. Joe told Thad not to say anything to them about his walking; while they were there, he went to a bench and sat down. They came and said, "How are things going, Joe?"

"Well," Joe said, "Thad and I thought that we would go into town and do some dancing tonight if you think that would be okay, Doctor."

He looked at Beverly and smiled; she did not smile back.

The doctor said, "We have heard what happened here, and we wanted to know if there was any additional damage to your body."

Joe said that he thought that the excitement had done him some good if anything. He looked at Thad and said, "What do you think?"

Thad just shook his head; he did not really know what to say. He realized what was happening. Joe did not want to lie to them, and in reality he was telling them the truth, but as he knew they did not believe him. They thought that he was just trying to make light of an impossible situation.

Beverly touched Joe on the arm and said, "Joe, you are going to have to face the truth. After this long a time, you probably will not ever walk again."

Joe said, "I refuse to believe that for one moment. But that is just between us, and you." The doctor asked Joe if he was exercising, and Joe said that he was. "These ropes will put iron in your arms, and, Doc, you should try it sometimes."

They could not jest about the problems that Joe had, and they did not know what to say to him so they said they would be back in a couple of weeks and left. Joe said, "I feel so bad about deceiving them, but we cannot let the word get out just yet about my legs."

Thad said, "At first I thought that you had lost your mind, and then I realized what you had in mind. I believe that someone really wants you dead. I do not know what the reason is that someone is trying to get rid of you, but I am here with you, and we will not quit until we have found out who and why."

Joe said, "Tonight I am leaving this place and go on the hunt for whoever it is."

Joe sat on his seat that evening for appearances' sake for those who might be looking at the camp; he sits there looking at his ranch where he has spent years working. Thad went into the barn and packed their stuff on a couple of horses with pack saddles and saddled their two best horses. By dark everything that they had was on the horses except for the tent, and they had to leave it for the appearances that Joe was still there.

What they know is that someone was watching them from up on the mountain. They could see the tent; they could see Joe sitting by the fire like he always did. Thad was not in appearance, but he must be around somewhere; the new men that they were expecting had not arrived yet, and they had to wait until they did come, then they could move against Joe after dark. Looking down from up on the mountain, they could see the old burnt-out house and close to it is the tack room, the blacksmith shop, the outhouse farther back from these buildings, on over from the blacksmith was a small corral for horses. This corral was for horses that needed special care, and then the big barn seemed to sit there alone. The corral was on the back of the barn and came up the other side almost to the front of the barn. This is where the tent was; this was where they slept, under the big tree, and the barn for shelter from the wind and the sun. On the other side of the tree is where the fire was and where this pitiful crippled man sat when they cooked their meals, and he swung on those ropes to get around.

"Well, he won't have to do that long. We will get him and that kid who helps him. Wonder how he overcame the other men, and especially that Indian. I didn't think any man alive could overcome him; it must have been a lot of luck on their part."

CHAPTER 4

Joe and Thad waited until it was getting dark, and Thad came out to the fire and pulled logs back out of the fire so it would burn down quicker; they did not want to leave a big fire burning after they left the area. And they did not want anyone to see them from the firelight; Thad and Joe went to the tent. Joe looked at the sky, and there were big billows of clouds, and they were moving slowly. When they covered the moon, there was full blackness in the open meadows. And if they kept under the trees for a ways, there was no way that they could be seen from the barn, let alone up on the mountain. Joe remembered that he used to sit in the darkness up on a mountain and watch the shadows move across the ground at night when the clouds covered the moon. There were times in the daylight when he was sitting on his horse out on a high bluff, and he would sit and watch the shadows move along the ground when the clouds would cover the sun and create the marvelous shadows across the ground. They moved out after full dark, and they went slow and stayed under the trees; it was like shadows moving, and from up on the mountain nobody was looking at shadows. They were watching the fire that slowly faded out during the night. They rode along the side of the meadow until the moon was covered with clouds, and then they moved across the meadow to the mountains on the other side of the valley, by then they were far enough away from the sentries that the horses could not be heard up on the mountain to the west of them. Joe told Thad that they would travel all night so they could get up in the rocky ground and could not be tracked by anybody. Joe still remembered the Indian that was with the men that shot him and burnt the house; he hoped that this was the only Indian in their camp. They were mostly good trackers and excellent fighters, and he did not want to come up against any more of them. There were places that they could travel for miles on rocky ledges and then onto packed ground. They came to a stream; this was one of the streams that fed Joe's ranch, and he knew this stream, and he knew where this stream would take them; he walked their horses into the stream and changed directions and headed back toward the ranch. Joe hoped that if the outlaws had someone who could track them as good as he could track; this maneuver might cause them some delay. He had not ridden for a long time, and he would like to get down every now and then to rest, and they needed to be a long way in front of anybody that might be following them. Joe knew that they would have to leave the immediate country and give the impression that they were leaving for good. Joe was going to take the battle to the ones that came hunting him. They know who he is, and where he is, or so they think that they know. But he is going to see what they look like and where they hole up when they are frightened, because he is certainly going to frighten them; men like to give the impression that they cannot be frightened, but Joe knew just as all men know, that this is a foolish notion. Given the right time, the right place, and the right set of rules any man can be turned into a quivering mass. And Joe had a few times done this to a full squad of soldiers.

When the early-morning breeze started moving along the western slope of the mountain, Joe knew it was time to start looking for the place that they were going to stop to build a fire and cook some food. Shelter their horses in a box cove, or a deep hollow, or a place that they could protect the horses and lie down and sleep for most of the day. It was a time to look over his back trail and see if anything was moving there; he knew that to a trained eye it was almost impossible to completely hide a trail while traveling at night. Joe was out on a point of the mountain where he could look down the mountain, as well as around the sides of the mountain both ways for a mile or so. Being up higher than the people who would be tracking him, he could look through the trees and catch glimpses of movement of riders or people walking long before they could see him, because looking up they were looking through trees that were a distance away from them. Joe was close to the same trees and looking out to more open country, and this was a beautiful country, but Joe was not admiring the country at this time; he was looking for some movement that would tell him that the enemy was coming after him. The trees blocked some of his view, but even through the trees, there is always a glimpse of movement; and sometimes that is easier to see than looking out through open country where there is so much to see. Sometimes a little shallow place or a ditch might be overlooked, and someone could approach totally undetected. But Joe lay in the shade of a great big oak tree and let his eyes slowly look over the country. Thad had set up camp and cooked breakfast using dry wood and put the small fire under a big leafy tree so the smoke would be broken up and could not be seen unless at a very close distance, but then you could smell the smoke before you see it. Joe would at any other time have seen the great beauty he was looking at in this part of the country. He had seen this same view and has lain in this very same place and admired this scene for hours; this was his land, but today he was looking for people, dust, or the birds and small animals that would be moving if anyone was coming through the land. He did not see anything, but still he waited until Thad spoke softly that breakfast was ready. Joe arose and moved back out of sight from the land below them before he stood up and turned to the camp and moved back in the brush and took a plate from Thad. He sat down on a log and ate his breakfast, and upon doing so, he told Thad to cover the fire with dirt and get some sleep; and he would stay on watch for a few hours, and then he would wake Thad up so he could stand watch for a few hours, and then they would trade off again. Thad rolled out in his sleeping bag; Joe straightened up the camp and packed everything up so if necessary they could move out in a moment and not leave anything behind. Joe went back to the place where he first lay; he took with him his bedroll and his rifle and some shells. Joe spread his blankets and lay down on them, facing the valley. The mountain was not too high, but there were ledges and some rocks that required that you come up by a winding route; Joe was lying there, not seeing anything. Suddenly, a quail flew up; it caught Joe's eye. This could mean nothing or maybe some animal stirred it up. A moment later, he saw a rabbit scurry out of the same area that the quail had flew from. Joe watched that area, and a few moments later a bird was flying around the knoll and started to land in a bush, and just as he was going to land he flew away in an awful hurry. Joe knew that someone was there. A full ten minutes later he saw an animal; it looked like a wolf, but Joe did not know of a wolf in this area of the country. Yes, one could have moved in, but this did not seem right that a wolf would be in the low lands in this time of the year, maybe in the winter when the animals had moved down off the high mountains but not now. The wolf was passing through where they had come to the stream; he followed their tracks to the water's edge and stopped and looked around, because the scent could not be followed on the water. Joe just waited; the wolf was a half mile away and could not follow them any farther; that was where they had hit the water and turned back to the right downstream. And came out a mile down the stream and come away from the stream through the next valley over and come up and around the mountain to where they were now, almost a circle so that he could do just what he was now doing. Watch and see just who was on his trail. He is a patient man when it comes to something like this; there was a time that he sat in the sun and waited for an Indian to make the first move; both of them were out of water, and Joe was wounded he was very low of ammunition. He did not know just how many Indians were alive just over the hill from him; he could see the only way that they could leave was to get water, and they could keep him pinned down where he was. If either one of them tried to get to the water, they were in danger of gunfire from the other side; Joe had known of Indians who could run in the desert for miles on one mouth full of water; this was something that very few white men could do. Joe sat in the sun and watched; he did not move; he did not do anything but watch for someone to make a run for an escape or a run for the water. After hours of waiting in the sun, he saw some movement in the other sink hole, then he saw a slight movement in one side of the sink. There was a whisper of movement, and he just saw a slight brown blemish on the ground; it was moving ever so slow toward the water. He rested his rifle on the mound of dried brown grass and held his breath and eased back on the trigger; and as the gun went off, a groan was herd, and then there was stillness. He settled back and waited some more; after a while, there came a hand up and a gun came over the edge of the mound and lay there in the sand. Joe still sat where he was, still a long time went by, and there was not movement on either side. Joe knew that the Indian had sent out another lesser man to test Joe and see if he could draw him out in the open so he could be shot. Joe thought that the big Indian was now by himself, and he would not have thrown out his only gun, so Joe just sat and waited; he wanted a drink of water more than he wanted anything in the world, except for his life. He knew that he sitting where he was sitting kept him alive, and nothing else would keep him alive he thought about digging in the sand to see if he could find any moisture, but he knew that any movement would take all the moisture out of his body, and he would be dead before the hour was out. Joe sat and waited; he saw the one that had crawled out being dragged back to the sink hole. He was dead; Joe did not have any doubt about that the big Indian just wanted to get him under the ground so he would not attract the buzzards; they would attract attention, and he did not want more white men coming to see what the birds were looking for. Joe knew that the energy that the big Indian would use to pull him back and to dig a hole would be a help to him because he would use up moisture in his own body. Joe waited some more; it seemed like an eternity, but it was about two hours, nothing happened; then he heard the same noise and knew that the big Indian was trying to do the same thing that the other Indian had tried. The big Indian was scooping sand to the side of the low place that was between him and Joe; he was going to try for the water by digging the low place and piling the sand up on the side. Joe sat still and waited; he knew that was his only chance to survive. The big Indian was almost to the water, and he ran into a rock and could not go any farther and kept in the low place. If he went, he would be exposed to Joe's gun, and he could not advance any farther. There was only a few feet from where he was to the water, to life. Joe wondered what he was going to do to reach the water; there were a few moments of waiting, and then there was a noise, and Joe saw a waterskin fly through the air, to the water. And there was a string attached; he was going to load the waterskin and pull it to him, and then he would have enough water to wait Joe out. *What am I going to do now?* thought Joe. *If he does get to that water, I am done.* For Joe started looking at the water and at the other man, or where the other man is hidden, the water was less than ten feet. And the place where the big Indian was lying was about fifty feet from Joe. *How can I stop the Indian from getting the water?* he thought. He has to pull that waterskin out of the water and across the rock, and then he had the whole ball of wax. Joe watched as the waterskin slowly filled with water and started to sink; after a while, the string tightened; the waterskin started moving toward the land. Joe might, with his last bullet, cut the string; and he might miss, but right now was not worth the chance. Joe waited until the last moment, and the string stuck on a rock and would not move; the waterskin was pouring out water on the ground. It was just inches from the grasp of the Indian; he pulled and pulled. The leather string was hung on a rock, maybe the white man was out of bullets. Maybe he would miss if he did have bullets; the Indian could not wait any longer. He was also out of bullets, and maybe the white man did not know it. He made a decision and jumped up and grabbed the waterskin and turned before the bullet from Joe hit him in the chest and took his life; he fell down in the shallow place. Joe waited a little while longer, and then he moved out of his place and held his rifle in front of him as though it was loaded and moved to where the Indian fell. He came to a point that he could see the feet of the Indian; he moved a little closer, and he found the Indian still alive but unable to move. He searched and found nobody else around. He checked the guns of the Indian and found that none of the guns had any bullets in them. Joe retrieved the water and drank a little of the water; he looked around and found a little food. He picked up his guns and his gear, looked back of the knoll, and found the horses along with his own that he thought had run off. He came back to the Indian, and he was dead; there was nothing else for Joe to do, so he left. He took the extra horses and supplies with him and headed home. He did not have very many battles with the Indians; they pretty much left him alone, and after this battle they stayed away from Joe and respected him as a great warrior.

Joe knew that this was another time to wait; one does not know what is going to happen if one passes the point in life that it is supposed to happen. The time was now for Joe to find out just who is going to be his enemy. It is hard to fight if one does not know who the enemy is. Joe watched the wolf, which just waited also; he looked up the stream and down the stream and did not know which way they had gone. He just sat down and waited; after a bit there was a rustle in the brush, and Joe saw five horses coming out of a ravine. Joe did not know that the ravine was there; a ravine such as this is a deep area that goes through the forest. Maybe at one time, water had washed out the ground and made a low place that you can travel without being noticed, and that is why the men came so close before he seen them, now what are they going to do. They should split up, and some go downstream, and some go upstream. That would split them up, and he and Thad could handle them much better that way. He watched well hidden and waited for them to decide what to do; he paid a lot of attention to the leader; also the Indian took his attention. He resembled the Indian that he had killed in the desert years ago. The Indian dismounted and stroked the wolf and then walked away from him; he went to the edge of the stream and looked across the stream, up the stream and down the stream. He came back to the leader and spoke for a few moments; the leader handed out some orders, and then they all dismounted and started a fire, cooked their lunch. While they were doing this, the Indian and the wolf went upstream to scout out the area. About a half hour, the Indian came back and shook his head no; they mounted and headed downstream, some on one side and some on the other. They do not want to split up, thought Joe. That also tells him something about them—they are very cautious and worried about him and Thad, and this is good for them. Joe went back to the camp and woke up Thad and told him what had happened and to get ready to move. Joe was going to lie down for one-half hour. He told Thad to wake him if he is not up by that time; they need to move quietly and undetected. They wiped out all of the prints of Joe walking around the camp. But left Thad's prints for them to find; he had an idea that would give them some time on these people, and they would set up their own way of doing these things; he never did like to run. Running was just not in him, but he wanted to even the odds. Joe was up in half hour, and they mounted, and Thad had fixed some biscuits and beans, and they ate on the way while in the saddle. Joe filled Thad in on what he had in mind for these guys behind them. Thad grinned and said he had never heard of such a thing, but it sounded good to him.

They moved out at a good pace, traveling in heavy leaves that leave a trail but not a clear trail. They came to a place that there was a narrow rock ledge, and Joe took the packhorses, and Thad moved his horse over; and he stepped his horse up on the ledge. Joe turned all of the rest of the horses to the left and started to climb a shallow bank that would top out on solid rock, after the horses were on solid rock. Joe dismounted and went back to the place that they left the heavy leaves, and he wiped out the tracks, but he left enough here and there so that they could find it. He really wanted it to look like an amateur had tried to wipe out the tracks but didn't know just how to do it. What Joe really wanted to do was disturb the tracks so they would not know that Thad had left the trail; Joe knew that from here on the ground would be so rocky and hard that they could not tell just how many horses were traveling together. Now Joe was looking for a narrow passage way up out of the low ground; he was passing through an area that was impassable from the bottom to the top, and sooner or later there would be a passageway that he could take the horses up to the next plateau or to the next level ground up the mountain. He came around the mountain, and there it was—a place that about three horses could travel side by side up a place that water had flowed down at some time and had kind of wiped this area clear of soil and left the rocks. But filled some of the places with dirt, enough so the horses could get footing over the rocks. He turned the horses up the narrow gully; it was a hard climb for the horses, but these were mountain horses, and they made the trip easy enough. He was glad that he had sturdy horses and not some of these light-framed speedy horses that were following him. When Joe got to the top, he looked around seeing what he wanted; he quickly tied the horses up just a little way from the top of the gully, except for his own mount. He found some large boulders close to the place where he came out of the gully, and he found a long pole and using this as a pry bar he loosened the boulders and moved them very close to the edge of the gully. He found some small logs and tree limbs and moved or threw them out into the gully ahead of the boulders. He moved his horse back a little way from the edge of the gully and tied him in the shade of a large tree, then Joe sat down and waited for the men and horses that were following him; he hoped that Thad had cleared his trail so the wolf did not sense him and his horse. Joe moved to the side of the gully, so he had the best look of the approach; he wanted to see them and get things ready before they came too close to him. He was concerned about that wolf; they were a very smart and wiry animal. He had run into them in the mountains near Canada. The nerve and the ability of this animal were uncanny; they moved like shadows through the forest, and they could smell a man or animal that they were hunting from a long way off. He wondered how the Indian had captured the wolf and tamed him. Things were passing through Joe's mind like maybe they had seen Thad's trail and turned off on it, instead of following his trail; maybe he had not fooled them for a minute. Maybe they were even now coming at him from his back; he set aside his thoughts. "Joe," he said to himself, "settle down and wait, and this is another time that you must wait and wait. Sometimes the one who moves first is the one who dies."

Joe pulled his hat down to shade his eyes from the sun and waited. About an hour later, he heard a movement; it was a horse hoof hitting something, and then he heard a saddle squeak just slightly. These men were good hunters; he had better remember this if he was going to survive this ordeal. Somebody paid good money for these men, and somebody paid, but whom? They were now very close. Wait, where is the wolf? He should be out in front of these men, but was he? Had Joe missed him? Joe scanned the gully very closely and both sides of the gully even a place that was impassable, and finally he saw the wolf; it looked like a shadow that would be there and then it would not be there. Joe knew that he had to wait and that if he showed himself too soon, the plan would not work; he put his rifle on the shadow and not on the gully. He knew that if that wolf made it up to the top, Joe would lose his horses and maybe his own life. The men were coming; they did not like the gully. It could be an ambush. Joe had thought of that, and he reasoned that they would still consider him a cripple, traveling with a boy. Back at their camp this morning, Joe left the prints of him lying on the edge of the cliff where he watched them, and they could see where Thad had cooked and walked around, saddled the horses, and made things ready; but Joe left no tracks of himself. He wanted to keep the idea that he was still a cripple for a while anyway. The wolf was having a hard time of it, but he kept coming. He was about halfway to Joe, and the men were waiting down below. One man cautiously moved into the gully and drew no fire; he motioned to the men that he could see the top and could not see anyone. He moved a few feet farther in the open, ready to dive into the rocks if need be. Joe did not want to kill anyone if he did not have to. He wanted the man, or men behind these men. If you stop the money, you stop men like these. The man in the gully stood still and looked all around; he had done his job. He motioned the rest of the men to come on. They came into view, just about the time the wolf was clearing the last narrow place; Joe raised his rifle and fired; the wolf fell into the gully dead. The men let out a yell and urged their mounts up the gully. Joe laid his rifle down and started pushing rocks into the gully; the men started firing at Joe but with the rocks and limbs coming down the gully and picking up loose rocks as they came; the men tried to turn their horses but too late. They jumped off and went for cover; the horses broke loose and ran down the gully. One man tried to stay on his horse, and Joe took aim and shot his hat off with a bullet, and he dived for cover. The horses went on to the bottom at a full gallop. Joe still had a couple of rocks to keep the men pinned down; he pushed the next rock after a period of time about when they would think it safe to move on up the gully; he slowed them down. To give Thad a chance to get the loose horses gathered up, Joe added a few bullets to let the men know that he was still here; he thought for a moment, and he spoke to them saying, "I could have killed most of you with the same bullets that I gave the wolf. You had better go back and tell your boss that the next time I am going to start killing." With that for them to think about, Joe went to his horse and gathered up the other horses and rode away; he went to the place that he had told Thad to meet him. When Joe arrived at the appointed place, Thad was not there to meet him, so Joe settled down to wait for Thad; he waited for two hours, and still Thad did not show up. Joe mounted his horse and started over the hill to where Thad should have caught up the loose horses from the other men. Joe was very cautious because he might run upon the men who by now would be walking to find their horses. Joe was coming over a rise and started over the next rise but stopped just under the rim and looked over the rim to check out the terrain before he started over. He stepped down and inched up the slope and looked over the top of the rise, he was looking at the men that were after him; they had stopped and set up camp in a cove in the other hill. They had a fire started and were getting ready to bed down for the night; they had no horses, and this gave Joe something to think about. It may be possible that they are going to stay there and send one person someplace to get more horses. And the rest could move out on foot the next morning. Joe went back to his horse and turned back the way that he had come until he was sure that he was far enough away from them so that they could not hear him. He made a wide circle around the camp and was looking for tracks of men walking, or of horses moving to, or away from the men. Joe did not know what he was going to find; he was hoping that he would find Thad with all of the horses. He did find the tracks of one man walking away from the camp; the prints were a long stride and deep into the sand. One man running away from the camp, the thing that bothered him was that the tracks were of a moccasin track, which left Joe to believe that the Indian was looking for the horses, or Thad, or was going for more horses. He knew that he had to find out, because Thad might be in big trouble, because he was no match for the Indian. Joe looked ahead and planned where the Indian might be going, and he calculated where Thad might be. So Joe turned off to the left and thought he might take a shorter route than the Indian had taken. When Joe turned a little to the left, he came to a rise in the ground; he stopped under a large tree and took out his field glasses and took a good look around the country. He was about to take his glasses down when he spotted something that moved and was not part of the natural country. He looked closer and kept moving his glasses over the underbrush, and he saw a movement again. He felt sure that this was a deer in the thick brush, but the longer that he looked at it, there was something different; he decided to move a little closer when it moved out into the open, and he saw that it was a horse. Not one that he knew, it did not belong to Thad, nor did it belong to the party that was searching for him. He mounted up and held to good cover and moved closer. Where he was the grass was thick and heavy; he moved with little noise. When he came close enough, he stopped and took his glasses and looked at the country over again. He finally saw the Indian move through an opening in the timber. Just a chance that he caught him, the Indian was moving away from him at a fast pace heading back toward Joe's ranch. Maybe after some of Joe's horses, they would certainly be the closest horses to get. Joe turned his attention back to the horse that was in the woods ahead of him; he could not see the horse now, but he knew about where he was. Joe tied his horse to a scrub bush, took his rifle and his rope, and headed out toward where the horse was last seen. The wind was gently blowing toward Joe, and he knew that the horse could not smell him and hopefully would not give an alarm. The one thing that would give Joe away was if he was heard; he was carrying a pair of moccasins in his saddlebag, that sometimes he wore when he was hunting, and he sat down and took off his boots and put them in the saddlebags. He put on the moccasins and started through the woods, stepping cautiously so that he would not break a stick or rustle a stone that the horse or horses could hear. He moved slowly and surely toward the spot. He stopped every few moments to listen and look around; he expected something to happen at any moment but nothing did. After a while, he saw there was an opening ahead of him and moved toward that; he came to the edge of the opening, and he heard low voices coming from the left side of the clearing. He turned that way and stopped behind some bushes and listened; he heard Thad's voice coming through the brush saying, "I am telling you that those men are killers, and they are hunting me and my boss. If they find us, they will kill us, and they will also kill you because they do not want any witnesses. My boss detained them and gave me a chance to get their runaway horses, to slow them up. We have no plans to keep the horses after we get away from them. We will turn the horses loose and let them go." Joe saw a man stand up; this man was a stranger. Joe did not know him, but he had Thad, and he moved toward that man. When he came close enough to see the camp, he saw Thad facing him; he sat tied up on a log. Joe stood up, and Thad saw him right away. Joe put his finger to his lips and made a motion to keep quiet. Thad nodded slightly and looked to the left and the right, and then back to Joe who nodded that he understood. Joe eased closer, and now he could see the horses and two men. Joe moved back into the brush and moved over to his left and went to where he could move in behind a large tree and get real close before he moved back out of the thick brush to where he could see. Thad moved about on the log as if he was uncomfortable or something, and both men turned to look at him, and Joe moved out in the edge of the clearing and spoke distinctly. "Do not move, and you will not get hurt."

Both men were dressed like the average cow puncher would dress; they did not have anything special about them. One man was about six feet tall and rather skinny. He had a two-day-growth beard on him, and he was dirty, the other man was dressed like his partner, but he was heavier in weight and about an inch shorter. He also was dirty, and they both had a look in their eyes that Joe did not like. Their eyes would shift from him to each other, and when he asked them questions, they would not look at him when they answered. They could look to the left of him or the right of him. The men did as they were told; Joe moved out a little more, and he ordered one of the men to drop his gun, stand up, and move around to Thad and cut him loose. The man started to move, and Joe said, "Stop and listen to me. We are running for our life. We do not want to hurt you or anyone else, but I will shoot, and I will kill if necessary, so move very slowly and make no wrong move. Now you." He turned and was looking at the other man. "Drop your gun and stand up and raise your hands and stand very still." The other man did as he was told; the first man had moved over as to go behind Thad and Joe said, "Hold it." He stopped. Joe said, "Thad, stand up and turn your back to me." Thad did as he was told, and Joe said, "Now untie him, and do not get in between us. I will take that action, as you are going to do us harm, am I clear?"

The man said, "Perfectly clear, stranger."

He untied Thad and moved back. "Now, Thad, where is your gun?" Thad motioned to the fire. Joe said, "Get your gun and then go and get our horses and move their guns over to where their horses are."

Thad did as he was told. Joe told the men that there were men about a mile from them to the west and an Indian who was walking away from them to the east to get fresh horses for the other men. "Now we are going to leave you your horses and your guns." One of them looked at the other one and made a motion with his hand, and Joe read the motion that he had better be very careful of these men; they are not to be trusted. "You can do as you wish, but if those men find you, they will kill you and take all that you have. If I were you, I would turn north and get out of here. Joe asked them, "By the way, what you are doing here anyway?"

One man said that they heard that there was cow-punching work to be done in this area and some good money to be made if a man wanted it."

Joe looked at the men and asked, "Where is this place supposed to be?"

The man said, "It was supposed to be to the east of them about twenty miles away."

Joe was thinking to himself that there is not any pasture over that way to handle enough cattle to need wranglers to handle them, but he did not say anything.

Joe asked, "Do you know what the brand of this ranch is?"

The man said, "That is why we stopped this young man and kept him because the same brand is on these horses that we saw him with." Joe said, "I do not know the brand yet. They have been chasing us, and we have not gotten close enough to see the brand, but I would advise you to go to the ranch before you let anyone see you. You can see what has happened to us. We were traveling along, and they started after us, and we were wary of anyone who would start tracking us, and we moved away. I don't know who they think we are, but we want no part of any trouble, that is none of our making."

Thad was behind the men, and he shook his head that he understood and moved away so Joe could handle it. The men said that maybe they could take the horses back to the ranch and find out what was going on.

Joe said, "That sounds like a good idea. Do you mind if we ride away with you? We want to turn north just a few more miles east of here, and we can part company there if that is all right with you."

The older man said, "This sounds like a great idea, and we are glad that this trouble between us is over."

Joe said, "I also am glad that there has not been any trouble between us."

They broke camp, and Joe moved over to Thad and said, "Stay with me no matter what happens." Thad nodded okay. They started to move out; the men were planning on Joe to lead the way and to stay behind them. Joe made as to start on, and as everybody mounted, Joe looked at Thad and said, "Boy, how many times do I have to tell you that is no way to tie your cinch. Get off that horse and do it right."

He turned to the men and said, "I am sorry. Just go around this low hill, and we will be along as soon as I get the boy out of this, man."

And he turned to Thad and winked and said rather roughly, "Listen to me again." And he winked at him.

Thad dismounted and turned to his horse, and Joe whispered, "Take your time." The men started to ride on; they would look foolish if they did not take the lead. As soon as they had moved out, Joe and Thad fell in behind. Joe did not want to turn his back on these men. They traveled to about where Joe had left his horses, and they stopped, and Joe told the men that if he was right in his thinking that the valley they were traveling in it would take them out into about where they might be going. "If we go any farther east, we will have to cross a mountain, but if we turn off here, we can travel around the end of the mountain. Best of luck to you."

Joe said, "Say who owns this spread anyway. I may have heard of him or them."

The man said, "He did not know the man's name. He had only heard of the jobs being offered."

Joe said, "Well, good luck, and be careful of some of the people around here." Joe and Thad moved out heading north; they went a few yards and stopped to listen. They heard the men talking and saying, "Maybe the horses that they now had would be worth much more than they could make at a ranch for a long time. Why not head north with these other guys and maybe come up with two more horses?"

Joe looked at Thad and smiled, but it was not a pretty smile. It was a smile of contempt of how some people are and how crooked they can become. Joe moved out at a good speed and left a clear trail for about a half mile and found the right place where the ground was so rocky that leaving a track was impossible. Joe turned east and moved a zigzag course down an dry old streambed for a half mile and then turned back south along to where they had left their other horses. They stopped every little bit to listen for the two horse thieves and finally smelled a fire; it was too early for anybody to camp, so Joe figured that the other men would wait close to sundown and follow the trail of Joe and Thad. And get a good idea where they were going to be traveling; this way after dark they could go on and try and catch Joe and Thad in their camp asleep and kill them and take their horses also. Joe and Thad dismounted and led their horses around the camp and traveled on south to pick up their supplies and horses. They rode on until well after dark and found a small hollow along a stream of water-fixed supper and cleaned up and repacked the supplies that they did not use for the meal. And had everything put away in case they needed to move in a hurry and tied their horses back into the hollow except for Joe's horse, and Joe kept him close to where he bedded down. Joe had raised this horse from birth, and he knew that this horse was better than a dog, to let Joe know if someone or any animal came close to the camp because he would jerk his head up and snort softly when something came close. Joe put a halter and rope on this horse and tied the end of the rope to his wrist and went to asleep. Along through the night, the horse tightened up on the rope as he lifted his head, but he never jerked his head up, and he did not disturb Joe's sleep. Joe arose the next morning well before daylight; he could hear the morning breeze coming off the mountain and rustling the leaves in the tops of the trees. Joe loved this time of the day and felt that he had missed something important if he missed the moving of wind in the predawn; he was up and moving just as the birds broke into their chorus. He glanced around as his horse jerked his head up and was looking east where the sun would be coming up. His horse started taking in air to snort loudly, and Joe spoke very softly to him, and Joe looked to where the horse was looking; out of the brush about fifty yards away came a black bear. He did not know that they were there; he stopped and stuck his nose up into the air and smelled; he did not like the smell of man and horse and turned and ran back into the brush. Bears can smell very well, but do not have great eyesight. Joe felt that there was little danger from the east because of the bear that was over there. Bears travel many miles, sometimes looking for food, so who really knows where this bear has come from? They would have to be careful traveling in any direction. Joe started a small fire, and he used the same rocks to border the fire that they had used last night; he wanted to eat and put the fire out before daylight; they were using a tree to break up the smoke. As the smoke rises up through a bushy tree even if the leaves have come down, it breaks up the trail of smoke, but in early-morning light it may still be seen, and there is no use in taking a chance. They have a long way to go before Joe would feel that they were safe from detection. Joe needed to find out who his enemy was in order to know from which direction that his enemy would come from. Right now he did not know. Thad and Joe had eaten and packed up the supplies, and Thad said, "Joe, we are getting low on meat. Should we kill a deer or something else? Or find someone to buy our meat from."

Joe said, "For the time being, we will make do and then. We will be far enough away in a couple of days to do whatever we wish. Right now we do not want to attract attention to ourselves."

They made ready and started due south; they traveled steady for most of the day, stopping every hour or so and checked the back trail. Joe wanted to confuse anyone that might be following their tracks, so he saddled the packhorses and the two of them rode and put the packs on their riding horses. A good tracker can tell if a horse is being ridden or traveling without a rider; one never puts a pack on a riding horse unless he has no other way of getting things done, but Joe trained every horse that he has to carry a pack, to ride double to pull a travois. When they came to a place that was rocky, they'd be unable to track the horses except for scratches of their shoes on the rocks. They would switch the horses in some way and when they came off the rocks onto dirt again, there would be a totally different pattern of tracks to follow, and that would confuse the tracker; he would spend time trying to figure out what was going on. Each horse has a different track, like a fingerprint, and someone tracking a horse finds out which horse is being ridden and which the packhorse is and if things change. He has to figure out what is going on, how many riders are there, and how many packhorses are there. Is he making a mistake, are there riders who are light, or heavy? What is going on? On one of these times, Joe took all of the horses but one packhorse, and Thad took the packhorse with a light load and riding him with the load moved away and set up an emergency storage place with food, ammunition. And even extra clothes for both of them and after the things were well hidden, he would meet Joe at another place and join back up with the rest of the horses. After they had three camps set up in places that would be important to them, if they were caught in a sudden storm, if they were cut off by the outlaws from their home camp to have a place to go, it could mean the difference between life and death for Joe and Thad. Anyone who might have followed them probably would never know why there were six horses at some times and only five at the other times. When Thad was riding the packhorse and setting up an emergency camp, Joe would put a pack on his saddle horse and see to it that Thad's horse walked beside the horse that Joe was riding. Because most of the time two people who are traveling together will either travel side by side, or one will follow right behind the other one. So following the tracks it will look like both men are together and maybe one of the packhorses is following right in the tracks of another horse; this might seem odd, but when one does not have a better reason, this one will do. After the three emergency base camps were set up, Joe stopped on a high knoll and took his glasses and looked all over the country. Way to the east, he could see a big plume of smoke; this was a rather large fire maybe a large camp or a house burning or maybe a wagon burning. Joe marked this place on a map that he had been making for years as he traveled around this country. Joe learned to make maps on the move when he was in the army; he would always point out enemy positions, high points that could be used as a lookout or a place that one could use to control cannon fire or watch for troop movements. So Joe in civilian life started drawing the maps of his country when he first came into the land. He had all the water sources on the map, all the lookout places, and even good campsites—three of which now were stocked with supplies and ammunition and extra guns and ropes. Joe stored wood in those places for the past months to use in the wintertime just in case that he would get stranded and need a place to spend a couple of days or even more. Now that Joe and Thad had the places stocked with supplies, they were ready to move out of the country, or at least leave the tracks that would fool anyone who would track them. They now were ready to kill and dry some meat for their campaign; this would also go into the three camps when the time was ready. Joe and Thad moved out of the mountains to the south and out into one of the large valleys; there was not good grass here like there was on Joe's ranch. It would hold some cattle for a short period of time; there were some places that had good grass back in the deep valleys where there was plenty of water. Joe had not told anyone of these places. Years ago, he had taken a rope and horses and pulled old dead trees down so they would lie across the mouth of these valleys, and it looked like the wind had blown them down in a storm. Most people would not walk back into these valleys and see if there was any grass that grew there; if a person did find one or even two of these valleys and some person had seen the grass, they would not think that someone would deliberately pull down the trees to keep others out. Joe would give anybody mostly anything that they needed, but he would try to protect his land; these were times that a man could not own all of the land. There was plenty of land, but most people would move in on a piece of land and not take care of it and put cattle or horses on it and ruin the land. Joe did not have time or men right now to improve this land or buy up these sections that have the water on them, and he is guarding them from the lazy person. Most cowboys do not like to get out of the saddle, and certainly none of the cowboys would like to take an axe and cut some trees out of the way just to go back into some valley to look for grass or water unless they were thirsty themselves, or maybe their horse was in dire need of water. Joe felt that the grass and water were pretty safe from discovery. Joe was not a stingy man; he would give help to any man that needed it; the man did not even have to ask Joe for help. He had gone out of his way many a time to give help to others; the Indians that were back in the mountains one time had needed some help; they were too proud to ask for help. Joe knew that they would come and steal what they needed, but they would not come and ask. He took them some cows through one of the hardest snowstorms that this country had ever seen. He tied ropes over the horns of three cows and tied them to horses and half dragged the cows through the snow to the Indian camp and presented the cows to the Indian chief as a token of peace between them and Joe. They knew that Joe was not weak, and they knew that Joe would fight them with a fierce rage if that was needed; they knew that Joe was trying to help them and let them keep their pride at the same time, and they honored Joe for the cows. Joe came to the camp half froze and had lost one horse in the coming. They took Joe in their camp and treated him until he was well and the storm let up, and they replaced his horse from one of the chief's own stock and sent him on his way back to his home with their gratitude. Joe had never had any problems from the Indians since then. One time Joe had some stock come up missing; he found that there had been a bear that tore down the fence and ran off some of his cows. He took his rifle and went on foot up in the rough mountain country to find his cows; he met the Indians bringing his cows back down the mountain and along with the cows they were bringing the hide from the bear as a token of friendship. Joe accepted the bearskin, and in trade he gave the Indians one of the cows as his gift to them; they laughed as Joe tied the bearskin onto the back of one of the terrified cows and led her back home. The cow was terrified, feeling that the bear was on her back. Joe smiled at the laughing Indians as he started for home with his other cows and one bucking, bawling cow that had its back covered with a bearskin, whose odor is making the cow very nervous. The Indians had told this story around the tribal fires for many years, and indeed may still be telling it to their children and grandchildren even today. This made Joe a legend among the tribe; this is a thing that the Indian liked, something that was worthy to tell and retell for years.

Joe was thinking of this as they rode along always keeping an eye out for any kind of danger that may come up on them. When something caught his attention our of the corner of his eye; they were in a stand of trees and were coming to an opening of the trees. Joe stopped and Thad, sensing that Joe was looking at something, stopped his horse and the packhorses and sat very still. He saw Joe looking off to their left; he looked off to their right and slowly moved his head so he could look straight ahead and kept slowly looking until he was looking in the same direction that Joe was looking; he could not see anything.

But he waited and still looking slowly from left to right and also ventured a look behind them. The trees put them in deep shadows, as if someone in the sunlight, and looking their direction, they would have to search the shadow of the trees very closely to see them and the horses sitting so still. Joe knew that Thad should be aware of everything around them; he kept his gaze on the spot where he saw a movement. His rifle was lying across his legs ready for a moment's use; Joe could pull a handgun about as quick as any man could, but

Joe was very fast with a rifle, and his horse had been trained for just such a time as now. When traveling if Joe would stop him and give him no further command, the horse would sit very still, and if Joe would raise the rifle and shoot, even over the horse's head, a thing which was even hurtful to the ears of a horse, this horse would sit very still. Joe was not sure of what made the movement; it was about two hundred yards away; out of the corner of one's eye is the best place that one can detect movement. When you are looking straight at something, you are looking for a larger movement, but the very slight movement is caught best out of the corner of the eye. If you wanted to move up on game, the game can still see you even if the head is turned away from you, when the animal turns his head slightly away from you, the vision is at the peak. A cat when watching for a prey turns his head away like it is ignoring the pray, but really the cat is watching the pray for the slightest movement. A cat can watch a prey for the swelling of the muscles that will tell the cat that the prey is getting ready to run; this gives the cat an edge on the prey. Joe saw another movement this time he knows what it is; in the grass, there is a deer; the deer is lying down, and every few moments the deer turns his head and look around. The movement is very slight; Joe does not know which way the deer is going to run, so he just waits. They need this deer for meat; Joe gets an idea. He slowly pulls on the right rein, and the horse moved his head to the right. The deer caught the movement and stood up looking around, as he turned his head and looked in the opposite direction. Joe had an instant to make his move; he brought the gun up and fired; the deer leaped forward and fell. Joe put another shell in his gun and waited to see if the deer was going to stay down or get up and run. If a deer is hit in a vital place and you run up on the deer that is shot, they still have the ability sometimes to run for quite a ways. Joe just sat there for about two minutes, and the deer did not move, so Joe and Thad moved out into the open and claimed the deer; they picked the deer up and placed it upon one of the pack animals. This was not a good place to dress out the deer; it is possible that the shot was heard, and someone might come and see what the shot was about. They were traveling again in about two minutes, and they did not stop until they came to a secluded spot and moved back out of sight. They came to a place that the hill above them was not a good place to travel. Joe did not want anyone to come by above them and smell the meat cooking; also there was some large flat rocks that they could cut the meat in strips and lay out on the rocks in the sun and jerk the meat or let it dry out in the sun. They started a fire and cooked as much of the meat as they could, while the rest of the meat dried out on the rocks. They laid out the skin, and while they waited on the meat to cure out, Joe scraped the hide and started stretching it. "There is no need to waste anything that God has given us," he told Thad. "You really put a lot of trust in God, don't you?" said Thad. Joe said, "Yes, I do, Thad, God is the only thing in our life that makes our life worth living, and he takes care of us in good times and in bad times alike."

Thad said, "My dad did not believe that God was worth traveling with. He said that a real man made his own luck, and a real man made his own way and asked no help from anyone."

Joe said, "Thad, I do not want to go against what your dad taught you, but yes, a man is to stand on his own two feet and take care of himself. But there is evil in this world that man cannot see, or hear, or even know when it is close. Thad, there is a spirit world all around us, and we need help to overcome this spirit world, or just to survive in the spirit world. This world is where the good and the evil of men really lurk, like those men who are out to kill us. They are driven by the evil part of this world. They do not know it, but they are driven by the evil spirit of this world. Now if we did not have God on our side, then we would not have any help to overcome the evil that they intend to do to us. But God can if he so desired overcome this evil that is about to overtake us, and he can put them in their place. We have to live our life according to the Bible, which are the teachings of God as to how we are to live our life. That is why I spend so much time reading the Bible and praying so that I know just what God wants me to do in any situation that I happen to come up to. Regardless of what the other fellow does, I have to do that which is right." Thad said that he had the Bible that his mom always read from when his dad was out of the house, but when she heard him coming, she would put the Bible away. Sometimes he would catch her reading and threaten to throw the Bible in the fireplace, but she told him that if he ever did she would take Thad and leave him here to burn in hell. "I do not know for sure what she meant, but it sure made Dad straighten up."

Joe grinned at that and did not comment; Joe stood and started turning the meat on the rocks. Thad jumped up to help him, just then Joe's horse jerked his head up and was looking off to the mountain. Joe grabbed his rifle and stepped out from the rocks to get a better look. He just caught a glimpse of something brown way up the mountain; he relaxed a little bit because he knew that it was a cat that had smelled the meat and blood and had come to check it out, also there was the smell of horses. But with the fire and the man smell, he probably would not come very close, but Joe would keep an eye on that fellow anyway. Joe was gaining his strength back in his legs; every time that he rode for a long period of time, he would get so sore; his legs would cramp, and there was nothing that he could do but get used to riding. He did not say anything to his friend about this; like everything else that bothered him, it was his battle and not Thad's; he was along because he was a good friend, who would do anything for Joe, but it was not his fight, and Joe had to keep him safe at all cost.

When he had Thad far enough away from any danger, then he would turn back and find out what is going on. He had to leave the area and make the enemy whoever that was believe that he had pulled up and run away. They would still try to track him down and kill him, but once he had Thad far enough away, then he would turn back and cut them off the trail and start them looking for him closer to their own home, much closer to their own home. They spent the day where they were drying the meat and getting it ready for storage in the pack so they could eat it or cook it more when they had a need for it. Joe told Thad to keep a close watch on the area, that he was going to back track their trail and see if anyone was following them; he needed to know if they got away clean. "If I am not back by dark, then settle in for the night and keep a fire going and keep cooking the meat. Remember that cat and keep the horses close to you. I should be back by morning. If I am not, then just keep going south until you come to a small valley on your right side. It will have a very small stream coming out of it. It will look like it is nothing, but turn into it and after you go about a quarter of a mile, you will see what I mean about the valley. It widens out, and there is a lot of grass, deer, and other animals—a great place to have a small ranch, or a farm, whatever a man would want. Camp beside the lake there, and I will come to you as soon as I shake these guys. The ground is very hard and rocky all around the mouth of the valley, and you should not leave any tracks so if anyone gets by me, they should not be able to follow you there. If by chance something would happen to me, just stay there. That valley belongs to me and is recorded in town. I have fixed up a paper and put it in the pack with the rest of my clothes and belongings. I have deeded that valley to you. All you need to do is take that paper to the recording office, and they will fix up a deed for you, and you will have your own ranch. I am going back and shake those guys loose from us, until I can figure just who we are fighting and what we should do."

Thad said, "Joe, I am going back with you and help you. I know how bad you are hurting, and I need to be with you to help you."

Joe very sternly said to Thad, "Look, son, this is my fight and not your fight. Now you do as I have told you. If something happens to me and they get me, someone had to be alive to tell what has happened so they cannot get away with it. If they get the both of us and that is what they want to do, then they have won the whole cake. Right now they think they have won the most of the cake, but I am going to make them wish that they had never tasted the cake to start with. My wife and baby girl need me to make things right for them. After I have done that, then my life can go on. But until they have been avenged of their deaths, nothing in my life can go on. These men, whoever they are, must be made to face the law. If they get away with this, some other family will have to face the same thing that I am facing now. They have to be exposed and brought to justice."

Joe packed some of the meat that was dry enough to keep in his saddlebag, some extra cartridges, and one of the larger canteens and mounted his horse and waved goodbye to Thad and rode out. He wanted to get away from camp and make sure that nobody was able to follow them; he would wipe out tracks and clean up the trail so they could not be followed and then maybe look around a bit. As Joe traveled back the same trail that he had came into this country, he stopped and took brush and wiped out all of the tracks that he and Thad had made. It took a long time because he would take a bushy limb and wipe out the tracks, and then he would move off the trail and pick up sand in a blanket and come back and sprinkle the sand over the rubbed-out tracks. Then he would spread fallen leaves over the sand to look like the rest of the ground. There were places the ground was hard, and he could not rub out the tracks; he would find a fallen bush or tree and cover the tracks, and then he would spread sand around the tree and under the fallen tree so someone would have to move the tree or bush in order to find the prints. Joe had covered his tracks and confused Indians before this, and he felt that he could do the same thing here. Joe covered the trail until he ran into some prints that were not theirs; these prints belonged to the two men that had the extra horses and who were supposed to take them to their rightful owners. They had come this way and had crossed their trail, maybe in the middle of the night or something, but Joe took out their tracks and left the other tracks plain to see. Joe wondered where the two men were; he moved away from the trail and covered the tracks of his own horse. Then he went back to where the ground was rocky and crossed the trail that he had covered and went into the direction of the two men. He did not want them to stumble on Thad; he moved a little to the right and found a high place and left his horse in a Laurel thicket. He took his field glasses and his rifle and went up the ridge to get a better look at the country. He stood behind a forked tree and put his glasses over a limb so he could rest his arms and started looking over the country. He traced back and forth; he finally saw the trail in a clearing. The two men and the horses had turned away from the trail that Joe had covered and were moving west; Joe did not know where they were going, and he felt that neither did the men. Joe started to turn away, and he caught sight of a movement in the trees across the valley from him. It was about a mile away; it was a small campfire. The people who had the fire were burning green wood, and the fire was putting off a lot of smoke. Joe moved his glasses carefully back and forth across the base of the hill; finally, he saw a horse raise his head. It was the big bay horse that Joe had taken away from the men who had been following him in the gully, and when he ran into the men that had captured Thad, he gave the men the horses to take back to their owners, and here they were across the valley from him. There was a bunch of horses over there. And a big fire like this did not look right; two men should not have that big of a fire. Joe was wondering about this, and he kept watching the smoke. A few minutes later, he saw a man go up the side of the mountain above the camp; and a few minutes later, another man came down the mountain to where the fire was. Joe turned his glasses higher up the mountain to try and get a look at what might be going on; finally, he spotted the man that had gone up the mountain. He was sitting out on a point of the mountain that could watch for any movement from anywhere in the valley. Joe was glad that he had not blundered out in that valley and been seen. What were they doing there looking for him and Thad? He did not think so. They had a lookout or maybe more than one. Now who are they looking for, or who are they hiding from? Joe did not know. Joe used his glasses to look some more, and he found another lookout, back the way that he had come; maybe these are guards to stop someone who gets too close. They could sit up there with rifles and keep anyone from getting close to them or close to who? Joe needed to know that. But at the same time, he needed to know that Thad was clear out of this area. This was good timber country; the trees were beautiful, and there were so many of them. But these men were not here for the timber; the two men that he had seen were men who were fighting men, not honest working men. He had seen too many men like these in the war. They did not fight for their country or for any cause; they fought for what they could get out of the war. When the heavy fighting was going on, they stayed around the edges and just shot whoever came close to them. He had one in his outfit, and as soon as he came to a large camp, he talked to the major in charge; and he got rid of those men. The major wanted a man for sniper duty, and this man did that job with pleasure. Joe had never shot a man from ambush; he always gave every man a chance to live or quit. When there was no other way, then he killed, but he took no pleasure in killing anyone. Joe marked this place in his mind, and he moved back in the heavy woods and moved on. What was happening there he could not find out now, but he could come back later. Joe came back to the place that he was removing their tracks and found that there was a lot of traffic in that area and the tracks of his horses were lost in the traffic. Joe moved away from the trail that was being used; there were horses going in both directions. Joe kept far enough away from the trail that he would not be seen or heard. But if a large group of horses would come along, he would know, and he would move back in the heavy woods and wait for the traffic to move away from him. He heard a group of horses coming and dismounted and moved his horse into heavy cover and waited until he could see the trail from where he was. He just waited, and as the men came into view, he noticed two of the men that had tracked him and some new men that he had never seen. Some of the men were working cowboys, and some of the men were gunmen looking for trouble. This was not a time for him to be discovered. He was getting a feeling that he was up against a large outfit, but what were they after and what were they doing here? To his knowledge, there was nothing in this area but trees and a little bit of grass.

CHAPTER 5

It was coming upon evening time, and Joe was going to try to get back to Thad before sunset if he could, but where was he going to go to get out of the traffic? And how many directions were the men traveling? Joe moved another half mile away from the outlaw trail; Joe is going to call them outlaws because honest men would not have that many hired guns for honest protection. The Indians now lived in small groups, and they did not want any trouble with the white man. And there was no other group of men that could give them trouble unless they were after the town; *I wonder if there is anything going on in town that these men would be interested in.* Joe decided that he would check on Thad, and then he would circle around these men and go into town. That would mean that he would expose himself by letting everyone know that he was well and could walk. That was something that Joe would have to let happen. Joe kept his horse at an easy pace because he wanted to hear anyone else before they saw him. It would serve no purpose to expose himself and get killed; that would help nobody. Joe crossed over a small hill, and he came upon another trail where a group of men had traveled; he crossed over their trail and stopped and wiped out his tracks, and then he kept going. At full dark, he stopped at a place that he could get back into, out of sight from all directions, where a large tree had been uprooted, and there he made a small fire and made him some coffee. And he chewed on some dried deer meat; he was beaten, and he knew that if he went to sleep in a comfortable place that maybe he would not hear someone soon enough. The night was cool, and he had put the fire out; he leaned at the base of a tree and took the halter rope of his horse in his hand and went to sleep. He knew that his horse could and would give a better warning than he would if he was wide awake. Joe lay down, and his mind was thinking about the things that have happened today and yesterday—about the men that they have encountered. He was puzzled about what it was all about. He felt sleep coming over him, and a picture of Maggie came into his mind. He remembered the time that he and Maggie were on a trip to Richmond, and most of the time they stayed in the wagon at night. But this one night, they were lying on some blankets beside the campfire and looking up at the sky and at the beautiful stars and how a few long stringlike clouds floated across the sky. The moon was just coming up over the mountain, and the light on the clouds was beautiful; Maggie reached a hand over and stroked his shoulder and trailed down to his stomach and said, "Why don't we just stay right here tonight? I think that the sky is so romantic."

Joe smiled at Maggie and said, "I believe this is one of your best ideas." Joe put his arm around Maggie and leaned over to her and gave Maggie a long lingering kiss, and nature took its course that night. Man and woman are beautiful together when love is the factor between them, and Joe and Maggie were two people in love. They had been married now for about two years, and it was about time that they had a child or two. And God gave them what they desired that night. Maggie had Ginny nine months later, and Joe was the proudest man in the world. What more could a man ask God for than what Joe had in his life? And now some evil men had taken away everything on this earth that Joe placed as important in his life. He lay there with tears in his eyes, looking up at the beautiful stars and some long threaded clouds floating overhead, and the moon was shining. The memories were flooding over Joe like waves of water; sleep was not coming to Joe. There was one thing after another coming into Joe's mind, and he could not stop them from coming. Joe decided that he had enough of this, and he would get up and go ahead and ride on tonight. Joe opened his eyes and was shocked that the night was gone and daylight was not far ahead of him. He had slept, and all that he had thought was his feelings instead was dreams; the night had passed so quickly that Joe thought that it had only been an hour or so. Joe arose and splashed some water over his face from his canteen, took a long drink, finished dressing, saddled his horse, rolled up his blanket, and started out to look for Thad. He pondered over the happening of the night, but tucked it in his mind as a good memory of Maggie. It seems that now all he has left is memories of Maggie and Ginny. Joe overtook Thad late in the afternoon just before Thad came to the valley that Joe wanted him to stay at. Joe had wiped out their tracks most of the way and left the rest of them to history. Joe found the opening to the valley. Thad said, "Are you sure this is the place? This does not look like the place that you talked about."

Joe said, "That is why I came back to show you because you can ride on by and never notice this place. I only found it one time when I shot a deer, and it ran into this place, and I tracked down the blood trail, or I would have never found it myself."

Joe dismounted and went back to where they turned into the valley and wiped out everything from a rocky place to the entrance of the valley. They moved on and came up to the lake; Thad looked around with a big smile on his face and said, "Joe, this is the most beautiful place in the world. I love it." Joe said, "I thought that you would. There is another way into this valley over on the other side of the old town of Bender."

Thad said, "Isn't that place a ghost town?"

Joe said, "That town was a boomer at one time; they thought they had a silver strike, with a little gold here and there. But the gold turned out to be iron pirate, and the silver was such a poor grade that it was worthless. There are some other buildings, but now there is just the one man who is setting up store in the old saloon. I do not think that there is anybody else living there. He sells food, and hardware not much, but he carries a little bit of any of the essentials that you would need. If you need anything before I get back, go out through that low gap in the mountain and down through that valley, and you will come to the town from the back side. If I were you, I would circle around and come in from the west side of town, and there would not be any questions. But if you come in from the east side of town, he would wonder where you came from. It is not time for anyone but you and me to know of this place. We might need it bad before all of this is over."

And Joe told him what he had seen back along the trail and the number of men that he had seen. "If I were you, I would build a corral for the horses, and over there at the base of the hill beside that stream would make a good place to put up the tent and would be a good place to stay. It is going to get cold before long, and you are going to need a warmer place than this tent to live in. There are plenty of good flat stone over next to the stream. I saw a large shelf and some cliffs along that hillside and plenty of sandstone lying around. I believe there is enough to make a good fireplace, and if you clean the dirt off over here on this little rise, you will find enough flat stone to make a good floor for your home and build a rock building to live in. I will be back in about a week, and if you will clean off enough space and use your packhorses to bring in enough stone, I will help you build the fireplace and chimney and start the foundation of the house. God gave you everything here to make a great home to live in."

Thad said, "Joe, you do not want me to be with you anymore."

Joe said, "I cannot think of anyone that I would rather have with me than you, but I want you to be happy, and I have a lot of people out there that want me dead for some reason, and I may not make it through this. But you are going to stay here and build you a life, and man, I want you to live that life for God. If you go out for supplies, one of the things that I want you to buy is a Bible." That said, "But, Joe, I have a Bible—the one that my mom had." Joe placed his hand on Thad's shoulder and said, "Son, my Bible was burnt up in the house along with my family, and I need a new one. When you go into Bender, take a little time and just listen and see what everyone is talking about. Don't do anything that is dangerous or take sides no matter what is said about me or anything else. Just stay in the background and listen, come back here as soon as you can and take time to cover your trail."

Joe sat down and ate supper and went to bed soon after because this might be the last night that he can sleep soundly knowing that he is safe. After a good night's sleep, Joe woke up well before daylight; the morning wind is feeling a chill in the air, which is coming down off the mountain. This makes a coat feel good on a morning like this, but Joe likes everything about this morning. How can you not like a day when you can look out over a piece of country that has everything, some low mountains or hills, depending on where you come from? But the trees are just starting to turn color, maybe a good rain, or definitely a frost will start the leaves of these trees to become a wonderful scenery of color, more colors than a person could name. Even right now, a person could not name all of the different colors of green; the grass is many different colors of green, the bushes are different, and all of the trees are different color of green. This just tells me that God has placed all of this here to show man that he made it all and made it all different. God tells us in everything that we look at who he is. He is a god that did not just make us a world. He made us a fabulous world. He did not just make things pretty. He made this world beautiful. This should tell us how God feels about man that he placed here on this earth. He saddled up and packed an extra blanket and a heavy jacket along with the rest of his gear on one of the packhorses because he was going to be out for a while. Thad still wanted to go with Joe to help keep him safe, but Joe was firm about Thad staying here. "If this campaign is going to last for a while, we will need a place for winter, and you know that it will get very cold in the winter. We need a cabin and a place to keep horses and some cattle. When we get ready, we will go back to the ranch and bring a herd of cattle back here and keep them safe also. We do not know what these people have in mind, so we must salvage all that we can. I am going back out and establish a camp and store some much-needed food and others in case we get cut off from this base camp. We will have options to go to. When the snow gets so deep, we will need to be able to make short journeys instead of having to come back here."

Joe saddled up and left the valley; he went over the mountain. It was a hard climb, but he had horses raised in this country that had the ability to survive in the country and were also able to get around in the deep snow. Joe noticed the horses that he had seen were tall and slim-built horses; they were good working horses, but they were not any good in the deep snow. Joe stopped at the top of the hill and studied the land before him; there did not seem to be anybody around, so Joe started down the other side of the mountain. Joe started making his way east; it seemed that the riders were coming and going to the east, so Joe decided to travel that way.

And see what he could find out. Joe was looking at the country; it had been a long time since Joe had been in this country. There were beautiful mountains and trees. But the grass was very thin, and there was very little water. The country was composed mostly of brush and briars. This was good for deer to hide in, but cattle could not live here for long. Joe traveled along the edge of the mountain and kept out of sight; every half hour, he would angle up on the mountain away and take his glasses and look out over the large valley. There was still nothing to see. Maybe Joe was wrong; maybe there was nothing in this area of the country, and he was chasing a bad idea. Along about dark, Joe came around a bend, and things changed; he started seeing cattle, just a few, browsing here and there. He took his glasses and took a look at the brand on these cows; now Joe nicked the ear of his cattle because there were not many different herds around this part of the country, and he did not go through the trouble of branding. His ear nick was registered and just as legal as a brand. The brand that he was looking at was a bar C bar; this is one that he had never heard of. These brands must be a new brand, or this brand was from some other part of the country; he had seen this brand on three of the horses that the first men that he had seen were riding. Joe wondered what was going on. Where did these cows come from? How many cows were moved in here? Who owned these cows? And where were the cows going? There was no grass in this area to last cows for more than a couple of months, and then this area would be ruined for pasture for years. Joe moved back up on the mountain so he could look at the cows and try to get a number and find out where the people were who owned the herd. He worked his way back up the mountain, and taking his glasses, he scanned the country until there was not enough light to see anymore. At about dark, he had topped out the mountain and was sitting out on a point looking over the country; he could see the cattle, and there were a lot of them. He also saw a herd of horses; he would estimate five thousand cows and about three hundred horses. This was a pretty big outfit for this country, but not big enough to support all of those guns. He had about 1,500 cows on his spread and was looking to bring in about the same amount of cows very soon to fill out his range. This herd looked like good stock, but they would not be good stock for very long. And as long as Joe controlled the water that he had, nobody could bring in this kind of herd and survive, and it hit Joe what was going on; he controlled the water, and he had no heir, what would happen to the water rights if something happened to Joe, and it could be proven that Joe was dead? Who would get his property then, what legally would happen to the ranch and the water rights if there was no heir? Joe had thought about making out a will and leaving all of his property to his family, but that would have done no good now, because Joe did not have a family.

Joe decided that he had to make some fast moves to protect his friends and his life before this went any farther. Joe made up his mind that whoever was doing this would not get by with it, and he would take steps to head this thing off and to put these people where they could not do this same thing to anyone else, or he would die trying. Joe watched until late in the night; he saw campfires close to the herd, with his glasses he could make out a few men; these would be the men that are taking care of the cattle and horses. These would be the honest cow hands, and he had no trouble with them. The person that he wanted was the one who was so protected over in the timber valley—the place that was so guarded. Joe slept for about two hours, and then he tightened his cinch and started on. He had to set up his emergency camps first; these had to be in place before anything else was going to happen. At daylight the next morning, Joe was miles away from the top of that ridge and was in a deep valley—a sheltered valley—where at one time there had been a great windstorm and had torn down a lot of big trees. This area was very difficult to travel through for anyone coming into this valley and seeing all of this destruction; anyone who did not know this area would turn around and go a safe way around this place. But Joe had shot a bear, and it started running. Joe knew that he had put a fatal shot into the bear, but it would try to get to its den and die there. But Joe had tracked the bear into this area and had gone into it on foot and finally found his bear; it was dead from his bullet. That bear had taken a calf of Joe's and had to be terminated. Once a bear finds easy pickings like calves, he will keep coming back for more. Now a black bear eats mostly fruits, nuts, ants, and things like that but given a juicy calf, he will kill it and just eat some of it and will move on to other things. Joe found the place that he was looking for; it was a small cave where water had eaten out some soft material and left a nice dry place that two or three people could stay in dry. And Joe was planning on storing some of the dry meat and bullets and a change of clothing and material to cut some wood and start a fire. Joe had stayed one night here, and he had found a rock that was about the same size of the opening; he had thrown a rope on it and pulled it to the front of the cave a couple of years ago, and now he was glad that he had done so. The reason he had done it to start with was that he might be in this area and need a quick shelter, and he did not want to crawl in here and find that a bear or a cat had found it first, because they do not like to share their caves with anyone. Joe stored his supplies; he staked out his horses and let them rest and eat while Joe looked around. There was no sign that anyone had been here in a long time, but Joe scouted around anyway. He walked up to the top of the ridge to get a good look at the area and found that there had been four horses traveling through there about three weeks ago or less; three weeks ago, there had been a hard rain and would have washed away these tracks, so it was less than that. Men are searching for him and Thad; well, since they have already seen this place and would not figure to come here again, this would be a good place to lie low if needed. This place was close to his ranch and close to Mr. Lincoln's ranch, so Joe would finish up here, spend the night, and go to Mr. Lincoln's ranch in the morning. Joe had a thought—they would have Mr. Lincoln staked out waiting for Joe; they would also have the town staked out waiting for him there also. He told Thad to go to Bender, not thinking that they would also have that place staked out; Joe broke out in a sweat. He may have sent Thad to town to get himself killed, but there was nothing that he could do about that right now. Thad was a smart young man; he knew that they would want to find him, and through him find Joe. There was nothing that Joe could do now but pray to God for protection for Thad. And he was doing just that as he was walking back down the hill to the cave; he was almost at the cave, and he still could not see his horses. He thought that this is good. *We are hidden better than I thought.* Just as he started to come out of the brush, he heard something; he stopped and listened. "I am telling you that those tracks were from the same horse that Joe Manning was riding when he left the ranch. I will remember that print for as long as I live." The other voice said, "I believe that we are trailing some hunter and not that guy; he is plumb out of the country now. I don't care what those other guys are saying. I tell you that he is gone like a rabbit scared to death and a good thing too because I would kill him and collect my reward and get out of this awful place and have some fun."

Joe stepped out in front of them; his rifle was held loosely in his left hand. "Howdy, fellows, what can I do for you and why are you tracking me?" Joe knew that he had startled them, and this was good, for a startled man will make mistakes, rather than the man who has his thoughts about him. The men stopped and went for their guns; the thought never crossed Joe's mind that there was two against one; he did not think—he just reacted. His muscles had a mind of their own; Joe did not have a choice. He drew and fired; he saw the look in the first man's eyes—the look of death. The man let out a gasp; he dropped his pistol and started to slide out of the saddle. He looked at Joe, and his eyes were glazing over, and he died; all of this happened in a second. Joe did not look at him. And Joe turned his gun on the second man and shot again, just as the man was clearing his holster with the gun; the man dropped his gun and toppled out of the saddle. He swung his gun back on the first man, but the first man was dead before he ever hit the ground. The other man was still alive, and Joe went to him and moved his gun, away from him; the man looked at Joe. He had a puzzled look on his face, and he said, "I did not know that you could shoot that good. They never told us."

Joe said, "Who sent you after me?"

The man looked at Joe and finally said, "Mr. Cole."

Joe asked, "Why is he trying to kill me?"

"He needs your land," said the man.

Joe asked, "Where are they now and how many men are there?" But there was no response; there would never be another response. The man was dead. Joe was hunkered down talking to the man; Joe sat there and looking around. There could be more men within earshot and have heard the firing, but Joe did not hear anything or see anything.

Well, Joe did not have a choice now; he had to go to town and take these men in to the sheriff and tell him what happened. Joe also knew that the friends of these men would be after him, and they would stay after him until he was killed or they were. The choice was not his; he did not take this fight to them, and they tracked him down and drew on him. Anyone can see that there were two of them and one of him, and anyone can see that they were both shot by a pistol and both of them was shot from the front. But the sheriff will want to hold Joe in town until there can be a hearing, and that would be the death of him. He loaded both men on their own horses and tied them down; getting his horses, he started for town. He rode up on the side of the mountain to avoid any travelers; he did not want advance notice that he was coming to town. He wanted to be the surprise for everyone, and that may be the only way that he will get out of town alive. Now it will be an all-out war; for the protection of Thad, he is going to have to lie to the sheriff and the townspeople because he is going to tell them that he is alone and Thad is no longer with him. Right at this moment that is the truth, but in reality it is not the truth. But in order to not put a death sentence on the head of Thad, he is going to lie to everyone; he knows that this kind of news will spread very quickly. The other side will hear it just as quickly in a day or two. At the most, everyone will know that Thad took off and left him. He can explain later, if Thad is still alive; and if he is not, then it would not matter anyway.

Joe needs to get word to Mr. Lincoln who he has to talk to, because he is also in danger along with his own family. Joe is searching the immediate area and has not found anyone else in this area, so maybe they just send two men teams to certain areas to search for him. Well, soon they will know that something is wrong in this area and will send more men to this area, but Joe will not be in this area. He is moving toward town and will get there late in the evening; he will circle around and come into town close to where Sheriff Toby Griffin's office is, so he will be shielded from the saloons on the other end of town. He is traveling at a good pace; he does not have to worry about covering his track. He just needs to make sure he does not run into a group of men and have to fight with them also. It would not do to have to take any more dead men into town at this time.

Joe reached the edge of town; it seems that it has been a long time since Joe has come to this little town of no name. People who have settled here it seems are from all parts of the country. No, that is not quite right. They had come from all parts of the world. There are so many people who have such a vastly different culture and different ways of living, different ways of looking at things. And they have melted into one group of people, a town which has no name; they have, through different opinions and different religious beliefs, come together and have formed a government. They have set down a set of laws to live by and govern their town and their people to make it safe and honest for every person who comes into their town. Joe is sitting on his horse and leading other horses—one of them is his packhorse; the other two are carrying their riders tied across the saddle facedown. Joe looked down the tree-lined street; he remembered the vote of the town council to leave the big oak tree along the street and never cut them unless they become dangerous to someone. To leave them for beauty of the town and for shade in the hot summer days. Most of them have homemade benches sitting around the trunk, under the branches where folks can stop and chat with each other anytime that they feel like it. This is a practice that almost everyone in town has taken advantage of; they come out of their hot stores and visit under the shade of the trees on a hot day when business is light. Joe helped some of these merchants build their stores and get their goods under shelter and away from the elements. He is sitting there thinking of how things have changed in his life; he heard horses approaching from behind him, and he broke out of his thoughts and urged the horses forward. He just had to cross the street, and he is in front of the sheriff's office. He is stepping down in front of the office when five men come around the bend of the road; he stiffened his body ready for trouble when they come into view. But here came the sheriff in front of a group of men, Joe relaxed a little because he does not know some of these men, and he is still on guard. Toby Griffin, the sheriff, yells at Joe, "Man, where have you been? We have been out scouring the hills for you and Thad. Joe, you are walking. When did this come about? Wow, I am so glad to see you. Joe, what is going on?"

He looked at the two dead men tied across their saddles. Joe noticed for the first time that three of the riders that were with him have separated themselves from the others and have moved to the far side and are facing Joe, and Joe is facing them, and his hand is menacingly close to his pistol. The sheriff can see in a moment that something is wrong. Everyone back down. He said, "Eddie, come out here and bring the shotgun."

The office door opened quickly, and Eddie, the deputy, came out the door and seeing something is wrong he stepped up beside the sheriff and turned the gun in the direction of the men that the sheriff is looking at. "What is going on?" And this time, he is looking directly at Joe. Joe said, "There is someone who is trying to finish the job of killing me off. They came back to the ranch and tried to kill me again as you already know. I tried to leave the country. Thad has already left the country. I had a couple of things that I needed to do and came back into the country. Yesterday, these two men came upon me and tried to finish the job, but they were not good enough to do it. I brought them in to you because that is the lawful thing to do. I am not going to do that anymore. The next time that some of those men—and he was looking at the three men sitting on their horses in the street—come after me, they will stay where they lay, because they are hunting me, and there are a bunch of them against one man. This group of men are really a bunch of brave men—and he pointed his finger at the men—tell your leader that from now on, if you come into my sights, I will pull the trigger, and you can lie and wait for the buzzards to clean up the country. I won't make this trip again." "Who are these men, Joe, and why are they after you?" asked the sheriff. Joe said, "I do not know, but they are from the same bunch that killed my wife, and my daughter, and burnt my house down a few weeks ago."

When Joe said the part about killing his wife and daughter, one of the men sitting in the street jerked back like someone slapped him in the face. But he did not say anything, Joe saw the reaction and went on. "You know, Sheriff, it takes a bunch of really brave men to shoot down an unarmed man working in his field and leaving him for dead. And then kill a defenseless woman and child in their own home. It takes a special kind of man to work for an outfit such as that."

Toby caught on to what Joe is saying, and he added, "When all of this is worked out and finished, everyone that has anything to do with hurting your family or that work for any outfit that does that kind of murder well. All parties will swing from the same kind of rope regardless of whether they were there or not. Because all of it will be of the same crime and the same punishment. I certainly would not want to be a part of that; I certainly would not want to swing for something that I did not even know about."

At this, Toby turned to the men that he had rode in with and thanked them for riding with him to try to find Joe. "It seemed that Joe did not need us to find him. You, men, go on over to the saloon and get a drink on the county." He turned to Joe and said, "What in the world is going on?"

Joe said, "I do not know for sure, but someone is out to kill me and maybe take over my land. There is a large herd of cattle over the mountain in a long valley to the east. I saw them the other day. They are carrying a bar C bar brand. I have never seen or heard of that brand before. There is not enough water or grass to handle a herd that size. It would take my place to handle a herd that size, or maybe my place and Mr. Lincoln's ranch also. I believe that they are in danger just the same as I am. Could you get them word? I am going to have to keep on the move in order to dodge the amount of men that are after me. Thad is gone. He . . ." Joe paused, and then he said, "I hope he will not be back until this is over." The sheriff said, "Where are you going, Joe, to be safe?"

"I do not know," said Joe. "Maybe west of here, find me a job at punching cows for a while. I would have to have thirty men to back me if they are after my place, and I sure cannot afford that."

"I do not know what I can do," said the sheriff. "I do not have anything to go on. I cannot arrest anyone if I cannot prove that they are the guilty ones, now can I?"

"I know what you are up against," said Joe.

"Where did you lose the tracks of the men that killed my family and burnt my house down?" asked Joe.

"I trailed them on past Mr. Lincoln's ranch, and they disappeared in the mountains beyond. I just thought that they kept on going and covered their tracks as they went. I am sorry, Joe, that I let you down." The sheriff hung his head.

Joe said, "I know that you tried, and that is all that I can ask of you. Is there anything happening here?" asked Joe.

"What do you mean?" said the sheriff. Joe said, "Oh, I don't know it is just that I have been out of touch with everybody and was just inquiring about news of the town." Toby said, "Oh, everything is about the same. Nothing much changes around here."

CHAPTER 6

Joe said, "I had better leave now. I am in the open too much here, with all that is going on now; I need to be going. I am pushing my luck staying in town this long. They could be coming to town right now and could lock up this place, and I could not get out of town alive, so I will see you."

Toby said, "What do you mean when I see you? Joe, you are going to have to stay in town until we have a hearing on these killings, you know that."

Joe said, "That would be a death warrant to me, and you know it, Toby. Figure out when you want to hold the hearing, and if I can get back here I will do it. If not, I will find a lawyer and send him back to take care of it for me."

Toby said, "Where will you get a lawyer?"

Joe said, "I believe I will go over to the state capital and change my land over to some way of protecting it against someone killing me and taking my land."

Toby said, "Can you do that, Joe?" He looked kind of surprised.

Joe said, "I do not know, but that is better than spending the rest of my life looking over my shoulder, if that is what is going on around here. I am leaving now. I don't even feel safe to eat at the diner. I am too exposed to gun fire. Tell the doctor and his nurse that I am doing all right now. I will see them when it is safe to come back into this part of the country."

Joe turned to mount up, and Toby said, "Joe, look down the street."

Joe followed his gaze and saw Beverly Waters coming toward them, smiling like a ray of sunlight. She was almost to them, and Joe just waited to see her. She picked up her pace when she came closer and stuck out her hand and grabbed Joe by the hand with a surprisingly strong grip; she said, "Joe, I have been so worried that something terrible has happened to you. Where have you been, and when did you start walking, how did it happen, how are you now?"

Joe said, "Slow down and give me a chance to answer your questions."

Beverly said, "My uncle is in town, and he is worried about you, and my aunt is ready to call the army and send them out to look for you. She said she was really not worried, but she just wanted to know how you were going to get around when you cannot even walk. She said that, but she really means that she is worried sick about you; they are at the diner and would love to see you. Why don't you just walk down there with me and talk to us for a minute?" Joe looked all around and decided that this would be his best chance to get all of this over with at one time. There are too many people in town for someone to just shoot him in the street, and he would have to get out of town anyway, so maybe after dark would be a better time. He took Beverly by the arm and grabbed the reins of his horses, and they walked down the street along the edge of the sidewalk, and he and Beverly stayed on the boards to the diner. Joe went into the diner after tying his horses to the hitch rail; he is still looking up and down the street; he is also looking at each window and between the buildings, but he has not seen anybody that looked out of the way. Mr. and Mrs. Lincoln are sitting at a table when Joe and Beverly walked into the diner. Every eye turned to see them as they come into the dark room after being out in the sunlight. Joe swept the room with his glance. He knew everyone there and the owner of the diner, its cook, waitress, and greeter; and she came out from behind the counter and grabbed Joe with a hug and told him how glad she is to see him walking. "Sit down and get the best meal of your life, Joe . . ." And she faltered. "Since . . ." She looked at Joe, and Joe patted her on the shoulder and said, "I know, Abbie, I know."

Mr. and Mrs. Lincoln were standing when Joe came to their table, and he hugged her and shook hands with Mr. Lincoln; they sat down, and he told them all that has been going on about the attack on his camp, how that when he was about to be killed that he lunged and found that he could use his legs. He did not make the event colorful; he did not need to. He just told of how many men came at them and how many were left standing at the end, how Thad had taken them into town, and then they left the area. He told them that he escorted Thad out of the area and told him not to come back. A lot of people were listening, and he knew that the tale would be repeated many times, so he did not add anything that would give him away later.

"What are you going to do now?" asked Abbie. "If it is any of my business."

"I am going to the state capital and try to find a way to protect my property even if I get killed."

They started eating, and he said in a very low voice, "Mr. Lincoln, I need to have a very private talk with you this evening. You also may be in danger."

Mrs. Lincoln and Beverly were talking about something and did not hear the remarks that he had said. Joe said, "I need to figure out a way of getting out of town without getting shot on the way. I do not know who my enemies are. I know what some of the men look like, and there are a bunch of them, far too many to just get rid of me."

Mr. Lincoln said in a voice loud enough for most of the people to hear, "Joe, come over here with me. I want to show you something. They have a new way of branding our cows that is better even than the way that you clip the ear of your cows."

They moved to the other side of the room where there were some select items of interest to the cow people who come into the diner. They were standing with their backs to the people, and Joe was telling Mr. Lincoln about the herd of cattle, and where it is, and about the camp of gunmen and cowboys in another camp, with the guard sentries out for protection. "Mr. Lincoln, I believe that they are going to need your property also, and that means that they will have to also get rid of you and all of your heirs, to take over your land and cattle. Why else would they need so many men? I cannot think of any other reason why they need so many men."

Ken Lincoln looked at Joe and said, "Now that makes sense. It just never did make sense that they would kill you and your family. I kept wondering why your family also. Even if they had some type of grudge against you, why kill your family? But now with this news that you have found, it does now make sense, and I have to do something to protect my family, all of my family. We have been thinking about going over to the railroad and taking a ride maybe to Washington DC or someplace and let these folks at least think that we and my men are in town. They can take care of the ranch while I am gone. They could even be a big help to you, but you are going over to the capital on some business." He was looking at Joe, and Joe slightly shook his head no. Ken caught on and said, "What better way to flush them out than to let them think that you were going to tie up your deed, pretty smart thinking. Joe, you always did have a good head on your shoulder."

They talked over the different things that had happened in the past, and how possibly that could have an effect on what was happening right now, and nothing else made any sense. But they left all the cards on the table, so to speak because neither one of them had any idea for sure what was actually happening. They decided that the best way to get out of town was to go to the hotel as to spend the night and head out in the morning, it was clouding up about dark, and it would probably be raining in the morning. Mr. and Mrs. Lincoln went with them to the hotel and Joe put his horses in the hotel barn, along with the other horses of the guest, with the instructions of the hustler to have his horses saddled and ready to go at daylight. The Lincolns went on up to their room, and Joe and Beverly sat in the lobby talking while making sure that both of them were well shielded from the street windows—behind the hotel registry desk so someone would have to come into the lobby in order to see them clearly. They visited exchanging details about what had happened to Joe and how he got the use of his legs, and how that God had taken care of him in giving him back his legs, and how her work was going on with Dr. Abernethy. It was quite apparent that she was very fond of Abb. And felt that he was a very skilled doctor, and he was quite a man also. Joe thought that he detected rather strong feelings between them and was glad that they were getting along quite well. He inquired about other people in the town that he knew and also asked about any strangers that the doctor had treated, especially bullet wounds, and found that there were not any. She finally excused herself and went upstairs to her room, and Joe found a couple of news papers in the lobby and busied himself with them. Joe caught the night clerk as he passed by and inquired about the cattle buyers that were in town. It seemed that there was just one at the moment, and he did business out of the saloon. Well, this was out of the question. Joe asked where he was staying and found that he was staying in the hotel. Joe asked the clerk to tell the buyer that he would like to see him when he comes into the lobby to pick up his room key. And when the night clerk went on about his business, Joe went back to reading his newspaper. A couple of hours later, a man rather late in years in his midfifties or early sixties, a short man, well built, with gray hair and a jolly type of face that could and did laugh a lot. Dressed in jeans, a gray cotton shirt buttoned at the collar, cowboy boots on, no spurs, with a casual type of black jacket on, and no hat came over to Joe and asked him if he was the man that wanted to talk to a cattle buyer. Joe stood up and greeted him. Joe was a head taller than the other man; they shook hands and sat back down. Joe asked him if he was interested in buying some stock.

The man said that he was. "So far," he said, "my trip here has netted me nothing worthwhile."

Joe asked, "If I might ask, why are you here? This is not the time that most ranchers would look to be selling off their herds." The man said that he had gotten a kind of idea that a large herd was coming to this area, and there did not seem to be any place for them to find pasture, and he did not have any place to be right at this moment. So he thought that he would spend some time here and see what was going to happen. But evidently his information was false because there is no herd here, and they seem to have fallen off the face of the earth. He said, "I have not asked any pointed questions. I have just listened, and some cattle have come this way, but they must have gone on through to some other place."

Joe told the man what had happened to him and his family; the man's face turned red and flushed. It was quite apparent that he was extremely angry and upset about this news. Joe asked him if he had moved money into this area, and he said that it was in the works right now. That he was planning to make this a central point for his company, and he would like to have a large amount of money in this area. Really in this bank so he could make any deals in this state, other states close by. Joe told him about the men he had seen a few miles out of town and made a suggestion that he hold off on the transfer of the money. Joe said, "I would like to sell you some cattle, but I do not know just how to do it. They are on my ranch. I have no men, and I cannot even get to the ranch safely to move the herd to the railroad loading pens. I could not even meet with you safely to close the deal, and I surely would not want to take a large amount of money in the shape that I am in now."

They talked for a long time; they came to know something about each other, their thoughts, and their values as to what kind of men each one of them were. And this cannot be done in a few moments, and they finally came to an agreement as to the terms, and the man told him that he had met a cattleman with a crew of men at the railroad yards who had nothing for his men to do right at this moment. He knew Dr. Abernethy, and he could be the broker for the two of them, taking care of the count of the cattle. Joe also told him about the herd that he wanted to cut out and move out with the main herd. He would be there to take the small herd away from them and move it to another location. This was a rather odd arrangement but a perfectly legal one; the arrangement of the money was also worked out at the same time. The buyer knew the herd of cattle and had already seen most of them, when he came out to Joe's ranch to talk to him about the sale. Folks told him some of what had happened and thought that Joe might want to sell his herd and leave this area; everyone thought that Joe would never walk again. But thankfully that has not happened, and they would take care of this deal, and nobody needed to know any difference, until it was too late to do anything about it.

Joe excused himself and went upstairs and tapped on the door of Beverly and apologized for coming to her room, but stated that he needed a word with her, and he would do the talking from the hallway. She said no, he would not stand in the hallway; she took his hand and almost pulled him into the room. He quickly told her what had happened downstairs and asked her if she would talk to Abb about this.

She said she would be glad to do anything for him.

Joe looked at Beverly, and he could see that her eyes were constantly looking into his eyes; she held onto his hand much longer than necessary to pull him into the room. Joe felt his heartbeat increase, but he dismissed it, because of his feelings for his late wife. Joe felt awkward with the feelings that he was having in himself, but he dismissed it, but he was having a hard time tearing himself away from those beautiful eyes of Beverly; Joe stepped back and started to leave. He was twisting his hat in his hands, not knowing just how to graciously leave. He thanked her and started to leave. She came to him and kissed him lightly on the lips and said, "Please take care of yourself. You are very special to me." And she stepped back with a kind of flushed look on her face. Joe also had a strange look on his face as he backed out in the hallway. Instead of going back down the stairs to the lobby, he turned and went down the backstairs and eased the door open to the rear of the hotel and stepped through closing the door quickly and silently. Stopping in the dark doorway, he stayed in the doorway for a long time listening and trying to see anything in the deep shadows of the night. Joe stepped down the three steps to the ground; it was grassy, and his boots made no noise as he slowly moved along the wall to the corner of the building. He removed his hat and looked around the corner of the hotel and could see nothing. He moved toward the hotel stable and working in a wide circle, he stayed back into the trees; this time of the night there were only small sounds like the frogs croaking, the crickets, and occasionally a hoot owl, or a night bird; there was music coming from the saloon, the sound of glasses, and some laughter occasionally. Joe moved through the woods and underbrush without a sound; he was coming around to the back of the stable, and he heard a cough, followed by a "Will you be quiet?" "I cannot help it. I am taking a cold." "If he hears you, it could be a fatal cough because if he doesn't shoot you, I will." Joe spotted them in a small building on the front side of the stable. Joe slipped through the back door of the stable, and every horse that he passed he rubbed the horse a moment and went on to the next; he found his horse. And true to form to a lazy man, the hostler only loosened the cinch of his horses but did not take the saddles off the animals. Joe tightened the cinches and eased the horses out of the rear door of the stable and out through the meadow. He walked beside his horses until he is a good way off and only then did he step into the saddle, because he did not want the hidden men to hear the creak of leather. Joe is very wary of anyone that is out in the night, because they probably are not his friends. Joe headed for his ranch; he did not think that they are ready for him to move any of his cattle, at least not tonight.

So he was working his way into the valley; he was staying along the edge of the mountain in the darkened shadows of the trees. The moon was not very bright, but if anyone was watching, they would not see him against the darkness of the trees; he is very cautious and intent on detecting any smell like smoke, coffee, even a cigarette; but so far he has not detected anything. At sun up, he is on the mountain about halfway up the mountain that is overlooking his valley and one of the herds of his cattle. Joe knew about how many cows are in this herd, and this is about how many that he wanted to move to the new location. Joe moved back into a little hollow and tied his horses close to a small stream that is coming down off the mountain, and he took his glasses and rifle and moved out on a ridge to look everything over. He lay down under a nice shady tree and started looking the land over, starting very close to him and sweeping back and forth and moving away from him until he has covered the entire area and nothing is seen out of the normal. The country is still the most beautiful place that God has made on his part of the world, and he felt blessed that God chose him to have this part of the country to take care of. He lay there for a couple of hours and relaxed his tired muscles, watching his cattle grazing on the rich green grass, with not a care in the world. He finally got up and started back to his horses, and he stopped; he smelled smoke from some place; he froze in place. He must find that fire before it is put out; he searched the valley again, and he can see nothing. He turned and looked up the mountain, searching back and forth; and he saw just a trickle of smoke coming out of the hollow higher up the mountain from where his horses are tied. Then he remembered that the guards over in the valley where the outlaws are camped had their guards high up in the mountain. If he had not come into this area in the night time, they would have seen him long before he gotten this close to them; he is going to have to remember to look higher up for the sentries that are covering any particular area. Joe started moving up the mountain; he took his time and moved with extreme caution. He must not step on a stick that will break. He must not step on a rock that will come loose and roll down the steep hill and make a noise; at night such sounds would alert the guards that someone was in their area because an animal would not normally make such sounds. Joe was taking his time through the underbrush and stopping every now and again, looking for tracks because he would not want to cross a path that they might be using; he is keenly aware of any sound or smell that might locate them for him. After he has gone up the mountain about one hundred yards, he started moving around the mountain into the hollow, being aware that at least one guard should be on the point behind him. And not knowing just when they change the guard, he would not know when someone would be coming from behind him. He found the path that they came down the mountain, but not around the mountain; maybe they were guarding the next point ahead of him and not the one behind him. Joe moved on down the mountain; he heard a horse stamp his foot probably fighting flies; he did not want to come up upon the horses first, so he moved back around the mountain to his left from where he had come. After he moved about thirty yards around the mountain away from the horses, then he moved lower down the mountain. He came to a rock cliff that he had not known that it was there, maybe this is why they are so high on the mountain; being above a rock cliff gave them security from someone coming up from below upon them. But it also locked them in so they could not descend farther down the hill if they were approached from above. So they would be guarding from someone coming at them from above, that is why they tied their horses above them. These men knew what they were doing; Joe was coming up against previous soldiers, because they knew how to fight and how to defend themselves. This did not make Joe feel any better; he was coming up against men that were trained the same as he had been trained, in the war. Could he know some of these men, could they have fought with him and turned bad, or had they fought against him and then turned bad? It did not matter; they had made their choice, and he had made his. God would be the judge between them. Joe was still moving around the mountain slowly, and without making any noise, he pulled back some heavy brush and looked at every angle that he could but did not see anything; he heard some snoring, and then someone must have punched the person because he grunted and said, "What are you doing? I was just trying to sleep."

The other man said, "I am sick of your snoring." And then the first one said, "If you are sick of my snoring, then get around the hill and take your watch. You forget that he told us last night that the man was going out of the country today. That is the reason they pulled most of the men out of here and put them on the hills around the town. They will get him today."

By this time, Joe was just a few feet from them, and he raised up his rifle and said in a calm voice, "Do not move if you want to live."

And he stepped into the circle of their camp with his rifle leveled at them, with the trigger of his rifle in his left hand. They looked at him, and he saw a look in their eyes that they were going to try him; he released the barrel with his right hand and moved it back to his holster. Joe was watching their eyes, and there was a twitch in the eyes of the man on the left, and Joe knew that he was ready to make his play, and the other man would be a second behind him. They both went for their guns about the same time, and Joe fired with the rifle at the man that twitched his eyes and drew his pistol and shot all about the same time. These were seasoned gunmen and paid killers; they knew that if they were arrested and tried, they would be hung from a rope. This type of a man would rather chance Joe's gun misfiring, or maybe Joe missing them when he shot, or maybe just wounding them; they had little to lose. They knew that they were pretty fast with a pistol, and they did not know how well Joe could shoot; besides he had one shot, and then he had to cock the gun again. One might be shot, but the other might get lead into Joe and live. But they were wrong when they moved their hand to draw their pistol; they became dead men. He shot one man in the face with the rifle and the other man in the chest with his pistol; the second man was trying to raise his gun again, and Joe shot him between the eyes. The one man who was standing with his back to the cliff fell over the edge of the cliff; he was dead and did not even know that he fell. Joe pushed the other man over the cliff to join the first one. Joe took both saddles and threw them over the cliff and kicked the camp gear over the edge. As he was throwing everything over the cliff, he picked up a pair of saddlebags. He felt them, and they were bulging, and he thought this guy sure packs heavy, but over the cliff they went. He drank the coffee and ate what food that had been prepared for their breakfast and threw all of this over the cliff after looking around the campsite and satisfied that everything was gone. And removing his boot prints around the campsite, he put the bridles and lead ropes on their horses and took both horses with him. He moved back around the hill and came down to where his horses were, and with three horses in tow, he went down and started the cattle drifting the way that he wanted them to go. He drove them slowly and left a trail of four horses spread out like four riders taking a herd out of their pasture. Joe drove the animals most of the day, and then he moved his horses over to a stream and let them drink and rest; he changed his saddle to his other horse, and still trailing the other horses, he moved the herd farther away from the area. He had been watching some thunderheads coming over the mountains and was banking on there being a good rain this evening and maybe tonight. He was going to keep traveling in the same direction until the rain hit, and then he would turn the herd toward his and Thad's valley, and it would be very difficult for someone to learn of the change of direction. If it would rain for a few hours, this area would be flowing with a few inches of water, and the tracks would be wiped out completely; the only problem with the cattle would be to turn them up the narrow opening of the valley. To do this, Joe would have to tie up the extra horses and work the cattle with just one horse and use the other three horses as a chute to help guide the cattle into the opening, but he would cross that bridge so to speak, when the time came. It started raining not too hard at first; Joe reached behind his saddle and removed his raincoat which he always carried along with his bedroll. It did not always rain, but Joe used the raincoat to lie down on the ground and lay his blanket on it at night to keep from getting his blanket from getting damp on the ground. The rain kept getting harder; he just hoped that it would not rain so hard that he would miss the notch that he had to turn through to get to the valley. He just hoped that Thad had something set up for a holding pen; he may not have had enough time to do it, and if he did not get the pen made, then they would just have to herd the cattle until they got used to the new location. Cattle would always feed their way back to a place that they were used to, the place that they called home, if they were turned loose, so he would have to keep them here. Now they are home, or this will be home until this mess is straightened out. Joe came through the woods and came out into the scrub brush valley, and sure enough there was water flowing over the ground, and it would soon seep into the ground after the rain stopped, maybe Joe would have the cattle through the gap in the mountain before the water stopped flowing. Joe turned the cattle to the right and headed them right up the stream of water. Most of the cattle were kept into the water; there might be a track or two left untouched, but he could take care of them without much trouble. The cows came up to the narrow entrance, and they just slowed up and came together and went through the narrow place. Joe said, "Thank you, Lord, for taking care of me and keeping my enemy from overcoming me."

He took the cattle and the horses to the lake and spread them out; he did not see any fire; the tent was dark, and the horses were standing there, and the packhorses were still loaded. He rushed to the tent and was very afraid of what he would find. Thad lay there on his blanket; he had been beaten pretty bad. Joe shook him, and he came around and looked at Joe and said, "I am sorry that I did not do a very good job of taking care of myself."

Joe started a fire and put some water on to boil; he unloaded the packhorses and brought the goods into the tent and stored them. He went out and tied all of the animals securely and came back in as the water started to boil. He took a clean rag and cleaned up the cuts and bruises and looked Thad over for anything that was more serious such as knife wounds or bullet wounds, but there were none. After he had cleaned Thad up and dressed the cuts on him, he asked, "What happened?"

Thad told him there were men in Bender who had known that he had worked for Joe. "And they tried to get me to tell them where you could be found, but I would not tell them anything. They worked me over pretty good, and finally the merchant came out with a shotgun and told them that four men beating up on one kid was more than he could handle. The merchant said, 'Now I am telling you that if you ever want to buy food or drink from me ever again, then you will leave right now, and you don't ever touch this boy again. Where are you going, young man?' Then I said, 'I am going anywhere away from here. I just came here to get some supplies to leave this country. People are too wicked for me here. Joe is also leaving out of here as soon as he is well enough to make the trip.'"

"They backed off and sat across the street, and after I was loaded up, the merchant told me that I was in no shape to travel, and he said,

'But if you don't leave here, they will kill you sure as certain.' I mounted up and forced myself to stay in the saddle until I was well out of sight, and then I tied my hands to the saddle horn and let the horse have his lead, and he brought me here. It was pouring rain before I turned the horse loose to find his own way home. But he brought me here, and I came too and untied my hands and crawled into the tent and this blanket. I do not know how long I have lain here until you came." Joe said, "Not very long because it was raining when I came into this valley, and there was plenty of water coming out of the gap when I brought the herd through the gap." Thad said, "You brought a herd of cattle in here today?" Joe said, "Yeah, the Lord and I sure did. Thad, I have fixed a bite to eat. You go ahead and eat, and I will ride a circle or two around the herd and keep them from straying. It should clear up in a bit, and I do not want any tracks out of this valley after the water stops flowing through the gap at the entrance of the valley." Joe made a circle around the herd, and they were all lying down. He had pushed them pretty hard today, and they were tired. Joe went back to the entrance of the valley and searched and could not find any tracks outside the entrance, so he turned around and came back and ate his supper. Thad was sleeping soundly; he looked bad and would be bruised for a while, but unless something was wrong inside, he would be okay. Joe was so sad that this had happened to Thad; this is one of the reasons that he wanted Thad to be here, and being here got him beaten up in spite of everything else. He must remember to thank the merchant in Bender the next time that he goes over that way. Joe must decide what to do next in a couple of days; his cattle will be sold and moved off the range that will leave the range open to anyone who wanted to use it. But that is not a problem; they can graze the grass, but they cannot own it. And Joe could always charge them for using his land without permission and collect grazing fees. Joe was sitting by the fire and thinking about the last evening, and he remembered the kiss that Beverly gave him and the look in her eyes, and he wondered what that was all about. He wondered about Ken Lincoln and how was he going to get out of the way of danger and keep his family safe at the same time. But of course if he was safe it would not pay anyone to harm his family; they thought that they had taken Joe out before they killed his family. If he had only taken a gun to the field with him, none of the rest of this would have happened. Joe remembers that some say there is a set time for each of us to die, but that time is God's time and not Satan's time for us to leave this world. Joe went out in the rain and checked the cows four times during the night, and they seemed content to stay right where they are; on the last trip out, it has stopped raining. He went down to the mouth of the valley and stretched their two ropes across the mouth of the valley at the close place to keep the cattle from coming through the entrance of the valley. But still far enough from the other end of the bottleneck so that nobody passing that way could see anything in the valley. At daylight he walked down through the bottleneck and listened for a long time and cannot hear anything. Then he remembered the path on the inside of the valley and went back through the bottleneck and turned to the right, and a few feet from the entrance, there is a faint path that goes up the side of the rock. He went almost to the top of the rock, and he removed his hat and lay down on the rock and inches up behind a bush and looked over the edge of the rock; there is nothing to be seen on the other side. He stayed there and studied the ground outside of the valley, and even through his glasses, he cannot see even one footprint of the cattle. The place that he turned to the right to come into the valley is so far away that he cannot see the tracks of the cattle even though he knew that they are there. And it would be logical to assume that the herd would have turned to the left instead of to the right and go on out into the scrubby valley and on into nothing. The water traveled for miles on the top of the ground, and farther out there are places that there is solid rock that the herd could turn out of the water and travel in about any direction. With his men's horses following the herd, it might appear that they had taken them and left the area, and maybe nobody will ever know that they died on duty instead of skipping out of the country with a herd of rustled beef. Maybe nobody will even care. Joe stayed there for a while, and then he thought of Thad and headed back to the tent to check on Thad who was sitting up and just looking around. Joe started a small fire and put on breakfast and soon had a meal ready; he gave Thad a cup of coffee to hold while the biscuits were cooking. Joe also fixed them some eggs and bacon; you never knew when the next meal would come along, and a man eats while he has a chance to eat. Joe and Thad made some plans on how to fix up the place because they are going to be staying here for a while. Joe grabbed some tools and went up on the rise to look it over; he made plans once to put a cabin up there and before that happened, he found and bought the homestead that they burnt out a few weeks ago. Joe found the markers that he placed here years ago, and taking his shovel, he started uncovering the flat stone that will be the floor of the cabin. After a bit, Thad hobbled out of the tent and started to rise up to see what Joe is doing. Joe pointed to a stump a little way off the place that he is working, and Thad sat down to watch. Before long, Joe has the rock uncovered and is cleaning out around the edges of the large flat stone; this is going to be the size of the cabin. Joe laid down the shovel that he was using to clean off the floor, and now he was ready for the stone to make the walls. He took one of the horses that the outlaws used and put a pack saddle on him and took him over to the edge of the woods; he found some slim poles. He cut them into certain lengths and dragged them over to Thad and cut some rawhide string from the doe skin that they had dried out and brought this over to Thad. And Joe explained to him how to make a drag to haul rock from the slide at the base of the mountain, over to the rock that is going to be the cabin floor. Thad and Joe laced the poles together and made a platform by taking the small poles of the platform and tying them to the two slightly larger poles for support and made the platform and hooked it to the long poles. This they hooked onto the pack saddle, and he led the horse over to the rocks, dragging the ends of the poles with the platform which is just off the ground. Joe loaded a bunch of rock on the platform and then led the horse over to the flat floor of the cabin and unloaded them and returned for another load. After he brought a few loads over to the cabin, he pulled the horse over to the side and tied him up to a tree. And he started stacking the first layer of stone around the perimeter of the stone floor, checking the corners and keeping the lines straight because they are going to be the walls, and they want the walls to be straight from corner to corner. Joe took the horse and the platform down to the edge of the creek to a mud bank and loaded the mud on the platform with a shovel and brought it back to the outside of the wall. He lifted up a rock and put down a layer of mud and then he laid the rock back down on the mud, pressing it down so that it squeezed out of all sides. "This," he explained to Thad, "will make a good seal from the weather." Joe started at one corner and built the corner up until it is high enough for what he wanted. He put a layer of rock and then a layer of more mud and more rocks, squeezing each rock down until it is seated well, and then he filled in all the cracks with the mud. After he put up a few rows of stones, he reached over the top and took hands full of mud, and with his hands he pressed the mud back into the seams between the stones and made a good smooth surface on the inside of the walls. Then he went to the next corner and did the same thing, making sure that each corner is square. He made sure that it is square by measuring each wall out to a certain distance and measured the other wall out the same distance, and then he measured from one wall to the other, and all of the measurements should be the same or close to it. After he has all the corners set to square, he measured from the north corner to the south corner and took the same string and measured from east to the west corners and made sure that the cabin is square. And when he is finished, the cabin will be square and evenly made. Joe wanted the cabin to be something he can be proud of. After he got the corners up so far, then he filled in the rest of the wall, and he had a wall built about five feet tall. Not tall enough but as tall as he wanted it for this round; he built up all four corners to about the same height, and then he finished the three walls also putting in windows on all three walls from the five-foot markup to the top of the wall. And then he came to the front of the cabin; by now it is time for a break and time to cook lunch and to go check on the cattle. He did not want them to be very close to the mouth of the entrance; he would not want someone to hear them if one would bawl. Joe took his horse and rounded up the cattle and drove them to the back of the valley and let them scatter out in that area. Joe came back to the cabin, and Thad said, "Joe, did you forget something?" Joe said, "What is that?" Thad said, "What about the fireplace?"

Joe smiled and said, "No, I did not forget the fireplace. I will start on it next." He had some long pieces of sandstone lying off to themselves in the floor of the cabin. Joe said, "Do you remember the special rocks that I have laid in the center of the floor all by themselves?" Thad said, "I wondered about that, but I figured you would let me know when you were ready for me to know."

Joe said, "I am going to build the fireplace and cookstove all in one. Remember, the winters get awful cold up here, and the summers are always cool at night, and not much cooking is done in the middle of the day. So the stove will also be a fireplace, and the chimney will go straight up through the roof and will put out heat all the way up."

Joe also said, "We have to put a window in all three sides of the house so nobody can sneak up on you if you do not want them to. The window will be about five-foot high inside and about six and a half high on the outside. Easy to look out, but hard to look in. The stove will have an oven to bake in, and it will be small so it won't burn so much wood. After that we will finish the rest of the wall and the locks for the roof joys that will hold the roof in place even with a strong wind. We will build the stove next. Maybe we can cook breakfast on it in the morning. We will still sleep in the tent until we get this thing finished, and then we will move in here. I will cut some poles, and while you are getting better you can make the bunk beds and table and some chairs. We want to be civilized now. Don't we, Thad?"

He nodded with a grin and said, "I do not think that I can make all of those things."

Joe said, "Sure you can, Thad, a man does not know what he can do until he tries it, and then he prays and get the Lord to help him and show him how to do it. We in our self can do very little, but when we allow Jesus to lead us and direct us, we can do just about anything, at least everything that is worthwhile."

Joe went over to the edge of the woods and selected just the right size of trees and cut them off and brought them to Thad. Along with some rawhide throngs and as he worked on the stone, he directed Thad on what to do and how to make the furniture. By evening, the stove was finished, and the chimney was about halfway finished. Joe took his time and did a good job; he made a stone at the side close to the bottom that slide open or closed to make a draft to help regulate the air moving up through the stove so they could regulate the heat and also would make it easy to clean out the firebox when needed. The firebox is separated from the oven by a thin stone that will take the heat and last for years to come. The fire would come up around the oven to heat; the top of the stove is made up of slats of stone where the fire can come up between them, and this will cook better than any campfire and will hold the fry pan or cooker on a level top. The chimney is designed to also throw off heat into the house and help keep it warm in the winter. But at the same time take the smoke out of the house, with very little wood burning at a time. Joe was very tired; he had not done this type of labor for a long time, and his muscles were complaining heartily, but he felt good at the rate that the job was going; they would soon have a place to stay and one that could not be burnt down around them. Joe was sad again when he thought of his wife and his daughter, but he would not allow his sadness to take over his life. It was almost dark, and Joe said he needed to look around again and make sure that everything was clear around them.

Joe went to the bottleneck area and found that the ropes were still in place and everything seems normal; he climbed to the top of the hill and looked over the top to the other side, and to his surprise there were three men who were sitting on their horses and looking around. One man said, "This seems like a good place to camp. I do not believe there is anyone even close to this area of the country. Those men took the cattle and left the country, but Mr. Cole will not rest until they are found and killed. Nobody walks out on him, especially when they have his money, and besides that they took a herd of cattle that he wanted and would have gotten as soon as we get rid of the Manning person. But we cannot go on any farther tonight, so let us camp here." Joe stayed there and watched them; he knew that if one of the horses whinnied or one of the cows bawled that they would find the entrance to the valley. What can he do to stop them from staying there? He had an idea; he went down to the stream and took the butt of his rifle and stirred up the stream and kept it muddy for a while. Right now would be the time that they would want to get water for their camp and for their coffee; it was getting so dark now that they probably could not see the difference between a clear stream and a muddy one. It was not full dark, and Joe went back up the path to the top of the ridge; he stayed there and watched the men sitting around the fire and the coffeepot on the fire. And one of the men checked the coffee and said, "It is done enough for me."

And he poured himself a cup and set the coffeepot down again on the fire; he took a drink and turned around and spewed it out of his mouth and said, "This is the worst coffee that I have ever drank."

Another man said, "I put the water from the stream into the pot and added the coffee. How can it get so bad?"

The other man said, "I don't know, but you go ahead and try it."

And he poured his coffee out on the ground. The second man put some coffee in his cup and tried it and did the same thing and said, "This taste is like drinking mud." The first man that tasted the coffee said, "Pour that out, and we can make another pot of coffee out of this canteen." The man who filled up the coffeepot said, "I just filled it up out of that stream."

The first man said, "You did what? This water is bad, and you took our only good water and put this bad water in it. We are going to have to move on. I haven't tasted water like this since I fell into the Missouri river after a river boat had just passed through, and I thought that this stream was clear water, but it sure tastes like mud to me. Maybe the recent rain has done something to the water and turned it bad. Let us saddle up and get out of here. There was a stream about two miles back from here, and I know that we can get some good water there. Pour out that canteen, and when we get back to the other stream. Wash it out good."

A heavyset man said, "Why can't we go in the morning?" He had not tried the coffee. "Because I want a cup of coffee, and I do not want to wait until in the morning. Besides that our horses have traveled a long time without water, and I want to get closer back to the camp and report that there is nothing in this area."

The heavyset man said, "What about Mr. Cole's money?"

The coffee drinker said, "Well, what about it if there is no tracks, then we cannot track them, can we?"

They saddled up their horses and crawled back into the saddle and started back up the trail. Joe felt good about his decision to dirty up the stream. He went back down the trail and picked up his horse and went back to the camp. He was grinning when he came into the camp, and Thad wanted to know what in the world would get Joe grinning like that, and Joe told him the whole story about what had happened. Thad said, "Joe, why didn't you shoot every one of them and get them off our backs?"

Joe just looked at Thad and said, "What has happened to you, boy? We do not just shoot people in the back and get rid of them. That is not what we are about. Now I know that they have hurt you and hurt you a lot. But you are going to be a lot better in a few days, and then we will get on with our life." Thad looked at Joe, and he had a lot of anger in his eyes. He said, "Joe, how can you just forgive them for what they have done? They have hurt you much more than they have hurt me. I just don't understand anymore."

Joe said, "Thad, you do not understand because this is the first time that you have had a real personal hurt that has hurt you and humiliated you at the same time. Son, we have to forgive other people for our own sake, as well as for their sake. I have not done wrong to anyone that I have not had to. There comes a time when there is no other way, but when there is another way, then I will not hurt any person. By the way, Thad, did you pick me up a Bible when you were at Bender?"

Thad said, "No, I did not have a chance to tell the merchant about that Bible. I was not thinking too clear when we talked."

Joe said, "That is just fine. I can get along just fine for right now. I am going to go to bed. The cattle are up in the upper end of the valley and bedded down, and I am really tired. I will wash out your cuts in the morning and make sure that you are okay then. Get some sleep and remember your prayers tonight. I told the people in town a great big lie the other day. I told them that you have left out of the country, that I forced you to leave. I was not totally lying because you left the ranch and came here, and I guess that could be considered another country. We will tell them different when this is all over because they think that I am going to the capital now anyway."

CHAPTER 7

The next morning, Joe was up early and started a fire in the new stove and cooked breakfast; it was faster cooking there than the campfire. The biscuits cooked great in the oven. Joe called Thad for breakfast, and he was a little slow coming out of the tent, but he was not slow at going after that first cup of coffee. Nor was he slow about devouring the plate of bacon and biscuits. Joe had already brought his first load of stone over to the new structure when Thad came to the work site. Thad had his work gloves on and was ready to go to work. He told Joe, "I feel good enough to work today. I will get the stone for you while you place the stone. How about that?" Joe said, "I will help you bring over another load of stone, and then we will get a load of mud, and then I will start working on the wall again."

By noon, they had the back wall finished with place sockets for the roof joys, and the side wall were almost finished; they stopped and grabbed a cup of coffee, a cold biscuit, and some hardtack. Joe said, "No apple pie today."

And instantly he thought of Maggie and her pies; nobody in the world could make pies like Maggie. Joe came off his seat and started back to work; Thad knew that some memory had struck Joe because of the look on his face; he did not say anything until later when he said something concerning the building, and Joe became his old self again. By evening time, the front of the wall was almost finished also. They quit and went into the woods and started cutting the poles for the roof and hauling them into the area of the cabin. Joe explained that they would take some of the reeds that were down by the lake and place these across the poles going in the opposite directions, and then they would cover the top of the roof with the floor out of the tent. Then they would cover that with mud; they would put the mud on thick enough so that it would sustain some sod from the grass back of the cabin where it was not going to hurt the grassy area in front of the cabin. Also they would want a vegetable garden in the back of the cabin anyway. Next year, they would put out the garden, if they were still here. Joe could not look that far ahead. Fact of the matter, Joe could not look as far ahead as tomorrow. They had to start thinking about food for the winter; they would have to lay in meat for the winter. The place that they were taking the grass out of would be the new cellar and storage house. Which would also be made of stone, but they would cut out the dirt floor and make the ground around the cellar so it would keep the water out of the cellar unless they hit some underground water. Then they would handle that when the time came. The next day they had the cabin finished except for the door. Thad did not have time to finish any of the furniture. Joe moved into the house with him, and they made the beds and laced the mattress with rope and wove it back and forth placing the tops of the reeds over the rope and placed upon the reed tops the grass that they had cut days earlier. They took pieces of extra blankets and sewed them into mats which they put on the beds. They were much softer than what they had been sleeping on. It felt strange to be in the cabin to have the solid walls around them and to be sleeping in a bed instead of on the ground; the floor was cold, colder than the ground. Joe told Thad that tomorrow he wanted Thad to go down to the lake and gather up all of the leaves that he could find of the reeds that they had used and bring them to the cabin. Thad asked, "What are you going to use them for?"

I am going to teach you how to weave us some rugs for the floor; they will be much warmer than this stone until we get a fire in here for a long time, then it will warm up. The next day, Joe spent the morning hours making a door for the cabin. Now it could be closed up and keep the wind out; more of the tent was used for the door, and another piece was used for the windows. Now the cabin was ready to move their stuff into. Joe made a table and two chairs for them to sit on to eat their meals, and he was teaching Thad about weaving. Thad took to weaving like a professional; he weaved a large rug. He weaved bottoms for each chair for them to sit on, and he weaved a rug to go in front of the door for them to wipe their boots on when they came in the cabin. He even weaved them a kind of broom because as the timber and walls dried out, stuff kept falling everywhere. Thad took the broom and wiped the ceiling down and the walls down, and this helped a lot. Joe said, "Now it is time that we took care of our stock." They built a gate at the entrance of the bottleneck to keep the cows from wandering out into the wilderness. The next job is for Thad to go into the woods along the back of the cabin and start hauling in logs that were fallen down. Dead logs to cut up for firewood and stacking the wood in a place that it will stay reasonably dry and close for them to get to it when the weather is bad. And it will be bad for a long time. It is time for Joe to go meet the cattle buyer and close the deal on the cattle; he is hoping that there is no trouble. He packed a horse with what he might need and saddled his favorite riding horse, and this time, he took a route out across the mountain so there will not be a trail for anyone to backtrack him to the valley. There is no trail to follow but a deer trail; following a deer trail will always take you somewhere, because the deer always know where they are going. By just taking out through the woods across a mountain, you might come to a place that is impassable and have to turn around and retrace your footsteps. But Joe has found that the deer travel from mountain to mountain, and there is a way that makes the easiest route to some other feeding grounds, and Joe took this route and later that evening he wound up in a remote valley far across the mountain. He knew the general direction that he wanted to go, and he did not want to be trailed by someone else, so he stayed off the easy traveled paths; and he is never bothered by other travelers. Man always takes the easy way, animals always take the safe way, and generally the two ways never cross paths. Joe stopped often and looked the country over; he found places that would be good to pasture cattle; he found water that would be there the whole year long and not run dry at certain times. He has always done this as he travels; this is how he found his home ranch, and this is how he found the valley that he just left. Now he has found a valley that is remote and beautiful; this valley is big enough to handle two hundred head of cattle or horses. And the water is plentiful, at one end of the valley is a large pond of water that overflows and comes down through the valley but does not leave the valley for some reason, and therefore someone passing the mouth of this valley might not know that there is any water near this place. He spent the night there and made a camp beside the stream of water and sure enough just at dusk the deer came out to graze in the meadow. He did not bother them, and they do not seem to be very frightened of him. That told him that nobody is hunting these deer. Joe made a mental map of this source of water and thought that he might buy this valley once this is over. He could run more cattle here and maybe finally link this land with the land that he now owns. He kept his horse on a rope close to him, and the kept the rope in his hand; his horse is his sentry, and Joe slept soundly. The nights are getting much colder, and Joe covered up good in his blankets without worry. He is awake the next morning before daylight; he made a small fire in a hole where a tree blew over at one time. He often sleeps in a place like this; the roots make a good windbreak and give him privacy from prying eyes, and his fire is hidden from anyone looking in the night. Joe saddled up and went out to the mouth of the valley. It started widening out, and he noticed the reason the water does not leave the valley is because at one time there was a disturbance under the ground, and the mouth of the valley is higher than the valley floor; so the water found a crack to travel underground. He went out into another valley; this area is clogged with heavy brush and heavy briars and vines—all an indication that there is not any water or very little water in this area. He might have passed up this valley, thinking that like the rest of this area, there is just no water here. Joe stopped in the heavy brush and took out his glasses and searched the mountains around him for possible early-morning fires. Places that a sentry might be placed and he found none; he looked for a while as the sun came up behind him. He found that this would be a good time to move across the valley. Someone looking in his direction would not wish to look into the sun, and he probably would go unnoticed to them. He crossed the valley, keeping to the trees as much as possible. On the other side of the valley, he is completely covered with trees. He noticed that these hickory trees would be a good area to come and get some nuts in the fall of the year and also a source of game that would like to take advantage of these nuts. He watched the country as he passed, with these large trees in such great quantity in this valley could mean that there is a water source not far underground; he is always looking for this type of thing. Joe stopped under one of the trees and looked under the leaves that have fallen and found some good hickory nuts, and he picked up a few handfuls and put them in his saddlebags. He soon moved on and started climbing the next hill keeping to the heavy trees; there are no leaves on the trees, but Joe is dressed in gray jacket and hat. He has brown chaps on his legs for warmth and his horse in a light brown with no white on him; the packhorse is almost a twin of the other horse. So Joe can pass through timber and not be as noticeable as most men would. He moved to the top of the hill; he stopped and looked all around again. He stayed just under the top of the ridge so he is not so noticeable, and he dismounted and walked to the top and started the same search with his glasses into the next valley. He knew just where he is now; he is in an area east of where the cattle are being held. He saw a very small trail of smoke several miles across the next valley, so they are watching there, maybe that is where their main camp is. The route that Joe is taking will give him a wide circle around the camp of the outlaws, and maybe he can find out a few things and not run into any trouble with them. He turned around and started back to his horses, and he froze. There are three men coming down the valley where he just crossed. They don't seem to be searching for anything; they just seem to be traveling. They come to the place that he crossed the valley, and as they passed his trail they were looking at something on the other hill and did not even look down at the ground and went right on past where he had come through. He watched them as they went out of sight. He stood there to make sure that they would not come back, and he mounted up and started on, then he thought of what they might be looking at on the hill, across from him. He brought his glasses up and started looking at the hill, and soon he saw what they were looking at; there were some buzzards circling in the sky above the hill. They might be going to check this out, but if they are how did they know about the birds? He swung his glasses to the west of him and started searching the top of the hill in front of him and found a second trickle of smoke coming which means that there are some more lookout post up there also, and it is coming up from the hill right in front of him. He would have run right into them if he had gone on. He went back to the top of the hill again and looked around; there was a way that he could get through if he came around the mountain on his right instead of on his left. Then he thought of the tracks of his horses where he crossed the valley; the men would not be looking at the hill when they came back. He had to get down there and take out his tracks before the men came back; he tied his horses and walked down the hill and out into the valley. The men would travel back the same route that they came, so he went out and covered the tracks of his horses with leaves; he turned back and started walking to his horse, and he heard the men coming back around the bend; he flattened against one of the big hickory trees and waited. The men were talking about having to go hunt down some dead animal just to satisfy some idiot who thought that he saw something. When is this going to end? Why did he ever come to this awful place. He wanted music, noise, and excitement; he is sick of these woods. Joe stood there as they pass, and one of the men said, "I wonder if there are any hickory nuts under

The engineer said for Joe to get back into the woods and go on about his way; the message will be sent, and he will wait for a reply and listen for one long and one short blast on the train whistle. Nobody else will know what he is doing but Joe. If there is no reply or the answer is no, then there will only be a small toot of the whistle when the train starts out.

Joe shook hands with him and went to his horse and mounted; he and Thad headed out in the woods and went back to where they had started from. When the train started under way there was a long whistle and then a short whistle, and the train kept going at full speed heading east. Joe knew that the telegraph was answered, and it was answered yes.

CHAPTER 12

Joe and Thad took turns sleeping that night, and when daylight came and the town was waking up, they ate a good breakfast; and when it's about time for the bank to open up, they moved down on the road and waited. Doctor was coming down the road; they moved out on the road. Thad was wearing a hat that belonged to one of the outlaws, and Joe was all slumped over his saddle horn, with the two extra horses and was coming down the road to meet him. He slowed and then came on; after all, he had seen this thing a hundred times. When he came closer, Joe rose up and pulled his gun and said, "I ought to kill you just like you killed my family. How in the world could you have done this to these people? But it is not going to happen to anyone else. "Thad, tie his hands to the saddle, and we will be on our way. Dr. Abernethy, you are going to hang for your crimes against the people of this place."

"You cannot hang me. You do not have the authority," said the doctor. "I have my rights, and I will not be hung by a lynch mob. My brother will not allow it to happen."

Joe said, "Gag him, and we will be on our way." The doctor said, "Are you going to take me to jail?" And those were his last words. Because Thad put a rag around his face and mouth, and they turned around and headed away from town; he was struggling and muttering against the gag when he saw that he was not headed back to town. Joe turned off the road and headed for the river, and he went into the water to mask their tracks; also this was the way that they wanted to go anyway. They traveled for hours in the water, and when they had passed the rocky places that they could have left the water without a trace, Joe kept going; he knew that the trackers would turn out on these rocky places and try to find his tracks later on. This would delay them for a while; they came to a small stream hardly wide enough for the horses to follow one another, and Joe turned off the river. He traveled for a few yards and dismounted still in the water and went back and wiped out the tracks in the mud and splashed water over the rubbed-out tracks and came back, mounted up, and kept going. The doctor kept trying to say something, but Joe just did not care about what he wanted, and he kept on going. They traveled for several hours, and finally Joe said to Thad to take his gag off and give him some water to keep him alive so he can kick real good when they hang him from a tree.

He started again that he had his rights to a trial, and Thad gagged him again, and they started on; they kept going through the water for a couple of miles, and finally Joe found a place that he could get out of the water and not leave many tracks. The ground was very sandy and he asked Thad to wipe out the tracks and then catch up with them for they were now on firm ground and it would be hard to know what kind of animal made the tracks. They were climbing into the mountains, and Joe found a low place in the mountain and went through; he wanted to stay under the trees so if there were any sentries in this area, they would not see them. At late evening, they came to the camp of the others, and Joe saw the guards; he waved to them, and they went on into the camp; the people wanted to know why the doctor was tied up and gagged. Joe told them that he was the one that had brought all of this on them. He took the gag off the doctor and put him rather roughly on the ground. His hands and feet will remain tied; the doctor was pleading to them that he was innocent, and he had done nothing wrong.

Beverly said, "Why did you send someone to take me and kill me? Why did you do that? Because the men told me as they were taking me to the ranch. They did not think that I would ever get loose from those big men, and they had nothing to worry about. They were even arguing that if they stopped which one could have me before they got to the ranch."

The doctor turned white as a sheet and said, "They would not say anything like that to you."

Beverly said, "What makes you think that they would not say anything to me?"

She got right in his face and screamed it.

The doctor said, "Because they had their orders." And he realized what he had said, and he dropped his head and said no more.

One of the men said, "What more do we need to know?"

"Wait," he said as he raised his head, "if you will not hang me, I will give you all of this money that I have."

Joe said, "What money? Everyone knows that a doctor does not have any money."

He said, "The money in the saddlebags."

Joe finished for him, "The money that you were going to use to pay your killers. Boys, I was not going to steal that money, but it seems that the doctor just gave us the money, and now I do not have to steal. It is ours anyway."

And they all laughed, except for the doctor. "Oh, by the way, Doctor, I hate to call you that, because a doctor, a real doctor, gives an oath to save lives not destroy lives. But we were not going to hang you anyway, that is illegal without a trial." One of the drovers said, "We can have a trial here. We would probably be on the jury anyway, so it could be legal." Joe said, "Where is the cattle of Mr. Lincoln and before you answer, I might have to leave this camp and who can tell what might happen to you then." "His cattle is mixed in with my herd."

Ed who was still very angry walked stiff legged at the doctor and said, "Your herd? That herd was stolen from my father, and I am going to take them back even if it means the death of my brother."

Joe added, "And your brother too."

Ed looked at Joe, who added that his brother is major. Joe added, "Thad and I heard all about that in the saloon last night, and about the money coming in last night on the train, and by the way I sent for a train load of soldiers to clean up this mess; we need some help, and they are the ones to do it for us. We have solved the mystery around all of this, and I am sure some of these men are wanted for crimes in many other places. So the soldiers are logically the only ones that could cover all the areas of the law. We talked that over with the buyer, and it was decided then." Lenny said, "How did you get the word to him, through his old friend the engineer who was running the engine when we transported the cattle; we met him last night, and he had the telegram sent in the name of the buyer, he knew most of the code."

He looked over at Beverly, and she did not look so good; he walked over to her and took her by the shoulders and turned her to face him. "How did you know that he sent the men to take you?"

She looked him in the eyes and said, "I did not know that, what I did know was that you were not lying, and he had to be lying. So I took a chance."

He took her in his arms and held her until she quit shaking, but let her go when he felt himself trembling, and she knew that was happening also. They all sat down to eat their evening meal, and there was a call of the whippoorwill bird, and Joe knew that one of the sentries had spotted something. He gave the command to break camp just in case, and he headed out toward the sentry. When he arrived at the sentry he was told that there was a group of men coming from the opposite direction from which they had come. "Evidently they are just searching this part of the country."

Joe said, "We will deploy the men and wait if they may pass us by, and they might not, but we will be ready to strike and run. We are not large enough to sustain a long fight. Keep watch and get ready to move out." Joe went back to the camp and spread the news; everyone was all ready to move out, and being late in the evening they might just do a hit and run. But there might be another bunch within hearing of this bunch, and that would be bad.

"Thad, go over the top of the hill and see if the way to the other valley is clear. We may go by the way of the upheaved valley and then over the hill. Their sentries could not spot us in that dense woods. See if we can get through before they reach us. You have about thirty minutes. You might have enough light to use your mirror." Thad jumped on his horse and flew out of there. Joe had to wait now, and it seemed that was getting harder to wait nowadays; there were so many men, and now Beverly was waiting, with him, and depending on him to make the right decision. While we are waiting on Thad, take brush and wipe this area as clear as you can. It just might be possible that they could pass through here and not even know that we have been here. One of the men punched Joe and pointed to the doctor who was taking a shining object out of his pocket and dropped it in an open space on the ground. "Move him and take no notice of the thing that he dropped. I will get it when he isn't looking. Let him think that he succeeded and maybe he won't try again." These men coming from the opposite direction do not know that we have him, and if they do not know, they may not look quite so hard. And if they keep going the same way, they will meet with the other people and report that we are not in this area. Tie his hands to the saddle horn and gag him good." When the man took him to his horse, Joe went to where he had dropped the object, and it was a pocket plaque of a doctor, and Joe put it in his pocket. They moved

back into the woods, and the sentries met them, and they pulled far
enough back so they could go either way. Thad came hurrying back and
said, "There is a larger bunch in the next valley moving the same way."
Joe went to each and every person and told them to walk their horses
and to keep the horses quiet. They were going to slip between the two
groups, and he would take them to another place to set up camp, a far
better place. They moved just under the top of the hill and started
moving around the hill and would stop every now and then and made
sure that they were not coming up on someone that they did not want
to meet. Finally, they heard the large body of men moving down in the
valley, and they stopped and waited until they had moved on; it was
almost dark, and they wanted to be out of hearing before they stopped,
and the other group would come across the top of the ridge and camp
with them. Joe hoped it would be dark, and they could not see their
tracks, but in the morning, they would surely see their tracks; so they
had to be secure before that time. They made good time shortly after
they passed the group of men. Joe motioned for everyone to mount
up, and he picked up the speed a little. They went out the ridge, and
as it ended they went down into the valley. This was where Joe had
seen the grove of nut trees. They passed on by and turned into the dry
valley, and it seemed that all there seemed to be was prickly brush.
Joe turned out into the middle of the valley, when he came this way
before he had traveled along the timberline to stay out of sight. But
this time, he was going back through the center of the valley; his horse
was kind of skittish; he dismounted to see what was the matter, and he
stepped in front of his horse, and there was nothing under his feet. He
grabbed the horse bridle as he was falling, and the horse jerked back
and saved him from falling into a hole. After he had steadied his horse,
he told everyone to stop and stand in their place. He picked up a rock
and threw the rock a couple of feet ahead of him, and he listened and
could not hear the rock hit the bottom of the hole; he finally heard it
hit and bounce off and fall some more. He struck a match, and there
was a hole about twenty feet across, and it was covered with brush and
fallen bushes; it looked like just regular brush. He knew that the men
would be following them, and they probably would be traveling fast
in order to catch them. He had an idea; he took a bright-colored cloth
from his saddlebags and tied it on a long slim pole and leaned out and
put it on a branch about ten foot over the hole then backed up and
told the men and women what he had found; they made a wide birth
around the hole. He told Jacob to brush away the tracks, leading away
from the hole.

CHAPTER 13

Jacob smiled and said, "All right, boss. I will lead them the right way." And they went carefully over to the edge of the timberline and went on. It was not long before they heard water falling and from then on, the scenery changed. There was plenty of water and grass. The valley he remembered was beautiful, just beyond there, he turned to the left and entered into the stream and headed up the stream for about half hour and turned up the mountain; his horse was on stone all of the way across the valley and for most of the way up the hill. He turned back and forth and made the steep climb easier on the horses and the riders. Especially the women when he crossed over the top of the ridge, then he started back down the hill until he came to some heavy brush and abruptly, he turned back up hill and through heavy brush. He went over the top of the hill and down into his valley where they had made the stone cabin. They dismounted and went into the cabin. They lit a fire and brought Beverly and the Lincolns in and made them comfortable, then he went outside and helped the men make camp and set up a shelter for them. He sent men back up on the top of the hill and set up sentry posts along the top of the ridge to watch for the outlaws. He rested the best that he could; they put the doctor in the root cellar, and Joe took the saddlebags into the cabin and tossed them in the corner along with the other saddlebags. Joe waited until breakfast the next morning, and he saddled up; he headed out to see what the cattle looked like, and he checked the opening to the valley, and there had been no tracks made after he had left. They seemed to be safe here except for the men who might be following them. He wanted to go back down the valley and look over the hole that he had seen last night. He had not seen anything like that in his lifetime; he stopped by the house and told them that he would be back in a few hours. Beverly asked if she could ride with him, and he said that it might be dangerous, and she could be in a lot of danger; she insisted that he take her, and he looked at Mrs. Lincoln. She nodded yes, and he said, "Okay, come on. But put on your riding clothes, and we may be a while."

She smiled and said that she could take whatever she needed to take. "I have been cooped up for far too long, and I need to get out and see something."

Joe said, "Okay, I will saddle you a horse. Be ready, and we will be off."

Joe and Beverly started off, and as they went up the hill, Joe asked Beverly if she remembered the big hole that they ran across last night.

She said, "Yes."

He said, "I believe that was the problem with the water around here." And he wanted to see for sure.

He said that if there was more water in this area that a ranch could hold ten times the cattle that it does now.

She said, "I do not understand."

He said, "It may be nothing, and it may be something really important."

They traveled on for a few miles; he stopped just before they topped out on the mountain and explained that you never go over a hill or mountain unless you see what is on the other side. You might not want to go over, until you see what is there.

He dismounted and walked to the top and looked over; he felt her as she moved up beside him. "Is there—" she started to say, and he placed his hand over her mouth; he pointed over the hill, and she could see movement among the trees, down along the river.

There were about twenty men over there, and they were hunting tracks along the river; he had been afraid of that, sometimes at night you think that you have covered every track, and sometimes you miss one or two.

Joe said, "We are going to have to miss the looking that we wanted to do. And get back to camp and set up for these guys, because it looks like we are in for it. Ride back to the camp and tell Lenny to get the men up here on the hill and let us set up a reception for these men."

Joe moved around the hill to where the sentries are, who have not seen the men yet; Joe told them, "When the men get here, set up a picket line and get ready for the outlaws who are following our tracks. If we can, we don't want anyone leaving here alive. I believe we can get them if we get in the first volley and make every shot count. I will move down the hillside and be shielded from the fire from our guys, and when they turn to flee, I will stop all of them that I can. When they turn to escape our guns, bring my horse, and we will follow them. Pick me up, and we will take care of all of them that we can." Joe heard the men coming up the mountain; he had been afraid of this; in an all-out battle, there will be men killed and wounded on both sides, and he did not want any of these men killed; they did not start this; they were not here on account of unlawful greed. This was thrust on them all by men who wanted something for nothing; they wanted their wealth taken from men who had worked and earned it, so now someone had to pay for the greed of someone else. Joe was down the mountain with his pistol in the holster, another one stuck down in his belt, and his rifle and some extra shells. If this was what they wanted, he was willing to give them all that they could handle. They were working up the river close to where his people came out of the river. He looked up the mountain and then down; he was about halfway; he found a place that their horses could not get real close to him, and he had a great place to shot at them. Unless there was a bullet that bounced off a rock or something, he was somewhat protected from the men from up above. If they came up the mountain here, they were in serious trouble. Was there another group of men behind this group, he did not know. There was one man down there that seemed to be the tracker; that man had to go; without him, they cannot find the tracks. The leader was a tall man who sat the saddle tall; Joe recognized him. That was Denver Cole—that was the man that killed his family. He raised his rifle and wanted to squeeze the trigger; he held it for a long time, but he could not do this. "Revenge is mine, said the Lord. I will repay."

If they come up the mountain, then that is a different thing. Suddenly, there was a shot fired from somewhere down below and to his right, then another shot from the same place. They turned and raced back down the river to where it went dry, and Joe followed them with his eyes. Through the trees he could not see much, but every now and then he could see a movement of men. They went to about where the big hole in the ground was, did they think that Joe's party went down over the edge? He did not think so, but maybe some of their men saw the cloth that Joe had hung in the brush and followed the supposed trail to their death. Maybe there were tracks that went over the edge. They might think that Joe's party is lost forever; the ground there is rocky, and maybe they cannot tell whose tracks those are. They would have to go down in that place to see for sure, are any of these men dedicated enough to do that? I wonder what they think the doctor did, was he killed and robbed like the first bunch of money? There were four horses that met the doctor on the road, and their two men are missing, Joe has so many things running through his mind. If they are not fooled, they will be right back and keep on tracking his group. He again must wait and see; he is standing on a point thrust out on the hill fully visible to the men above but not visible to the men below. The men up above probably cannot see the outlaws below. Joe turned and looked up; he could see some of the men standing up; he motioned that they had come and went back there; he pointed in the direction of the men where they are now. He was intent on what they were doing, and he heard a rustle of leaves, so slight he knew that Thad had come down to be with him. He turned to tell Thad because nobody else could move that quiet, and there standing at his elbow was Beverly, smiling up at him. He said, "Beverly, you must go back up there and be as safe as you can."

She said, "My place is with my man, because if something happens to you, I want it to happen to me also."

He was overwhelmed with a feeling of love that he had never had before; this woman was willing to risk everything just to be with him. He did not have anything to say; he just took her hand in his and went back to looking at the outlaws to find out what they were going to do. After the longest time, they moved on down the valley and out of sight. What is going to happen now? Were they safe? Their trail it seemed has vanished into a hole in the ground. Would he have believed that happened? He thought about how he felt at the edge of the hole and how easy he could have fallen except for his horse, who had stopped; he would have fallen, and the others would have followed maybe. Was this God's way of protecting them? Was this God's way of ending this thing and keeping him from doing any more killing? He did not know what his next move should be; he just stood there, and Beverly whispered, "Joe, what do we do next?"

Joe said, "I have been standing here thinking about that very thing. Is this God's way of keeping them off us? Are they down there waiting to see what is going to happen next? They have to have this money or their men are going to leave them and walk off. Their men will not stay without money; they might go into town and rob the bank or destroy the town for that matter. They will certainly kill those who have promised them all of the money; they might take the cattle for their money. I really do not know."

Beverly said, "Joe, we have to trust God to take care of us."

He said that he would do just that. "We need to get back to town and see what is going on."

Beverly asked, "Could the army have had time to get there by now?"

Joe looked at her and said, "I do not know, but maybe that is what we should do. The people of the town need to be made aware of what is happening. They need to protect themselves from whatever is going to happen. With our group and the townspeople, we could put up a pretty good battle."

They walked hand in hand up the mountainside; their horses were waiting for them, and they told the men what had happened and what they thought they should do. Ken and Lenny agreed with them, and they mounted up and moved down the hill to the stone house and packed up the horses. Joe put all the money on a packhorse, put the doctor on his own horse, and they went out through the mouth of the valley and headed straight for town. If they are doing things normal, they have all the men around them and on sentry duty at their home base. So we should not run into any sentries on our way to town. We will come into town from the west and travel along the mountain until we get safely into the town itself. They arrived in town late in the evening. Joe, Ken, and Beverly went into the mercantile to see Samuel Edwards in his back room and asked him if he could get the different merchants in town along with the sheriff to come to his store without telling them who is here. "Remember please do not tell them who is here and what you want them for. Will you do that for us and the whole town?"

Samuel said he would do that and have them over here in minutes. "Just wait here."

Joe slipped out the back door and told the men what they had done. "Thad, kind of look around and see who is in town and let me know please."

Thad nodded and left; Joe went back into the store. Lenny came into the back door and said, "There is something going on out there. Men are gathering behind the other stores and across the street. I don't understand it. Aren't we the good guys? Is this town turned against us, and what have we done that is so bad? The gang is out in the woods looking for us, and we walked into a trap in the town."

Joe said, "Let me get out of here. Bring all the men in here and just hole up. Don't go outside no matter what, and don't let them get too close. Try not to shoot anyone unless you just have to and try to pick a stranger if you do. I am going to the telegraph office and see what I can do; there must be someone on the way to help us, unless they have turned every one against us. When I have done what I can do, I will come back the same way that I went out, so don't shoot me. Now these folks can shoot, and they will if they are convinced that they are in the right side. I do not know what they have been told, but I am going to find out and try to stop it."

He stepped outside and went through the horses and disappeared; one minute he was there, and the next he was gone—one of the things that Thad had told him and it works. Never go where the other person thinks that you are going to go, go somewhere else. He was first going to the diner to see what was going on; he knew that he could trust Abbie. If no other person in the town would trust him, he was sure that she would. He went to the back door and knocked; a moment later, she came with a rifle and opened the door. He did not know what to expect, but she broke into a smile and said, "Get in here before you get shot."

Joe came into the diner and said, "Abbie, what is going on with my friends in town? it seems that they have all turned against me."

She said, "Dr. Abernethy's brother said you killed his brother and stole all the money that they had, also you have kidnapped Beverly, and they think that you have killed her also. Also you are holding the Lincoln folks as your prisoner, and you will kill them as soon as you can get their money also. The people around here kind of believe that you are going loco, and they want to stop you. They do not want to kill you if they can help it, but there are some in that crowd that would shoot you in a heartbeat, and that is quick." "Abbie, could you talk to some of the board members of this town and see if you could get them over to the store and talk to the Lincolns, Beverly, and the doctor because they are all there, and they know what is going on."

She said, "I will go to each one of them personally and tell them privately what you have said." She grabbed her coat and said, "Joe, you stay here and have a piece of apple pie and a hot cup of coffee. I am going to find the town council, and I am going to tell each and every one of them what I think of what they are doing to you. You have been a member of this community for years, and they are taking the word of a stranger over you. I don't know about folks sometimes, they just run off and do not think. Now don't you move. I will be right back."

"And I will bring them over here for you to talk to." After she left, Joe was thinking that if someone came by here, he would have to kill them or get killed, and he did not want any more bloodshed over this. He went out the back door and around the outbuildings and into the woods; he moved very slow and careful; he was moving toward the sheriff's office. He did not know why he was going there, but he wanted all the information that he could get. This seemed the only way for him to get out of this trouble and back to a normal life. He moved around town in the woods; he did not hear the birds singing; he was listening for any sound that a human would make; his whole being was to stay alive and hear someone before they heard him. He was almost there; he was behind a large tree and watching the back of the sheriff's office, and someone spoke softly to him. He turned around, and there was Thad. He said, "I did not know whether to touch you or to speak to you. There was no sound you have this down path. Now I don't think that I can move as quiet as you are now."

Joe said, "You are a good teacher, Thad. I just watched you and followed suit. I always was pretty quiet, but you showed me what I was doing wrong. I am going up to the sheriff's office and see what I can hear." "I tried and could not hear from under the floor," said Thad. Joe said, "I know of a place that the sound comes through the wall," and he moved off. Thad stayed where he was; Joe went to the side wall of the jail and put his ear to the wall. He could hear two voices talking—one of them wanted to pull out and leave.

"We aren't going to get any money," said one.

And the other said, "We are going to get everything that we want if we just stay here and wait."

"Where are we going to get the money that we want?" said the other voice. The first voice that Joe heard said, "From the bank." The sheriff said, "Just you wait. We are not going to hold up the bank. That is out and final." The first one said, "You think that you are faster than I am, Mr. Griffin?"

There was a pause, and Toby said, "No, Denver, I do not think that I am faster than you are. But no buts about it. The money shipment is coming in on the train tonight and we are going to take the guards out before they get to the bank and take the money. Then we will ride out of town and people will think that Joe Manning did the robbery."

Denver said, "But he is supposed to be in the store and locked in there by the people of this town."

The strange voice said, "Well, we will have to make sure that they are distracted by maybe a fire on one of the buildings, and he could and will get away."

Then Denver said, "Why would he run if he had a chance? Sheriff, you are supposed to be so sweet on the lady at the diner, what is her name, Abbie. Well, let her tell Joe what we have planned and tell him to get out of town or he will get killed. We can track him and his gang and take care of them once and for all. Then we will be free to go on with the original plan and take those ranches and have those herds of cattle for ourselves." "That sounds like a good plan, Denver, but maybe we should not kill Joe. Just kill all of them, and he will be a hunted man for the rest of his days, that would be better than killing him. He would never prove his innocence; he would just be a hunted man."

Joe sat there leaning against the wall in between large wooden boxes; he could not be seen unless someone walked by and just looked in his direction. He had heard enough to know what they were planning to do, but how to stop them was another question. He and Thad need to get back to the store and tell the rest of the men and decide what to do, to stop them or to prevent the guards from getting killed so he would not be blamed of more murders. Joe went back to where Thad is, and together they went back to the store. When they got to the store, men are behind the store as well as in front of it. Joe pulled back into the woods to rethink what they should do. It is getting late in the evening, and they decided to wait until full dark to enter the store. They must find a better place to hole up and wait; they waited until there was a change of guards. The first guards were strangers. The new guards were two strangers, and the owner of the store, and one other town person. Joe motioned to Thad and as soon as the first guards were gone, they moved a little closer to the guards; they looked all around and could not see anyone else. So they quietly moved up to within five feet of the men, and Joe said to the men who were still standing, "I am Joe. Do not move or you will get shot."

They stiffened, and Joe said, "There are two guns on you. Please don't make us shoot. Starting with you on the left, take your left hand down and remove your right gun and drop it to the ground behind you, and the same with your left gun." After this was done he told the next and the next, until all of them had been disarmed.

Joe told Samuel Edwards to go behind them and tie each one of them up tight."

He used cords that Thad handed him; nothing was said until all three of the guards were tied up, and Joe went to Samuel and tied up his hands. He said to Samuel, "I am ashamed of you thinking that I had done the things that they told you about me." Samuel said, "There was so many of them that told the same story that it was hard not to believe what they said."

"Let us go into the store, and you can talk to some of the men that I was supposed to have killed." Samuel turned around and said, "Where is Beverly Waters? They said that you killed the doctor and her." "Well, you can ask her when we get inside. She probably will be the one guarding the good doctor, who is a ring leader in this game of theirs. Major is the doctor's brother, and they wanted to have all the land in this area and all of the cattle. And they were going to bring in outlaws from the big cities and house them here and charge them a large price to live here. Now what do you think they would eventually do with all of you town people, who by their stories would move out one by one and never be heard of again."

Samuel looked at the men beside him and asked if this true. The men did not say anything one man just hung his head, and the other two looked straight ahead.

Samuel said, "Joe, I am sorry that I doubted you for a moment. I can see by them that you are right, but what do we do now?"

Joe said to Samuel, "The doctor, the sheriff, Abbie at the diner are all in it, and I do not know how many more are in it. Maybe the telegraph operator, I have sent word for the army to come here and take charge of this town and sort out who is who."

They went into the store, and Samuel looked around at the people. Joe said, "Beverly, come here please. Samuel wants to see you and the doctor who I killed. Ken and Mrs. Lincoln, I am supposed to have taken your land and cattle and killed you also. We need to figure out what is going on and decide what we are going to do about it. These were the guards out back. Lenny, why don't you take your crew and wait out in the woods? They may send out another set of guards, and we will surely need to move tonight."

As Lenny moved back to the door, Joe told him what they had planned to do about robbing the money and blaming him. "I will keep the rest in the store to show force if they attack. If they do attack, move back and protect yourself and your men. We do not want them to get shot."

Lenny said, "We will do whatever is necessary for everyone."

Joe laid a hand on his shoulder and said, "Please keep yourself and them safe."

Samuel said, "What can I do to help?"

Joe said, "If they think that you know something, they will kill you in a moment. Well, I do not think that they wanted me on the guard duty tonight so if I show out front, they will not question that, and maybe I can talk to some of the others, when I tell them what I have learned, they will feel the same as I do now."

Joe said, "I do not think that all of them will feel the same as you, because there have been so many things going on in this town for everyone to be clean. Maybe each of you do not know about the others."

Samuel said, "Maybe I can find out. Remember, Joe, we play poker with each other. You get to know something about a poker player, and maybe I can run a bluff and see who raises the bet, and who folds their cards."

Joe said, "Maybe but please be careful. I want to go out the back. Is that all right with you?" Joe said, "Take your gun with you, you may need it, and remember who you are up against."

Samuel left, and Joe wondered if he let a gang member go free, but he had to take a chance. They were here and here they would stay for a while; Joe asked Beverly if they could get something to eat, and she disappeared and a few minutes later she brought him a bowl of beans. He dived into the beans and about the time he finished them she came back with a steak, potato, and a biscuit covered with butter and honey. He looked at her and smiled and asked her how long that took to cook. "We fixed this for you while you were out." His prisoners were piling up, and he did not want this to happen; he did not have the men or food to take care of prisoners. There was a commotion outside. Joe went to the window, and Major was out there with a group of men, and he hollered for Joe to come out. Joe said, "I can hear you just fine from here."

He said, "Can I come in?"

Joe told him that if he took his coat off and dropped his gun, he could come on in.

Joe slid the bolt back when he came close to the door, just then a shot rang out, and he slumped down at the door. Joe opened the door and pulled him inside the store, and Beverly ran to him, but he was already dead. Dr. Abernethy was trying to yell through his gag and jerked his arms and body, trying to get loose. Joe walked over to him and said, "He was shot from behind by one of his own men. They did not want him to be in here talking to us." Abernethy quit struggling and just looked at Joe. "You run with a real nice crowd, Abb. How do you like them now?" He just put his head down. "Now you know how the families of the people that you have had killed feel, not very pleasant, is it? Like my family, if I was a different kind of person I would pull my gun and put a hole in your head, but I am not that type of person. That shot was ordered by the sheriff." Joe said, "I heard him and Denver Cole plotting against someone earlier today in the sheriff's office, but I did not know who it was. It seemed that your brother wanted to end this thing and leave, but they are going to try and steal the next money shipment and lay it on to me. "And go ahead with the plan to steal the land, of course they will kill everyone who has been caught, and that means all of you. We have caught other people, and they have killed them all."

One of the men was trying to speak; the others were trying to shut him up, but Joe moved in and stopped them. He pulled the gag off the man, and he said, "If I tell you everything, will you let me go?"

Joe said, "I do not know. Tell me first, and we will see."

"This was all started by the doctor and the sheriff, and they contacted Major and Denver Cole to gather men and come in here and do the dirty work, which they did, and the doctor was going to supply the money. Denver was going to bring in more cattle, and a very large ranch was going to be set up. And later on the hotels, gambling houses, and other stuff would be set up for the guest, and they planned to make millions. And all of us who worked for them would get a cut of the action. Which would mean thousands of dollars for all of us who worked for them after it was started. They had the law on our side, and no outside people would ever know about this deal."

Joe asked him, "What about the town people?"

He said, "Well, as time went on, they would either be brought into the organization, or they would leave the area, and we would take over their businesses and run them under the original name."

Joe said, "You mean the townspeople would be six feet under ground; well yes, that was my understanding."

Joe said, "You have not told me anything that I did not already know."

"But you promised," said the outlaw, "that you would let me go."

Joe said, "I said to tell me something, and we would see. You have not told me anything that I did not already know."

"That is all that I know," said the outlaw. "I am not one of the killers. I only take messages back and forth."

"From who to who?" asked Joe.

He said, "From the doctor and the sheriff out to the camp, or over to the ranch, and that is all that I know."

Joe said, "Well, you do not know enough." And Joe replaced his gag.

CHAPTER 14

Ken got Joe's attention and said, "Look at that." He pointed to four men who just rode up to the saloon; they dismounted and walked inside.

Joe said, "What about them?"

Ken said, "They are military, or they are just recent military because they rode in turned into the hitch rack, dismounted at the same moment, just like the one man was giving unheard orders for them to do it on cue. They may be an advance patrol; the army may be very close to us. How can we get them word about what is about to happen with the money?"

Joe said, "Thad, will you come here?"

Thad said, "Sure."

Joe said, "Will you go out with me another time? We need to make contact with those soldiers."

Thad said, "I sure will."

Joe said, "If you can get to the road on the west end of town and wait for them to leave and tell them what is going on. And tell them where we are and tell them about the money that is coming in tonight and what we overheard, and we will let them take over and stop this madness. The money is the first thing that they will have to have in order to hold their men together. If they get the money, then they will have something to work with. If not, they will hit this town and take everything that they can and burn it down, to hide their work. Just like they did with my house. This seemed to be their method of operation. I will go to the east end of town and watch for them to come that way. We do not know where they are camping, the main body of men. This way, we should come in contact with them and hopefully stop any more bloodshed."

Ken said, "What do you want me to do?"

Joe said, "If Samuel comes back, maybe he can get to the saloon and talk to them there. Please don't let anyone leave here. They might just rush this place. We do not know what to expect. If I find Lenny, I will have him move his men closer to this store, just in case they try something. We might have trouble getting back in, but we will be very close if we cannot get back in to you." At this, he looked at Beverly, and she nodded that she understood. "You might want to feed the doctor a little, but don't let him talk to the other men, and don't untie his hands. And don't believe anything that he tells you because he will say anything at this point to get out of hanging."

"But, Joe," said Mrs. Lincoln, "the doctor did not kill anyone that goes against everything that a doctor stands for."

Joe said, "Mrs. Lincoln, when you pay someone to pull the trigger and kill another human being, it is just the same as pulling the trigger yourself. In fact it is worse because you are involving another person as well as yourself."

She nodded her head and said, "I always felt that a doctor is someone very special."

Mr. Lincoln looked around and said, "Honey, a good doctor is someone very special, but someone like this piece of trash will taint a hundred good doctors and give them a bad name. No, he is not anything special. Maybe he was at one time, but when he turned outlaw, he is not any better than the lowest of them. If he could get loose, he would kill now."

They were talking about the doctor like he was not even there; he remembered the time when he walked into a house. He was treated like a king, a savior. He was looked up to by everyone, and now they were talking about him like he was nothing. If he could just get loose and get back to the men he would wipe out every one of these people. They called him trash, him, who helped them through all kinds of problems, and half of the time they did not even pay him, or paid him when they got the money. He had to pay for what he bought on the spot. Had it not been for the money that his father left him when he died, he would have had nothing to try and build an empire with. Even his own brother came out here to try to get some of the money; he told his brother what he and the sheriff were planning, and he wanted to have a part of it. Why did the sheriff have to shoot him? He had just about sawed through the bindings on his arms with an old piece of glass that he found lying on the floor. If he could get his hands free and get over to one of the men, maybe they could get out of here. Here comes Beverly with something to eat. His hands are almost free. He will grab her and make her shield him from the rest until he gets one of the men loose, and then he will hold her in front of him and leave this place. Maybe his men are guarding outside of the store and can take him to the sheriff and then they can get free of this town. He knew that Joe has one part of his money and maybe all of it. This money will pay the men and keep them working for him; he does not know where Thad and Joe went. They saw something out front, and then they put their heads together and left. Saying that they would be back if they could, if he catches them they will never get back here or anywhere either, he will put them in the ground. Beverly had made some soup for the doctor and was bringing it to him. She was looking right and left as she approached him for something to set the hot coffee on. And the hot soup was in her hands he jerked his arms loose and made a grab for her; she tried to step back, but he grabbed her legs and was trying to pull her down, just before she fell, she dumped the hot soup and the hot coffee on him; he screamed and rolled away from her. She jumped back, and as he was trying to get up, she heard a gun cock just behind her, and Mrs. Lincoln who had been watching the street to let the men get a break said in a calm voice, "If you want to live, stay very still and do not move."

He said, "I am scalded. What do you expect me to do?"

Mrs. Lincoln said, "Lie very still or die. Those are your choices. You have already had supper."

Beverly looked at her with wonder in her face. Mrs. Lincoln looked at her and said, "I have shot Indians while nursing a sick baby, and I surely think I can handle this piece of garbage."

She looked at the other men and said, "It would do you good to remember that also. Right now I would just as soon shoot you as not."

Ken came and took the gun out of her hand and said, "Go rest, honey, you have had a long day, and it is not over yet. Abb, if I were you, I would do what I could to handle those burns because in just about two minutes you are going to be tied up again, and this time, we will use rawhide. You will not find it as comfortable as the cord that was on your wrist before. Beverly, go get one of the men to tie him up or if you want hold the gun, and I will tie him up."

She said, "Give me this gun after what he and the others have done to you and to Joe, I just wish that he would try something. I have never killed a man before, but if I have to kill someone I would just as soon start with him."

Abernathy just looked at her and said, "What have I done to you?" "Well, sending me out to be killed for one thing, if that is not enough then trying to have my uncle and aunt killed, and if that is not enough, then trying to kill Joe, the man that I love is a plenty."

Ken chuckled and said, "Man, if I were you, I would not even bat an eye because that might just get you shot, and by the way she can knock a freckle off a house fly."

Joe was on the east end of town and was sitting his horse and waiting for the soldiers to come out of town. He heard horses coming from the east of town and watching from a heavy thicket; he counted ten riders coming; they were some of the outlaws, and they were headed for town. At the same time the soldiers were coming from town, the outlaws stopped in the middle of the road and was waiting for the soldiers who were dressed in regular clothing, but Joe had ridden for the army and could spot a soldier as far as he could see one. The men who were waiting said, "I wonder who they are." And another one said, "It doesn't matter who they are. We cannot let them go out there. We have our orders." Joe pulled his rifle and waited. Nowadays he always carried a bullet in the chamber; all he had to do was cock the hammer, and he was ready for the first one that went for his gun; he would be dead because Joe was not going to let them kill the soldiers if he could help it. The leader said, "Three of you, move to either side of the road and flank them." The men started to move out, and Joe yelled for them to stop, or they would open up on them. Being by himself, he wanted a little edge; they were very surprised to have some men out in the brush; they did not know how many or where, but they were not going to give up either. They went for their guns and started firing in all directions. The soldiers cleared the saddles and began firing back; Joe was taking toll on them also; bullets were crashing all around Joe. He came out of the saddle and started moving around them to cut off any retreat that they might try to make; he knew there were empty saddles in the road. The shooting had slowed down—he guessed because the men were finding cover getting behind rocks, trees, and bushes, anything that would hide them. Joe was glad that he had not been hit, but he felt his side where it was hurting, and his hand came away bloody, so he had been hit and did not know it. He thought that he had bumped into a broken limb or something that had jabbed him in the side. The shooting from the soldiers was just once in a while; the shooting from the road was a lot more; he had almost reached the road when he heard more horses. He was afraid that it was more outlaws, and he did not know how to handle them; he stumbled and fell just as a bullet hit the tree that he was beside; he rolled over and fired with his pistol; his rifle was under him. He took the man in the face with a bullet. Then the firing started much greater, and the firing from the coming horsemen was really intense, then he heard the bugle; and he knew that the army had arrived. He stuffed a handkerchief in his side and tied his belt around the place. Just as three soldiers came crashing through the underbrush, they looked at Joe and at the dead man in front of him and said, "What is going on here?"

Joe asked them to take him to the commander, and they helped him up, and he went along with them.

The captain was sitting his horse in the middle of the road, and Joe came walking up just as the other soldiers came up from the other direction. The sergeant who was in charge of the patrol said while looking at Joe, "Was you the one that challenged the outlaws?"

Joe said, "I could not let you walk into that trap now, could I? These men have been killing all that got in their way. It did not matter who they were. I overheard them talking at the jail this afternoon. One of them is the sheriff, who now is running things along with Denver Cole, the town doctor, and Abbie in the diner. And this is all that we know about, the last count that we had was about forty hired guns. Some of them have sniper rifles, and we have whittled them down somewhat. The doctor is tied up with some of my people in the town store, and they even have the town people swung over on their side. But anyway, tonight there is a shipment of money coming in on the train, and they are planning on killing the three guards and taking the money, and they have made the plans to put the blame on me. But if I am with you guys, then that would be pretty hard to prove now, would it not?"

The captain said, "If you will stay with us, we will make sure that you are not charged with any robbery."

Joe said, "But they will kill the guards without hesitation. We need to try to save them." "Where will they hit them?" asked the captain.

Joe said, "I do not know for sure, but I think that they will come out of the sheriff's office and take them there, who would expect that. I do not believe the guards would. I have a little problem. I need to get back to town and get my side looked after; I took a bullet in the side."

The captain called for the company doctor to come forward and look after this man. The doctor looked at Joe's side and said, "The bullet went clear through. I will put a bandage on it, and it will be all right."

"Where is your horse?" asked the captain. Joe said, "Over there in the brush." The captain sent a soldier over after Joe's horse.

He brought it back and said, "There was a pile of shell casings all around the horse."

The captain said, "You mean you sat up there and shot it out with them."

Joe said, "I had to be that high up in order to see them, and if I had been on the ground, I could not have seen anything."

The captain said, "You have been under fire before."

Joe nodded his head yes; the sergeant came to Joe and said, "I believe that I have seen you before."

Joe said, "I doubt it but maybe. Were you in the war?"

The sergeant said, "Yes, I was, but that was a long time ago. I had a man pull me out of a burning building and patched me up and carried me on his back for about two miles to an aid station, and I believe that man was you."

Joe said, "What happened in the war is long past. It might have been me, but if it was, you owe me nothing. We all did things that were pretty bizarre in those days. I think that you will remember that."

The sergeant said, "We can talk about this some other time. Right now, I have two men who took a bullet and need my attention."

Joe asked, "What about the outlaws, how many came through it?" Sergeant said, "Well, none came through, after they turned and fired on the troop, we let them have it in the back." The captain said, "We need to be moving. They surely heard the shots from town. Who knows that we are coming?"

"I sent you word," said Joe, "and I told the people with me, but nobody else should know. We might move around with little or no resistance if we keep off the main road. I sent a young man the other direction to stop the squad if they were going out of town the other direction. So he will be out ahead of us somewhere." They started out for town; they moved into the woods and spread out to move in the woods without bumping into each other. Joe took the lead and directed them around behind the outbuildings and away from sight of the town; they moved slowly and silently when they came up behind the store. Joe found Thad waiting for them, and he was shocked to see how many that there were. Joe asked if there was anything that was different in the town.

Thad said that people were moving around, but he did not know what was going on. "There are three men behind the store, but they are just sitting there and look like they don't care anymore."

Joe said, "Well, let us take care of them. Captain, if you will just sit quiet and wait a couple of moments, Thad and I will get rid of the sentries, and then we can get our people and prisoners out of there and take them to safety. Is that all right, sir?"

The captain said, "I have a couple of guys that are as quiet as a mouse in the woods. Why don't you take them with you?"

Joe nodded yes, and two men dismounted and took off anything that would make a noise. Joe, Thad, and the two soldiers moved out and came up on the sentries in a couple of moments and had them in iron's courtesy of the army, and soldiers took them to the rear of the column to hold out of sight and sound from the town. Joe went into the store and brought everyone out; the soldiers went in and took out the prisoners, taking them also to the rear of the column for safekeeping.

Beverly noticed the bandages on Joe and wanted to know what happened; the army doctor informed her that it was nothing to get upset about. She turned to the doctor and said, "I am not upset. I just wanted to know what had happened."

The doctor said, "I know how women get hysterical when something happens. I thought that I would help you keep calm."

Mr. Lincoln said, "Look at the town doctor, and that will tell you how this woman gets excited when he attacked her."

Joe said, "What?"

She was smiling now. "Don't get hysterical." She turned to Mrs. Lincoln and said, "You know how men are when something happens. They get all upset and hysterical." And they both laughed.

The captain called his men together and sent some men to the railroad station and told them to lock it up. When someone comes to the station from town, they cannot return. They can get on the train, but they cannot come back to town until after the money train has come and gone. He sent men to be stationed all along the route that the money would travel from the train to the bank. He explained to the people with him that a law officer needs to be caught in the act of a robbery by an independent group of people to make an arrest airtight. "And we want to get all of them dead or alive. It is up to them. But we will make every effort to keep the railroad guards safe, and if something goes wrong, we want you guys right here with me so I can state the fact that you are completely innocent. We already have pretty good proof that Joe is all right because he stopped an ambush. But we want to do this by the numbers. I hope that all of you understand." Everyone said that they do understand. Joe said, "I just want this over with so we can get on with our lives." Beverly said, "Yes," and she smiled at Joe, who smiled back.

A while later, they heard the train whistle; and a little later, they heard the wagon coming down the road. They were close enough to see the lights of the sheriff's office, and suddenly, the door opened, and men started out, and they yell at the wagon. The men pulled the team to a halt; there was a shout and gunfire.

CHAPTER 15

Joe broke loose and ran to the road; there was a lot of gunfire for a few seconds, and then there was silence. Joe came around the corner, and someone yelled, "There is another one!" And the sergeant yelled, "Cease fire! That is Joe." And the guns went down.

Joe stopped, and he saw that the three guards were safe, and there were men lying all over the road; he went closer, and in the light, he could see one of the men was Denver Cole. One man had a badge on, and all of them were dead. He turned and walked back to the place where the captain was standing with his men, and he said, "Is everything to your liking?"

Joe said, "They will not be causing any more trouble to this town or any other town. What about the outlaws in the mountains? You don't have enough men to get them out of there, without losing a lot of your men." The captain said, "Joe, the money was not the only thing that the train was hauling. We are just the advance force. On the train tonight is a full battalion of men and horses, judges, and lawyers to try to sort this thing out. We are going to set up a very large circle around this whole country and start tightening it up until we know of every cowboy, gunfighter, cow, horse, mule, and rabbit out there in the woods. We have more outlaws here right now than had been in any one place in years. The governor has ordered the arrest and jailing of each of them. The ring leaders, it seems, are captured or dead. So we just have to round up all of the rest of them." Joe said, "There is a bunch at a small town called Bender." The captain said, "Not any more. They are now on a train headed east. They will be back here when the others are up for trial. Sergeant, lock down this town and have double guard on every road, every trail. They cannot come in until you stop them and disarm them, but nobody leaves this town for any reason."

"Yes, sir," said the sergeant, "it will be done gladly. Have a good night's sleep, my good friend Joe. I know that it was you."

"What was that about?" said Beverly.

"Oh, nothing," said Joe.

The captain said, "It seems that Mr. Manning is a closed-mouth man. My sergeant said that Joe is the man that saved his life and carried him to safety during the war, and Joe will not admit to anything." Beverly looked at Joe with much love and took hold of his hand and said, "Well, that sounds like the Joe Manning that I am getting to know and love. He doesn't feel that anything that he does is of any great value, but he places great value on what everybody else does."

Joe looked at Beverly seriously and took hold of both of her hands and said, "I know that it has been a short time since my wife and daughter have passed away, but it seems like years, but I would like to do something very important to you if you will consent after this mess is cleaned up. Because I want to spend the rest of my life with you, trying to make you happy. I believe that Maggie would understand and bless us."

Big tears welled up in Beverly's eyes and she said, "I would be the proudest woman in the world to have you as my husband, and yes, I believe that Maggie would understand and give you her blessings. If it were in reverse, Joe, I would want you to find a good woman and be happy. You certainly deserve it."

The town was locked down for the night. In the morning, there was a house-to-house search, and the town leaders were found bound and gagged, and the soldiers released them. The town people were told what was going on and who the guilty party was; they went to their houses ashamed; some went to their stores and opened for business. When the opportunity came, they told Joe and Beverly how ashamed they were forever doubting Joe and were deeply ashamed. They were told by Joe that it is all right. "We all make mistakes sometimes." The small army closed in on the outlaws; it took weeks to gather all of them. After the soldiers rousted out the outlaws at the different ranches and camps, the sentries were killed or captured as were the outlaws. The most of them elected to fight it out, and they died with a bullet in them rather than waiting for the hangman to do the job. The wounded that could not do anything but surrender were brought to trial. The judges and the attorneys had their trial and presented the evidence, and after a rather speedy trial, they were hung. The doctor, who many of the town people had once loved, felt that he had betrayed them; was ordered to should spend the rest of his life in a prison where he could doctor people just like himself. He said that he would rather be hung than spend the rest of his life in a prison cell. But the choice was not his. Some were sent to prison for a long term, like the people back east who knew what was going on and sending money to finance this venture. And a couple were put on probation like Abbie, who did what she did for love of the sheriff. Joe asked the court to be lenient with her; when she left Joe in the diner, she went to try and get the council to make things right with Joe. But she was tied up with the rest of the council; the telegraph officer who only reported to the sheriff what messages came in and what messages went out—he lost his job but did not go to jail. Joe turned the money over to the court, and they awarded him a good chunk of the money to rebuild his ranch; the Lincolns were awarded money for their losses; some of the drovers went to work for them at their ranch. Beverly was awarded an amount for her trouble and trials. The cattle herd that had been rustled from Ed's dad was sold to Joe and moved to his ranch. Joe has made the plans to build a nice bunkhouse with a kitchen and all of the fixings, which his foreman will oversee the building of this. Joe is making plans for a nice home just around the bend in the valley from where his house was burnt; that place is going to be kept in a fenced in area. Joe wanted his new house to be made out of lumber; there are sawmills back east that can cut anything that Joe wanted and ship it to him. And of course the freight bill will be a wedding gift of the cattle buyer, and there is a great big load of bricks to put on the outside of the house. It will be the only house in the territory to be built like this, and this is a wedding gift of a grateful son of an ex-railroad man. Lenny bought a small herd and moved them to his dad's ranch and took some of his men with him and started ranching there. Thad moved in on the property that Joe gave him and is living in the stone house in the valley; his herd is growing on the rich grass there. Joe took the rest of the drovers along with Jacob as his foreman to look after his ranch. Jacob has hung up his gun; one of his men said, "Jacob, what will you do if you need a gun?"

Jacob said, "Why would I need a gun?"

The man said, "Well, what if you ran into a bear?"

Jacob said that if he runs into a bear, instead of shooting it he will just find that rabbit of Joe's and let the rabbit club that bear and keep him safe. Besides he has a crew of veterans to keep him safe.

Joe is turning the running of the spread and the building of the bunkhouse over to Jacob227. After the bunkhouse is built, then they are going to build him a house, and he is not going to worry about it.

Because after the wedding, Joe is going on a long trip and doesn't want to be bothered by cattle for a while. Now there is a wedding being planned that is going to be the biggest shindig that this country has ever seen; the governor is planning to attend, and Joe's pastor who is all upset about being a small town pastor who is going to preside over the biggest wedding this country has ever seen. With a full military honors and everything, what is he going to say to all of these people? Joe and Beverly just want this over with so they can get away and be together. After all, this was supposed to be their small church wedding, which was going to be short and sweet. But it kind of got out of control, and they had to go along with it; the town felt so bad about letting Joe down, and they wanted to make it up to them. The sergeant who Joe rescued just wanted to be helpful, and he had his major contact the governor about this hero who saved him and saved this town and this area and so on. Until this town gets the wedding all sorted out, Beverly hung her beautiful new wedding gown in her hotel room, and Joe hung his honorary military uniform in his hotel room. And Beverly grabbed Joe by the arm and said, "Let us take a ride and you can show me the country, and we can stop anywhere that we want and look at things. Or talk about things, or just visit with each other for a couple of hours or whatever that we would like to do. My plans were that we would have already been married."

Joe took her by the arm and said, "You had best get into your riding clothes, because we have a lot of looking and stuff around here to see, some place."

Thad said, "Should I kind of go along with you just in case there might be trouble?"

Both of them said at the same time, "No. Thad, you stay here and try on your new suit, or something."

They rode off into the country. As they were riding along, Beverly said, "Joe, where would you like to ride today?"

Joe said, "Let us just follow our nose and see where it takes us." They rode east of the town and wound up at the campsite where Joe and Beverly first kissed each other; they figured it was time to let the horses take a rest; they turned their horses loose and went over to the shade and sat down on a fallen log. Joe looked out over the mountains at the beautiful trees and the land in general; he reached over and took Beverly's hand, looking at this beautiful bride-to-be of his and said,

"Just think, one of these days there will be more people in this land than we would ever want."

Beverly leaned over and kissed Joe and said, "Maybe but not today." And she threw her arms around his neck, and they sat there on the log and kissed each other and touched each other and allowed the horses to have a good long rest. Joe was getting kind of worked up, and he said, "I believe that we should ride on for a while. How do you feel about it?"

Beverly said, "I think maybe we should. We can wait another day or two, can't we?"

Joe took her in his arms and said, "I have waited a lifetime for you already it seems." They rode across the mountain, and Joe said, "Wait a minute, while we are here, if you don't mind, I want to look at something that might be important to us."

She said, "What are you talking about?"

Joe said, "Remember that great big hole in the ground that I wanted to check out one day. I believe today would be a good day to do it."

Beverly said, "Whatever you would like to do."

Joe said, "It would only take about an hour of our time, and it might be important to us." They rode up to the edge of the large disturbance, and they dismounted. Joe took his lariat off his saddle and hooked one end of it to his saddle and then took Beverly's rope and tied the two together. He looked for and found a water birch tree and pulled off some of the dry bark and took a dry stick and wrapped the bark around the stick and found an old pine tree and took some resin that was dry, and he scraped some of it off and rubbed in on the bark. And said, "Now I have a torch if I need one." And he told Beverly that he was going down on the rope, and if he needed a lift back up, he would yell at her, and she could back his horse up and lift him out of the hole."

Beverly touched his arm and kissed him on the cheek and said, "Joe, please be careful and don't break a leg or something. I need you to be very healthy."

She said that while looking Joe in the eyes. Joe kind of smiled and looked at her and nodded his head affirmative; he started down in the hole; he can walk after sliding down the rope for about ten feet. He has to be careful because there is broken rock and large holes between the rocks at times; he looked at the solid walls on the edge of the hole and noticed the different layers of strata. He kept descending down the slide of broken stone. Finally, he comes to the bottom, by now it is so dark that he has to light the torch. He is standing beside a small river. It is a larger river than he saw at the top of the hole; he thought to himself that other streams also come into this hole as well. This is a great source of water that someone could tap into and furnish unlimited amount of irrigation for livestock. He was looking down at the water, and he could see some specks shining under the water; he reached down and picked up a few pieces and held them in his hand while he was looking at the tunnel that the river flowed through. He was wondering where it came out, and he could not remember a river surfacing anywhere in this whole country. Joe rubbed the stones on his pants leg and put them in his pocket without looking at them again. He started back up the slide toward the rope, as soon as he reached the rope he put his gloves back on and started pulling himself up as he walked, and soon he was at the vertical last ten feet. He called to Beverly and said, "Back the horse up and pull me up, please."

She said, "Are you sure you want to come out of your hole?"

He said, "Please, honey." She did as he asked her to do, and he came up to the top and said, "Thank you, horse, for pulling me up."

He turned around and took Beverly in his arms and said, "Thank you so much for getting me out of there."

She said, "I thought about leaving you, but I could not think of anyone who could take your place at the wedding, so I pulled you up."

He said, "What am I getting myself into anyway?" She punched him on the shoulder, and he took her into his arms, and they stood there kissing and holding each other for a long time, and neither one of them wanted to part. He told her about the large river running down there and what it could mean for every person in this whole region if they could just tap into that water and bring it to the surface.

She said, "How?"

Joe said, "Windmills." They got back on their horses and headed back to town, riding slowly and talking, and they came back after dark; as they each went into their hotel rooms, they wanted to clean up and then go eat their supper. Joe started to take his pants off, and he remembered the stones that he put into his pocket. He took them out and started to put them on the table, and he looked at them and was shocked. He held them up to the light and said, "Well, I be darned. Look at what I just found."

When he changed pants, he put the same stones back in his pocket. They were eating supper, and he looked around the dining room.

There was nobody close to them, and he leaned over to Beverly and said, "I am going to show you something, and I do not want you to say anything until we are away from everyone, okay?"

She nodded her head; he laid the stones in her hand; she looked at them and said, "What am I looking at?"

Joe said, "Gold nuggets, I found down in the hole."

Beverly said, "How many?" He said, "I do not know. I just seen some and picked them up and dried them off and put them in my pocket. I did not even look at them until I got into the hotel room. I have no idea what we have found, maybe nothing, but I am going to buy that land."

She said, "Yes, you must in order to protect ourselves."

He said, "Remember, not a word to anyone, okay?"

She shook her head again; the next day they left before daylight, and this time, they rode west of the town; they angled north to the base of a mountain range and after going for a few miles, they turned their horses away from the mountains. And keeping a close eye on the range, they traveled south most of the day and kept turning easterly; they were looking for some low ground that might be a place that the river would surface, but they never did find any place that the river came back to the surface. It was a hard ride, and they only stopped to eat lunch and love on each other for a while.

Joe said that after their honeymoon, they could go to the capital and go over the army's survey records and try to find that river.

Again they were gone all day and again came back after dark.

The pastor said, "Now, Joe, I think that you should stay here tomorrow."

Joe said, "Why should I do that, Pastor?"

The pastor said, "Tomorrow is the day of the wedding."

Beverly hugged the pastor and said, "Pastor, we even unsaddled the horses this evening." And they went hand in hand up the stairs to their rooms to change for supper at the diner. The wedding was a great success; people traveled for miles on horses, buggies, wagons, but especially the train to come to the wedding. It was the event of the year. Beverly in her beautiful flowing long white gown overlain with very intricate beautiful lace, and a long train trailing after her, was the envy of every woman that was to see her; she absolutely glowed with joy and love. There was a shine in her eyes and a spring in her step like a queen coming to the palace of her love.

CHAPTER 16

Joe in his awarded soldier's dress uniform looked very handsome; he looked a little uncomfortable and out of place until he looked around and saw Beverly, and then a change came over him. He stood straighter, and his eyes brightened; his face shone, and there was a smile on his face that made the women cry with joy, and the men just grinned at him. Each of them just glowed when they looked at the other. This was just before the ceremony was to start (a stolen glance at each other).

The governor made a splendid entrance when he came into the church with the smartly dressed men who traveled with him; he shook hands with Joe and waved to the people and would have made a speech but the usher nudged him into a seat. The music started, and Joe turned and looked down the aisle, and here came the most beautiful woman that he has ever seen; he broke out in a large smile, which matched the smile that Beverly had on her face. She was walking on the arm of the sergeant whom Joe had saved in the war. He stopped just a step short of Joe, and Beverly took one more step and took Joe's outstretched hand. They squeezed their hands and looked lovingly at each other; after the pastor swallowed hard and had prayer, he was ready to begin with his part of the ceremony. And then their vows were exchanged in which they both promised to each other their complete love and devotion to each other; the pastor pronounced them man and wife. Joe took her in his arms, and they kissed; they walked together down the aisle looking at their smiling friends. They were ready to get out of there, but there was still a reception, and the governor was going to make a speech. But nobody knew this would happen, but it was sort of planned so that after the wedding and before all of the speeches and so forth. There was a man who came running in and announced that the train had to make a sudden departure, and they were forced to leave early; nobody can prove anything, but the cattle buyer had a big smile on his face. They were told in front of everyone that they had to leave immediately, "Just you two, come on, all of your luggage has already been put on the train." Joe looked over at the cattle buyer, and he saw a thumbs-up and a big grin; his son looked at the governor and shrugged his shoulders and said, "I do not know what happened," and he poked his dad in the ribs. They left on the buggy that was parked at the front door and ran out saying goodbye to everyone as they left. When they were on their private car and the door closed, Beverly said, "What just happened?"

Joe smiled and said, "I just love that man." And he took her in his arms and kissed his new wife, and she understood what just happened and was very happy. And they are planning on going someplace for a long time and just get acquainted with each other. Nothing at this moment is more important that this moment and the rest of their lives. Joe and Beverly loved each other more than the world could ever know; they held each other and kissed each other and intimately loved each other and were not ashamed. Their love is a love that will last though their life. They traveled on the train and knowing that they could go anywhere the tracks were laid for free, for the rest of their life. They went to the eastern shore and left the train and took a ship and went on a cruise to Paris, France, where they visited all of the sights or those old and wonderful cities; Joe was intrigued with the people who they met, and I am sure that many of the people will remember the Manning couple. After the visit to the cities, they went back to the ship.

On board ship, they met new people and saw all the marvelous things that were to see on a ship. They would sit on the deck and watch the ocean; it was a marvelous thing to watch the waves and the motion of the ship, but they could not go for a minute or more without touching each other. They held hands as they walked and the other folks that met them would smile, and after they passed another couple, they looked behind them—at Joe and Beverly holding hands; the other couple just had to hold hands themselves. Love is a contagious thing, when other people are around those that love, they seem to want to love their spouse or loved one. One day for a moment only,

Joe was comparing the love that he had for Maggie to the love that he had for Beverly, and they were both deep love, but they were so vastly different and just as deep as any love could be. Joe was sad that Maggie and Ginny had to die, but he was so happy that he had Beverly in his life now. Joe and Beverly went to shows, to concerts, they even went into the gambling casino, and Joe played some poker; he lost a little and won a little. Beverly was sitting on a chair watching what was going on; she knew a little about the game but not much. A gentleman came over to her and said, "Do you play?"

Beverly looked up at a very tall man who wore a white suit, a black string tie; he was smiling at her through his white whiskers and a white chin whiskers. He looked for all the world like a picture of a southern gentleman. Beverly said, "I know a little about it but not very much."

He said, "May I sit down here, and I will explain it to you."

Beverly moved over a little closer to Joe, and the man sat down on the other side of her; he started telling her what was going on with the players. He was talking in low tones, but Joe could still hear him; the game kept going, and he was walking Beverly through the game. Joe started to win a few hands, and the player directly across the table was getting angry. There was a banker at the table who worked for the ship line. He was watching the game very carefully. Joe was watching the dealer, and he saw a card come off the bottom of the deck. The banker looked at a couple of men who were standing close by and who had been getting drinks and so forth for the gamblers; he also looked at the dealer; the men moved quietly to either side of the dealer. Joe also heard this man tell Beverly that the dealer was bottom dealing and a card cheat. The dealer heard what he said; he started to rise and reach in his pocket. The two men grabbed his arms and checked and removed two guns from him and also checked his arms for card holders and also found those. The banker said, "How much money did you start with?"

The gambler said, "All of it."

The banker said, "I will give you back what you started with, and then I will divide the rest of the money equally with all of the players, and you, sir, will be locked in your cabin until we come to some place that we can put you ashore, and you will never gamble on any ship again ever. We will notify every line of your identity and your card cheating."

The banker looked at the players and said, "Gentlemen, you shall continue playing and my company regrets that this happened. We had our suspicions, but we could not be sure until now."

The play continued, and everything went along fine, but Joe wanted to quit and spend some time with his new wife instead of playing poker. Joe turned around and looked at the elderly gentleman and extended his hand and said, "How are you? My name is Joe. I believe you have met my wife and have been schooling her in the art of poker."

The man said, "My name is of no importance, but I am glad to have met such a lovely lady and a very gracious lady to allow me to sit beside her and talk with her."

Joe said, "You have very good eyes. I was sitting directly across from the cheater, and I saw the bottom deal. The banker caught it, and you also caught it. I perceive you are a gambler."

The gentleman said, "I used to be a gambler at one sad time in my life, but that has faded into the past."

Joe said, "Well, I am not a gambler, and I do not want to be. I want the odds to be in my favor and the game to be in our daily life and not around a table."

The old gentleman said, "For someone who does not play the game, you have a very good eye and a good mind that understands the game."

Joe said, "I understand people, and the cards speak for themselves."

The old gentleman said, "I would not want to set into a serious game with you, Mr. Joe, because you do not play the odds. You play the players."

And Joe said, "I do not believe that I can play cards that I cannot see, but I can play the people who I can see."

With this, Joe and Beverly bid the older gentleman farewell and left the casino. Beverly said, "I wonder who that fellow was. He seemed so nice to me, and he was so intent on the game. I do not believe that he sat down with me to explain the game, but he sat down with me to watch the game."

Joe said, "I seem to remember a gentleman whose trademark as a gambler was the gentleman who could read cards like he could see the face of the cards that each player was holding." He finally quit gambling and started a detective bureau to expose crooked gamblers, and that may have been his detectives who were working the game."

Beverly said, "Well, how did you do in the game?"

Joe said, "With what I won and the share of the cheat's pot, I believe I have won enough for me to afford to buy you dinner this evening in the most elegant roadhouse in this town."

She laughed and punched Joe in the ribs and said, "You will take me to the best restaurant in this great floating city."

They walked on down the deck of the beautiful ship, nodding to the other passengers that they met coming the other way.

Things in the town were getting back to normal after the wedding was over, and all of the dignitaries had left on the train. Lenny and his men went back to his ranch on the train. Thad bought supplies and went back to the valley to his cattle and his rock house. Jacob took Joe's men back to the ranch and started building the house that Joe had lain out; they laid a good foundation for the house to set on at the edge of the hill. And close to the forest setback in a small cove where the wind would reach some but the hard wind of winter would not bother the house. They built a solid wood frame and covered the entire frame including the roof with wooden boards; they put brick on the walls after installing the windows and the doors. Good wooden shingles or shakes were put on the roof; the house was now watertight. They began building the inside of the house; the kitchen had a sink with a pump on the side piped into the spring on the knoll behind the old house. In the kitchen, instead of building shelves along the wall, one of the men said he was in a great mansion in the south one day, and he saw cabinets built in the kitchen.

One of the men asked him, "Who let him in the back door?"

He said, "The cook did. How else was I going to deliver the groceries from the store?" Everyone laughed, but they became serious and said, "We have the time, and we have the lumber, why not?"

The worker explained how they looked, and the men built Beverly kitchen cabinets. The men also worked on the bunkhouse while they were working on Joe's house; they had a place to sleep anyway. They knew that Joe left orders to build the bunkhouse first, but they wanted to make sure that Joe's house would be finished when he and Beverly came back.

The bunkhouse was coming along fine; the weather was getting colder, so they knew that winter was not going to be very far behind them. They finally finished it up and set up the kitchen, and they were ready for winter.

Jacob sent a crew of men to drag close to the house area dry logs so they could be cut up and then chopped into kinlin wood. Men took time out to cut hay and stack it in the fields and build log fences around each stack to keep the cattle out until the snow covered the ground, and they then would open a stack of hay and allow the cows to eat of the hay because they could not get to the grass. They searched out the deep valleys where the snow would not get so deep and the wind would not make the snow pile up so deep. And they kept the cattle out of these areas and allow the grass to grow better, and they could move a herd of cattle into these areas and let them graze on this grass also in the bad weather, plus the cattle would have some shelter from the freezing weather. Jacob was not as knowing about the land as Joe was, and he had to travel the hills and the valleys until he knew the land; he knew where he could put a herd of cattle and how long he could let them graze; he knew where the herds had to be when the weather became so bitter cold. He also in three little valleys put up a small cabin in each of them so he could put a couple of men in them, and they could watch over the herd of cattle that was in that valley at that time. These were stocked with a stove, a couple of bunk beds, and plenty of wood; they each were stocked with food and plenty of warm blankets—everything that a man who was caught out in the weather might need to survive a severe storm. Jacob went over across the mountain to the east and found a large valley; he thought that he might move a herd of cattle over there, but there was no water to water the herd with. He knew then why Joe had never used this valley; he thought this is a shame that so much land is wasted because there is no water to feed the land. Jacob sat on his horse on top of a ridge that looked out over the majority of Joe's ranch and just looked at the beauty of the land. He could see the small mountains or hills from where he sat; it looked like there was just one hill after another as far as he could see, and he knew what he could not see was the vast flat land that lay between each of these hills. There were streams and rivers between some of these hills. The grass that was in these valleys was bountiful enough to feed the beef it took to feed the whole country. And look at the places that could grow crops to also feed the people of this country. Jacob said to himself, "I will never leave this country when Joe comes back, and if he ever runs me off, I think that I will find me a piece of this country and plant myself and grow with this country, and hang my gun up forever."

CHAPTER 17

Joe and Beverly came home, and the town went wild; Beverly said, "Shouldn't somebody put a name on this town?"

The people said, "Why should we?" Beverly said, "When someone asked me where I was from, I could not tell them proudly where I was from because there was no name. When you said 'the town,' they would look at you and walk off, and I am proud of this place whatever it is called."

Someone said, "Maybe we should call a town meeting and talk about it. The railroad is here, and we may be traveling some place."

Beverly said, "What if one of you want to tell other people to tell them about your business, where would you tell them to come to?"

Joe spoke up and said, "It is hard sometimes to get a railroad ticket to this town because you cannot tell them where you are going. They look on their list of places, and they do not see town."

The folks started talking at the train station where they met Joe and Beverly, and as they walked down through town, Joe heard a lot of different names like George Washington; one person wanted to name it after his wife, Dorky; another wanted to name it City. Joe and Beverly looked at each other and grinned; they knew that as soon as they could get to the livery stable and rent a buckboard, they were heading home. But Joe had a thought. He looked at Beverly and said, "Have you thought about putting furniture in our new house, that we haven't seen yet."

Beverly said, "How could I do that? I don't even know what would go with what, Joe. I have to see the house to know what to buy."

Joe said, "I am sorry, but this is the first time that I have even thought about it. I feel kind of ashamed of myself." But he put his arms around her and said, "We have been kind of busy."

She smiled and kissed him and patted him and said, "Husband, let us get home and look things over and see what we really do need."

They walked on to the buckboard, and he helped her in and went around to the other side, and they headed out to the ranch. The closer Joe came to the ranch, the more excited he became; he drove by landmarks that he had passed so many times, and they brought back memories; they finally came within sight of the ranch and could see the house, and Joe said, "What a mansion, I thought that we were going to get a house, not a mansion." Beverly said, "There were a lot of people grateful to you for all that you did to stop those bunch of killers from destroying every person in this country." They pulled up in front of the house and left the buckboard and started up the steps to the house, and one of the cowboys saw them and let out a war whoop, and they all came running. Jacob just stood there and grinned. Joe turned to his men and said, "This is fantastic. Now I know you guys can do more than ride horses and drink liquor. Maybe we should stop being ranchers and start building houses for other people."

With the look that he received on their faces, Joe said, "I am just kidding. Nothing is going to get me up and out of this beautiful house and off this ranch ever again."

With these words, there was a great cheer from all the men. Joe and Beverly went into the house and looked at it; it was beautiful, and there was enough furniture in the house for them to move in.

Joe asked, "Where did all of this furniture come from?"

Jacob said, "The people of the town and Mr. and Mrs. Lincoln all brought different pieces of furniture to get you started. When your new furniture comes, we will take all of these things back to their rightful owners."

Joe looked at Beverly, and she was dabbing her eyes; she said, "These people cannot be beaten; they are the best neighbors in the world."

Joe and Jacob walk out on the porch, and Joe asked Jacob saying, "How is Thad doing these days?"

Jacob said, "I was over that way a few weeks ago, and I saw Thad, and he had ran into a young lady that lives somewhere close to Bender, and I believe that he is smitten. The young lady was all Thad could talk about."

Joe said, "I am going to ride over there and have a talk with him as soon as I can."

Jacob said, "You know that real big valley just a couple of mountains over?"

And Joe shook his head yes, he did know, and Jacob said, "If we could figure some way of watering that valley, then you could have three times the pasture that you have now."

Joe said, "I already know of a way of doing just that, but it is going to take some time and money, but we are going to do just that."

Jacob said, "You're always one step ahead of all the rest of us, but I cannot figure out just how to make water run uphill."

Joe looked at Jacob and said, "Defy gravity." And he smiled at Jacob, who was scratching his head.

Joe went into the house and hugged Beverly and said, "Thad has a girlfriend. He found her over close to Bender. I am going back to town and take the buckboard back and pick up our two horses. They are still at the livery stable. I will be back after a while."

He gave her a kiss and patted her on the fanny and said, "I will be back about dark, don't go away."

Beverly looked at Joe and squeezed him and said, "Just try and get rid of me. It won't be worth the effort even to try."

Joe hugged her and put his hat on, and for the first time in months, he strapped his gun on and left the house. Beverly noticed the gun and thought, *now we are away back to the world that started from*, and she hoped that Joe would never have to draw that gun to defend himself ever again. Joe drove into town and went to the livery stable and turned the buggy back in and went to their horses and started saddling them. A man walked up to Joe and said, "Would you like to sell those horses?"

Joe turned around and said, "No, sir, I really would not. These horses are very special to me, and I will always keep them."

The man said, "I would not say always," and Joe looked at him closely; he was a man that was a couple of inches taller than Joe, broad in the shoulders, features like they were chiseled out of granite, he had hair that was black and starting to get gray at the temples. His clothing was a combination of western boots, Levy pants, a white shirt, and a suit coat; and the thing that set him apart was a colt pistol which sat in a holster that was positioned for a quick draw.

Joe said, "Mister, I just got back into town, and I do not want any trouble out of you, but do not push me too far."

With that, he took the reins of both horses, and he walked out of the livery stable and mounted up and started off; the man spoke again, and Joe got the meaning very clear. "I always get what I set out to get, and don't think that I will not."

Joe kept riding without looking back; he stopped at the mercantile store and went in. Sam met him at the counter and said, "My friend, what can I do for you today?"

Joe asked Sam if he knew the man that he met at the livery stable.

Sam said, "He came around here a few weeks ago and is hanging around. He has a big mouth, but I don't think that he is going to harm anyone."

Joe said, "I would not be so sure. Have you got anyone lined up to be the next sheriff?" Sam said, "I was thinking of asking Murphy, that is the man's name, to consider taking the job, seeing as he has nothing else to do."

Joe said, "If I would have a vote in that, I would vote absolutely no."

Sam said, "Then we will not consider it, but we do need someone."

Joe said, "Someone will come along. I feel sure."

Joe picked up a few things that Jacob told him about that they needed, and he went back outside. Sam followed him out and was standing on the porch. Joe tied the sack of things on Beverly's horse, around the saddle horn. And just as Joe started to mount up on his horse, the stranger came down the street and yelled, "Stop." Joe did not mount up, but as he did turn, he took the throng off his gun's hammer. The man noticed what Joe had done, and he stopped; he said, "Mister, you had better not do that."

Joe said, "What do you want?" The man said, "I want those horses, and I aim to have them, and I do not care whether I buy them off you, or I just take them off you." They were standing there, looking at each other.

Sam said, "Mister, I believe that you should look at me just for a moment." The man said, "Why should I do that?"

Sam said, "Because if you twitch a finger toward your gun, I will blow you in half with this scattergun."

The stranger's face turned a sickly pale, and he raised his hands in the air. Joe walked to him and took his gun out of his holster and said, "Mister, Sam just saved your life." The man said, "No, he saved your life."

Joe stepped back and drew his gun, which was the same lightning speed that the other outlaws had witnessed just before they died. Joe smiled and pointed it at the stranger's nose and said, "Can you draw this good?" Again the man's face grew pale.

Joe asked him if he had any belongings here in town. He said all that he had was at the train station.

Joe said, "What are you doing here anyway?" And the man said that he came here to meet the sheriff, but he doesn't seem to be around, so he wanted a horse to go out to the sheriff's ranch."

Joe said, "You came very close to meeting the sheriff when you started to draw against me, but if you really do want to meet him I will walk you up to the graveyard. That is where he is buried."

The man said, "What happened to him?" Joe said, "He and some of his buddies tried to rob the bank payroll, and the army blew them away."

"Now if you want to stay healthy, you will walk to the railroad station." He followed the man to the station and asked the ticket agent when the next train was due. He said in about an hour.

Joe said, "Give this man a ticket to the farthest point that you can give him one."

The man said, "You cannot do that to me."

Joe looked at him for a little bit and said, "You are right. I cannot do that to you."

And Joe said, "Do you know where the army took all of those other guys a while back that did not want to leave our town?"

The agent looked at Joe and then at the stranger and said, "Is that where he wants to go?"

Joe said, "That is exactly where he wants to go. You can give him a one-way ticket there and call ahead and make sure that he is met at the train station and is escorted to the finest hotel room that they have."

He turned to the man and said, "The men that worked for the sheriff left this town and went to this other town and are staying there. My understanding is that their present job is going to take a long time to finish. Would you like to go to the farthest point away from here, or would you like to go there?"

The man said, "If I have a choice, I will go where the other men have gone."

Joe said, "You have made a wise decision."

Joe and Sam waited for the train; the man asked for his gun back, and Joe said, "No, you are not going to get this gun back." The man barely moved his jacket, and Joe pointed the gun at him and said, "Open the front of your coat."

The man started to open his coat with his left hand, and Joe said, "No, you open your coat with your right hand and you sit on your left hand, or I might get nervous and blow it off." The man did as he was told, and he had a small gun in a shoulder holster. Joe cocked the man's pistol that he took from him and told Sam to remove the other gun.

Joe said, "Now I am going to ask one time only, and if you lie to me, you will be loaded on the train in a blanket. Do you have any more weapons, and I am going to search you."

The man said, "In my right boot, there is a derringer."

Sam said, "You are just the same as all the rest of them murdering, thieving outlaws. They all got what they belong."

The man said, "What are you talking about? Where are you sending me?"

Joe smiled and said, "With all of your buddies. That is where."

The man started to lunge at Joe; he was ready for something, and Joe came down on his head with the pistol and knocked him out. While they were getting some rope to tie him up, Joe went through his coat pocket and found a wanted poster on the man wanted for murder. He had a price on his head for five thousand dollars, and Joe said, "We have just found the money we needed for a new schoolhouse for the kids."

He showed Sam and the ticket agent the wanted poster, and the agent said, "I will send the telegram right now to everyone that needs to know about this."

They heard the train coming, and Joe went out to the landing so he could tell the conductor what was going on. He met the conductor, and the conductor said, "Wait just a minute, Joe."

He went back into the train and out came the cattle buyer and hugged Joe and said, "How in the world are you and Beverly doing? We were wondering how your trip was, how is your ranch coming along, what are you up to now?"

Joe said, "Trip fine, house finished, loading up trash on your train." And he smiled at the cattle buyer who looked really puzzled.

Joe said, "Found a man who was looking for the ranch of the sheriff and was going to force me to give him my horses, so we thought we would give him a nice trip on your train to a new hotel he can stay at for free."

"Plus there is a big enough price on his head to build us a new school in town." The cattle buyer said, "When are you all going to do something about a name for that town?"

Joe said, "We thought maybe we could call it the cattle buyer."

And they laughed, and the cattle buyer said, "I do not think that the teacher or the student in your new school would like that now, do you?"

Joe just laughed and said, "When we came home, we proposed to the town that they come up with a name for the town, and they are working on it."

Sam came over and said, "They had a meeting and decided to call it Jameson."

Joe said, "Now I am not complaining, but how did you come up with the name Jameson, who is Jameson?"

Sam said, "That is just everyone wanted to name the town after someone they knew and that hurt other people's feelings. Someone finally came up with the name Jameson, and others asked who he is or was, and nobody could think of anyone with that name, and so Jameson it is."

The cattle buyer laughed heartily and said, "I have never heard of a better way to pick a name for a town, any town."

Joe heard someone yell at him, and he looked at the engine, and there were two people hanging out the engine window, waving to him; he told the cattle buyer that he would be back in a moment. The buyer looked at the engine and said, "Joe, you had better take a moment and go and say hi to those men. They have been pestering me to death as to when you and Beverly were coming back to town, er, Jameson."

Joe went to the engine and shook hands with them and talked to them for a couple of moments and came back. They shook hands all around, and the cattle buyer went back into the car, and the conductor waved to the engineer, and as they left there was a healthy blow on the whistle, and then a short toot. Joe remembered the signal they were going to blow if the telegram was received by the cattle buyer when he called for the army to come into town months ago. Joe smiled to himself; Sam looked at Joe and said, "What has made you look so smug just now?"

Joe told him what the train whistle was all about, and Sam just smiled. Joe went back to the store with Sam. Joe shook hands with Sam and got on his horse and started back to the ranch; Joe looked over the beautiful country and noticed the leaves are in full bloom; there is every color in the thoughts of man, but these colors come from the mind of God. Joe cannot look at the great forest, but what he does not think of God. He knows that God could have made a universe for us that was just black and white. But God did not just make it full of color, of beautiful sounds, but he put mountains, hills, valleys, and such a variety of everything that a man cannot ever get used to all of the wonders of God. Joe is just waiting to get home and get Beverly up on her horse and go across the mountain and see Thad. Joe headed home to see Beverly, his new ranch house, and all that God has allowed him to have. On the ride home, he again looked at the country over, and what a country it is. He watched the eagles soaring across the sky; he watched the hawks darting along the mountain. The deer that is eating in a secluded glen, taking a bite of grass and lifting her head and looking all around for danger as she chewed the food. Joe thought to himself that this would be a very good habit for a man to do, each thing that a man does to look up and ponder about possible lurking danger. Because man has an enemy that is stalking this world like a lion seeking who he might devour, and that would be Satan. I know that you cannot see Satan or hear him, but you know that he is always near, so we can look for the signs of Satan and be very aware of him and stay very close to the Lord because that is the only protection that we have in this world. Joe came into the ranch, and Beverly saw Joe coming up the road, and she is already dressed in her riding outfit. She met Joe on the porch and said, "I am ready, where are we going today?"

Joe said, "Let us go and look at our cattle, and then I would like to go over to the valley and see Thad."

They mounted up and started out for the valley that belonged to Thad; it was a beautiful day. The sun was warm for the season; the air was still some color in the leaves especially the maple leaves. Joe and Beverly took coats with them just to be safe; you could never know when there would be a storm and bring some really cold weather. They told Jacob where they were going so he would know just in case.

Joe said, "Isn't this just about the prettiest day that you have ever seen?" Beverly looked at Joe and said, "From where I sit, it could not look any better." Joe felt uncomfortable for her to say that in front of Jacob so he put his heel into his horse and moved out. Beverly, with a smile on her face, followed; and when she came up behind Joe, she pinched him on the back of the leg. He looked at her and smiled all over himself. They traveled over the hills and finally came to the valley; they started through the bottleneck and found a gate across the pass; Joe dismounted and opened the gate and let Beverly through, and then he closed the gate. Thad had planted and harvested a garden since Joe had been here; he looked the place over with some pride like his own son had done this. They rode pretty close to the house, and Joe yelled hello to the house, and Thad said from behind them, "Hello, Joe and Beverly." They jumped and said, "Thad, how did you get behind us?"

He said, "I was standing here when you opened and closed the gate. You just did not see me."

Joe said, "One of these days, you are going to give someone a heart attack."

Thad just smiled and said, "I figure that your hearts are pretty solid. Come on into the house and see how you like it."

They talked for a while, and Joe asked Thad why he changed the bunk beds for a single wider bed.

CHAPTER 18

Thad said, "I felt that it would do me a lot more good this way."

Joe said, "What if I come over for a visit, where will I sleep?"

Thad said, "Probably outside because I will have someone with me before very long."

Joe said, "Tell me about her." Thad said, "Wait a couple of days, and I will bring her over to the ranch, and I will let you meet her."

Beverly said, "Where did you meet her? Where does she live?"

Thad said, "I went over to Bender to pick up some supplies at the store, and she was in the store. We bumped into each other near one of the counters. She said, 'Why don't you look where you are going?' I said, 'I am sorry, but you backed into me, and you should be the one who is sorry.'"

She looked real mad until she saw me, and she said, "I thought that you were my brother. He is always in my way."

"We started talking, and I carried her groceries home for her, and she and her mom invited me to stay for the noon meal. They are very nice people. They moved here from back east and are farmers. They seem to like me a lot. I have made a few trips over to Bender to see her, and finally I asked her to marry me. Her name is Malinda Connors. She said, 'yes.'"

Joe said, "That is fantastic, Thad. We just wanted to see how you were doing and make sure that you were safe. We had better get back across the hills before it gets too late. We will be looking forward to seeing you in a few days."

They went outside, and Joe said, "It is really getting colder. We had better hurry and get home."

Thad said, "Let me open the gate for you while you are getting your coats on and cinching up."

They mounted up and started out. It was late in the afternoon. Beverly asked Joe, "Do you think that we can get home before dark?"

Joe said, "No, I think it will be dark by the time we get across the mountains, but once then we will be on our own range, and we will not have any trouble."

They were almost across the mountains when it started snowing. Joe stopped and said, "Let me have your lead line, and you hold onto the reins, and that way, we will be able to stay together if the snow gets heavy."

Beverly unhooked the lead rope from the saddle horn and handed it to Joe and said, "I will be right behind you, big boy."

Joe started out at a pretty good speed to get as far as fast as he could; he knew the country very well, and he headed straight for the ranch house. The snow was blowing, and Beverly put her head down and let her hat shield some of the cold wind from her face and ears. She had gloves on, but her hands and her legs were getting very cold, but she knew that Joe had to keep his head up to see, and it was colder on him. All of a sudden, Joe slowed up and turned to the left; he took them into a shielded place on the hillside and started up the mountain; he traveled for about thirty minutes, and then he stopped. He came back and helped Beverly off the horse and led her into a sheltered area and said, "Stand here." He moved off about five feet and pulled a slab of rock down. He took her and led her into a small cave, took some blankets, and put them around her shoulders and legs and said, "I will have a fire going in a couple of minutes."

Beverly said, "What is this place, where are we?"

Joe said, "This is one of many places all over these mountains that I have supplies stored for just this type of reason." Joe built a good fire from some wood that was stored in the cave and went outside and brought some heavier wood from the outside and piled it close to them. Joe said, "We could stay here for days if we had to, but this storm will blow itself out by tomorrow, and then we will go back home."

They both shared the same blankets and needless to say they both stayed pretty warm. Beverly slept with her head on Joe's shoulder, and

Joe napped waking every so often and putting more wood on the fire. The next morning at daylight, they looked outside and found a world that was beautiful; the snow covered the whole earth as far as they could see. The trees were covered on one side where the strong wind had blown the snow against the side of it. The limbs on all of the trees held snow on them; it was a sight to behold. The temperature was warming up as the sun started coming across the mountain. Joe was looking around at the supplies that he had stored in this cave, and he found some coffee and a coffeepot. He went out and filled it with snow and put some coffee in the pot and put it on the fire. After a bit, they had coffee. Joe always carried a cup in his saddlebags. They sat huddled in their blanket and sipped their coffee and were content. After a while, they put the fire out and mounted up on their horses and headed on home. Joe reached over and caught hold of Beverly's hand and said, "Hope this will be the worst night of our lives."

She looked at him and said, "I do not think that it was a bad night because we were together."

They rode into the ranch house and were met with men who were so worried about them. Beverly said, "You, old women, what was there to be so worried about? We were just fine. It was just a little snow."

The men looked at each other and did not know what to say to her; they looked at Joe and he said, "Don't worry, Beverly took very good care of me."

They went into the house, holding hands and smiling to each other.

Joe had been thinking about the underground river that they had found in the back country; he told Beverly he was going to take Ed and Jacob with him to the underground river and do some exploring. They took plenty of rope, lights, and extra food and canteens. The weather was much warmer, and they had a pleasant ride through the hills and looking over the country. The trees were bare of leaves, but it was a great time to really look over the hills. Joe showed them the different hills and valley when they stopped to let the horses rest on the top of one of the hills. You could look over the tops of the hills as far as the eye could see. I turned into a blue haze way off in the distance. Joe explained to these two men that with more water, they could have a much larger territory to graze a much larger herd of cattle. Ed said, "Where do you plan to get this water, Joe?"

Joe said, "I plan to get this water from under the ground and pump it up with windmills. The wind blows through these valleys most of the time."

Ed said, "Maybe we can dam up the water during the windy times and irrigate with it when the season of little wind or no wind."

Jacob said, "Joe, I have some experience building dams. I have built some very large ones."

Ed, looking at Jacob, said, "Yes, but did they hold enough water to fill a coffeepot."

They good-naturedly laughed at that, but Joe tucked this bit of knowledge back for future use. They came to the place where it looked like the earth had a great disturbance at one time, and it fell into a great hole. The small stream that was coming down the very fertile valley just fell into the hole, and the valley beyond it was nothing but scrub brush and a dry nothing. Joe took the horses around to one side and showed them where he had gone into the hole.

Joe said, "Jacob, Ed and I will go down, and I want to travel a way down the lower river." Jacob said, "There is a river down there? Where is it coming from?"

Joe said, "I do not know, also I do not know where it is going."

Jacob said, "Man, I would like to look at this. When can I get a chance to go down there?" Ed said, "Joe, if it does not matter to you, I really feel funny going down into a hole in the ground."

Jacob said, "Joe, I would count it an honor to go down there with you."

Joe said, "Come on, Jacob, hook up one of the long ropes on the saddle horn, and when we get ready to come back up, you can haul us up to the top." Ed said, "That will suit me just fine, do you really mind that I do not go?" "No, I do not. I believe that I have found the man that I need to take care of this project," Joe said, looking at Jacob, who was just beaming. They took lanterns and a backpack each and let themselves down on the rope until they could get to the broken rock that made up a gradual slope down to the level of the river. They had lit their lanterns before they started down, and as soon as they left the rope, Joe started down the slide rock and Jacob said, "Joe, look here behind you," and Joe turned around and saw what Jacob was talking about. There was a space in between the solid rock of the top and the broken rock that they were standing on. Jacob said, "With just a little work, I believe that a man could make a hole big enough for men to go through there and travel upstream and explore that area."

Joe said, "That would be a great idea, but first let us explore what is down this river first and try to see where this river goes."

They moved on down the broken rock to the edge of the underground river; they looked at the large cavern over; it was about ten feet high, and in some places it comes down to about six feet high. They traveled about they would guess five miles, and the river kept going in the same general direction. It seemed like it was going directly toward the ranch headquarters. Joe said, "I wonder where this river comes to the surface or if it ever does." Jacob said, "If you are really wondering, I can take a crew of men, and we can get a compass and some other equipment and survey the river and see where it goes."

Joe said, "I was just wondering if there was a storm back where this river starts. I wonder how high the water would get in here, and would it be safe for men to be in here."

Joe glanced down at his feet and saw a shiny object and bent over and picked it up and pulled his fingers through the sand and plowed up a few more of the same thing. He showed Jacob, and he said, "You are picking up gold nuggets without even trying." They spent a few moments and ran their fingers through the sand, and there was a few of them. Jacob said, "Maybe we should go upstream first and find out where these are coming from. But, boss, I do think that I would not say anything about finding gold, or there will be people crawling over your land, and you will not be able to stop them."

Joe said, "Let us get out of here and tell Ed what is going on and the three of us plan what we are going to do." Jacob said, "Joe, do you think that Ed will tell anyone about the gold you found down here?"

Joe said, "I trust Ed just like I trust you. We cannot start distrusting each other over gold, now can we?"

Jacob looked ashamed and said, "Joe, I am sorry about what I just said. Can we just drop it?"

They went back to the rope, and Joe called to Ed and said, "Go ahead and pull me up." Ed pulled the horse forward until Joe came up to the top of the hole, then they backed the horse back, and Joe let the rope down for Jacob who came up as the horse was pulled forward. They coiled up the rope and fastened it to the saddle. Joe told Ed about the gold that is down there and about what they talked about mapping the river in both directions to see where it starts from and where it is going. They mount up and ride back to the ranch as they stopped on the top of one of the hills, and Joe turned to Jacob and told him to pick a man to go with him and travel up the river on the surface and try to find where it goes underground. That will let us know something maybe. "Ed, I want you to pick a couple of men to come over here and build a ladder long enough to go down in the hole. I do not want them to put the ladder in the hole but just build it, okay?"

Ed said, "I will have the ladder built tomorrow."

Jacob said, "I will pick a man and get back in the country and map out all that I can find." Joe said, "Guys, I want a lid put on this thing. I do not want an army of people in here looking for gold. If we find anything worthwhile, I will take care of all of you, men. I have about everything I want in this world, and if there is something worthwhile, I will share it with every one of you."

Both men seemed well pleased with what Joe had just told them. Joe went into the house and told his bride what he had found out and what he was going to do in order to get more water for the ranch. They sat and talked about it. Beverly has very little knowledge about such things, but when Joe explained what he is talking about, she has such wisdom about possible solutions. Joe said he wanted to go to the capital and see what the army has in maps of this area. She asked the question, "Do you really want the army going down to the river and find what you do not want anyone to find."

Joe said, "I really need to buy that whole area and lock it up before anything happens. I will go to Richmond and find out how much it is going to cost me purchase that whole area. Maybe I can tie our land to the land that Thad owns."

Beverly said, "Why don't you mine enough gold out of there to pay for the land?"

Joe said, "I do not believe that I want to take anything out of there until we own the land that might set up a legal battle. I am going over to the capital and talk to the right people and see how much the land is worth. The actual land could not be worth much."

Beverly looked at Joe, and a smile came to her lips, and she said, "Joe, I just remembered the money that the government gave me after the trial is in an account at the capital, and we have not touched it."

Joe looked at her and exclaimed in amazement, and he said, "Yes, and some of the money that was awarded to me is still in there also. Beverly, what do you say we put all of that money into land and water rights and buy that whole area and get the whole underwater area."

Beverly said, "Joe, we do not want to be unchristian about this, but I believe God has given that area of land to us because when we were running from Satan and the outlaws that was a part of the deliverance that God used to defeat them because that was the beginning of the end for them. So maybe God has given us that land so we can use it for the betterment of other less fortunate people."

Joe came over to Beverly and put his arms around her and held her to him and put all of his love into this tender moment. And looking into the beautiful and tender eyes of Beverly, he said, "You are so good. Honey, you want only the best for the unfortunate folks around us, and I love you so much for that tenderness. I agree with you we have so much and others have so little, so yes, let us buy that land, and we will use it however God leads us to use it."

Joe went out to the blacksmith shop and found Ed and told him they were going over to the capital and see what they could do about the land. He said, "Remember to say nothing about what we are going to do. Beverly and I want to use the land, water, and anything else for the betterment of the people who will come to this country and try to get a start. What we are doing could be very important to many people, so we must allow God to lead us in what happens from this time onward. Do you agree about this?"

Ed was listening to Joe and was looking off to the hills around us, and he said, "Joe, I am proud to be a part of you two because you look at what you are doing and see how much it means to the country around you. You are looking at the people who you do not know, people who are living some other part of this world, who maybe have not even heard of this country, and you are planning to help them. I believe this could be the most important trip you will ever make. You go ahead, boss, and I will do my part here at home, and I will try to make sure that everything here is secure and safe."

Joe shook hands with Ed and said, "Ed, I do not worry about you, and I do not worry about all of this because I am leaving everything in the Lord's hands, and in your hands it could not be safer."

Joe went back into the house, and Beverly already had their clothes packed and was ready to leave. They prepared themselves and called for the buggy to be brought around; Joe put their bags in the buggy, and they got in and drove to Jameson to catch the train to the capital.

When they drove into Jameson, they drove to the train depot and purchased their tickets and left their bags at the depot and found that it would be about an hour before the train would come. Joe said, "Let us go to the diner and get some lunch. I will take the buggy to the stable and leave it there until we get back."

When Joe was coming back to the, diner there was some folks there and they were looking kind of lost. Beverly was sitting at a table and watching them. Joe sat down, and Beverly leaned over to Joe and said, "I do not believe that they have any money to eat. Joe, they were counting their money and shaking their heads. The three kids with them look like they are pretty hungry."

Joe walked over to the man standing near the door with his family, and Joe said, "Can I be of help to you folks, is there anything that I can do for you?"

The stranger looked up at Joe, and he is ashamed, and he said, "My family is hungry, and it seems that I do not have enough money to feed them. That is all right. We will just leave and no problems, sir."

Joe looked at the man and his family and said, "Mister, take your family over to a table and sit down, and I will talk to Abby, the owner of this restaurant, and I would be honored to take care of the bill for your family. I have in the past had some problems and some of my neighbors have helped me and now I would like to extend the mercies of God to you and your family."

The man said, "You do not know how hard it is for me to let another man feed me and my family, but right now I do not have any other recourse but to accept your help. May God bless you for your kind charity."

Joe said, "Sir, it would please me if you did not accept this as charity but as a gift from a friend or a Christian brother, but if it insults you, then you can pay it back. The next time that you see someone who needs a friend to help them, you can pay me back by helping them."

The man smiled and said, "Sir, I take that as a loan, and I will pay it back to you many times if I can possibly do it. Would you shake hands with me on this agreement?"

Joe was smiling and put a hand on the shoulder of the stranger and said, "I would count it as an honor to shake your hand."

They shook hands, and the family sat down at one of the tables, and Joe went over to the counter and talked to Abby about the arrangement that he has with the man. Joe leaned in to Abby and whispered to her, "If they skimp on the order, then you give them a generous portions, and I will pay you extra for all of it, okay?"

Abby looked at Joe and reminded him of what he had done for her when she was in so much trouble and said, "You do not have to worry about a thing. And, Joe, you will only pay the bill that I charge you. Is that understood?"

Joe said, "I am not sure of what you just said, but I will go along what you said, okay."

Joe gave his and Beverly's food order to Abby while he was standing there and talking to her then he went back to his table. As he was walking back to his table, he passed the stranger and his family. The man spoke to Joe, and he introduced his family to Joe and Joe waved to Beverly she came over to their table and he introduced her and they all visited there until Abby came out with Joe's order, and they excused themselves and went back to their table. Joe and Beverly held hands across the table, and Joe said a prayer asking God to bless them and their food. As Joe raised his head, he saw the man at the other table looking at them. The man had a very thoughtful look on his face and when their food was brought to the table. He talked to his family, and after a little struggle with the children they each took hands, and he bowed his head and prayed. Joe felt like he maybe had some effect on the family, and he thanked God for the privilege.

After Joe and Beverly ate their meal, Joe went to the counter to pay Abby for the meal for both families. She said she thought that the bill would be two dollars, and Joe leaned across the counter and said, "That is not enough for all of both of our families."

Abby looked at Joe with large eyes and a smile on her face, and she said, "What two families, Joe? There was just you and Beverly so that is the cost as we agreed on, remember?"

Joe looked at her, then he looked at Beverly, and he said, "Well, I guess that I agreed now, but didn't we have another understanding." He reached across and took Abby by the shoulders and pulled her to him and gave her a big kiss on the cheek, and he patted her on the other cheek and said, "Friend, you have this one, but there is always tomorrow."

Abby smiling at them said, "Joe, it is hard to get anything over on you, but I have this one."

Joe and Beverly left the restaurant, and Joe knew that Abby was trying to make up for the time that she betrayed him, but he knew that she had been lied to about him. They went to the train station and waited on the train; they talked and sat on the bench outside on the platform. The train station was painted red and some black trim, but the platform and the bench had never been painted. Joe was looking down the tracks, and it was beautiful; there were trees lining the tracks as far as he could see. It looked like way down the tracks the rails kept getting closer together, and as far as he could see, the rails were no wider than his hand. Now Joe knew that this was not true, but he was interested as to why this false image was the way that it was. Beverly was looking at him and knew that he was concentrating on something, but she would not say anything for a while, but Joe started frowning, and she asked Joe what was wrong. Joe turned to her for a moment and smiled at her and put his arm around her and said, "If you were a school teacher, I would tell you but you would think me dumb or stupid." Beverly said, "Joe, I would never say or think something like that." Joe looked at her and said, "Look down that railroad track and tell me what you see."

Beverly looked down the track and said, "Joe I see a mystery one that has baffled me all of my life, those tracks look normal here in front of us but the farther away they are, the closer they get, and I have never been able to figure that out." Joe laughed and said, "That is exactly what I have been sitting here and thinking about. Maybe I am not so dumb after all."

Beverly said, "Joe, you are the smartest man that I have ever met. You could never be dumb."

Joe was looking at Beverly when she said that, and he dropped his head and looked back down the railroad track; he finally turned back to Beverly and said, "I really do not feel very smart. I make so many mistakes. If it was not for God, I would really make a mess out of everything, and I know that."

Beverly put her arm around his and leaned her head over on his shoulder, and he reached over with his hand and patted her leg. She placed one of her hands over his hand, and they just sat there for a while, and finally she said, "Honey, I think that everyone feels the same way that you do. I know that I certainly do. When I am around you, I feel that you are so much smarter than I am. I just try to somehow keep up with you, and there is a very small area that I can even come close to staying with you."

There was nothing said for a long time, and then they heard the train coming; the rails started to make a noise, and then they could hear the big engine chugging, and then finally they saw it coming. Joe finally stood up, and when it came to a stop at the end of the track, there was yelling from the engine. Joe walked down to the engine and spoke to the engineer, the fireman, and the conductor came up the track to say hi to Joe. It seemed that every time that the train came this way that the three of them were on board. They talked and joked for a bit, and then they all got aboard, and the conductor said all aboard, and they left with a large black puff of smoke and headed down the track. Joe and Beverly had a good seat away from the smoke of the train, and they had an enjoyable to the end of this engine's run, and they changed trains. The conductor and the fireman carried their luggage over to the other train, and the conductor told the new conductor that he had better take very good care of these VIP, or there would be a lot of trouble. The two conductors moved a short distance from Joe and Beverly, and Joe was feeling kind of bad because of what the friends of his was doing to them. The new conductor said, "Folks, I will see to it that you have the best seats that are on the train."

Joe said, "You do not have to do that. We can just sit anywhere. The man stopped and looked at the two of them and said, "That is great because I have a place that is just begging for someone to stay with it, would you please come with me?"

Joe decided just to let it happen and keep his mouth shut. They moved to the best Pullman car on the whole train. They were left for a few moments, and the waiter from the dining car came to them with a bottle of champagne, and Joe thanked him and told him that they did not drink any alcohols, but he really appreciated the thought. But if the waiter had a hot coffee, they could use a cup each. The man left and later came with a tray a pot of coffee, cream, and two cups and poured the coffee and asked, "How do you like your coffee?" Joe said, "The coffee tasted great and was just the way that we liked it." The man left bowing as he backs out the door. Joe and Beverly were rather tickled at the actions of the waiter. Joe said, "He acts like we are something special, but we know that we are only who God wants us to be."

Beverly said, "Joe, I think that the stories about what you did to the outlaws have reached all of the ears in this area of the country, and they just want to show you how much they appreciate what you did."

They sat back and talked about all of the things that brought them together, and they could see how things from the start would put them together. It seemed that things could not possibly happen this way, but they did.

Joe said, "My first family was destroyed by evil, and I do not understand that. But God gave you to me, and now I have the start of another family, and I thank him for you and for the rest of our life."

Beverly put her hand in his and leaned over against Joe, and silently thanked God for giving her another chance for happiness. The train gets to the capital the next morning and she and Joe were glad to get out of the train and walk for a little bit. Their luggage was sent to the Empire hotel, and they wanted to get something to eat and just walk a while and let their body settle down and plan what they were going to do about the land that they want to buy.

They spent the night in the hotel, and the place was very nice, but their minds were on the business that they came to do. Joe went to the lawyer friend that was working here, they ate breakfast and looked around for a while.

Beverly said, "Joe, while we are here maybe we should look at some furniture for our new house." Joe agreed to look and see what they would need. Beverly looked over the different styles of furniture, and they decided on the style that they wanted and ordered the furniture and accessories that they needed, and Joe made arrangements for the shipment. Joe walked with Beverly to the office of the lawyer, and they were received graciously by the secretary and then openly by the lawyer the way that friends should be. Joe showed the lawyer what land and water that he wanted to buy from the government; it is not exactly that the government owned the land. But he was required to pay for the land to ensure that the division of land grants required money to be paid for them to keep track of who owned what portion of the country in the state. Joe was a soldier of the army of the north, and he was given courtesy with the government of the state of Virginia. Joe was looked down upon still by certain people because he fought for the north, but Joe was born in a family in the state of West Virginia, and these people disagreed with the people of the state of Virginia.

They concluded their business and the land that Joe wanted was recorded and Joe had in his the legal maps and papers showing that Joe owned the land for miles in every direction from his ranch to the land that he had given to Thad. He bought to within miles of the ranch of Ken Lincoln. He wanted no dispute from anyone as to who owned the land around the great hole and the underground river. Joe and Beverly took the next train back to Jameson the ride was long, and hard they were glad to be home, while they were getting the luggage taken to the end of the train station walkway. Joe went to the stable and harnessed the horses hitched them to the buggy. Then he brought it to the station and picked up Beverly and the luggage. They had a pleasant drive to their ranch, and when they arrived home, their luggage was taken to their bedroom. Supper was on the table waiting on them. Joe walked into the house and said, "How did you know that we were on the way home?"

Jacob said, "One of the boys was leaving town and saw you get off the train; he hurried home, and we fixed supper so you would not have to Beverly we knew that you would be tired from the trip."

Beverly went over and gave Jacob a big hug and she kissed him on the cheek. Jacob stepped back one step and his face turned red, and he said, "I might just cook your meal every day."

Everyone got a good laugh at Jacob for his face turning red, but it was all in good fun. The hands all left, and Joe and Beverly went in and had supper, both enjoying it very much. Afterward they went up to bed and slept soundly in their own beds; traveling is a little hard, and coming home is wonderful. The next morning while Beverly was fixing breakfast, Joe went to the bunkhouse and talked with Ed about what was going on at the ranch. Also what was going on at the sink hole; he filled Joe in on the ranch and said, "Jacob was telling him what he found, but it did not make sense to him, so he would let Jacob tell Joe himself." Jacob came into the house, and Joe was waiting for him in his office, and Jacob sat down and was telling Joe the survey that they had taken over the mountain. They found no water, but they traced an old river that looked like it had not had water in it for many, many years; large trees had grown up in the old riverbed. They followed it for about forty miles and then turned back after they came to some farms and a small town which received its water from a different direction. He told Joe that they went underground by placing the ladder down to through the large disturbance in the ground. They traveled all day and kept check on the route that the water was traveling, and the direction was about the same as the old water course that they had followed on the surface. They picked up gold nuggets all along the way and kept them in a bag; he placed the bag on Joe's desk. Joe picked it up and set it back down on the desk. Joe said, "What do you think about putting some of the men down in the hole to mine or pan the gold that is along the river we will need quite a bit of money to buy windmills and to build dams to hold the water for hard dry times."

A portion of the gold will go to each man, and a portion will go to the ranch. Jacob said, "Joe, if the men go to town and start spending a lot of gold, it is going to start a stampede; and someone will find out where the gold is coming from, and you will have to have an army to keep them out."

Joe said, "This has been worrying me also, but what do we do. I want to be fair with the men at the same time."

CHAPTER 19

Jacob said, "Ed and I were talking about this while you were up at the capital, and we came up with an idea. What if you buy some tracts of land for each man and tell them that this is what they are working for instead of giving them the money. You can also set up for them an account to build them a house and furnish them with a small herd. The longer they work for it, the more they will receive. If they tell anyone, they will not get anything. If they leave, they will not get anything unless there is a legitimate reason, and then they will only get what they have earned."

Joe was thinking about what Jacob had said, and he posed a question to Jacob what about the man who cannot go underground, those who are afraid to go underground. Jacob said, "I have not even thought about this problem."

Joe said, "How about this? Some of the men who want or can go underground and the others who work the ranch, who must work harder because they are shorthanded, get the equal amount of the benefits. I feel that would be kind of equal all around."

Joe continued, "I want you and Ed to come back into my office as soon as the both of you can get loose from your duties. Jacob said, "I will tell Ed, and we will be back as soon as we can."

Joe was sitting at his desk and working on some bills and also the payroll for his men. There was a knock on the door, and he looked up and Ed and Jacob was standing there; he waved them to come in and sit down. He finished up the columns up before he lost the figures and had to do it over again; he put the papers aside and looked up at his two friends and employees. Joe said, "Have you been talking about my possible proposal?"

Ed said, "Boss, you tell us what you want, and we will see to it that it is done."

Joe said, "Guys, I do not want to make it an order. This is something that cannot be done as an order. If the men do not have a choice in it, then it will not work for any of us."

Jacob said, "What if the men say to start with that they will not promise or agree to promise and then go against you on secrecy of the project."

Joe said, "That is the kind of choice we will have to take. What I want to do is something that will benefit this whole country around us. I believe that God will honor and protect what we are going to do. Because I believe that when you do something to help other people as well as helping yourself, then God will take a part with you."

Ed said, "Like fighting the outlaws not just for ourselves but for the town and all of the innocent people who would be affected if we had not done what we did."

Joe said, "Yes, kind of like that. I do not know if there is a word for it, but when men who live for Satan and work for Satan come against God's people, then God's people must fight the evil that Satan has placed against them. I know that God placed his forces with us to defeat the forces that Satan placed with the outlaws to help them."

Jacob looked at Joe and Ed; then he looked down at his hands and said, "I had never thought about that. I knew that we did what was legally right, but it really bothered me every time that I had to take a life, even when they were shooting at me."

Joe looked at both men and said, "I died a little every time that I took a life. It was just like when I was in the army in the war. I died a little when I gave an order to kill, or I killed someone myself. But God knows our heart, and he does not hold that against us. We were fighting Satan and not people, so do not let it bother you too long when you have to come against evil because we cannot let evil take over God's world."

Both men looked at Joe and Ed said, "Joe, you should be a preacher because you sure make things like this clear when you speak, and you make us feel a lot different after you speak."

Joe shook his head no and said, "I am certainly not a preacher. I feel that I am just barely a Christian, so do not put something into nothing. Now for the topic at hand, I want the four of us to agree on this thing."

Ed and Jacob looked at each other and then at Joe, and Ed said, "The four of us."

Joe said, "Come on in, Beverly."

And the men knew who the fourth person was. Joe explained to Beverly what they had been talking about including the proposal for all of the men. Beverly listened intently and said nothing until Joe had finished, and she said, "Have you guys come to an agreement?"

Joe said, "We or I feel that God will kind of help us keep this a secret until the right time to reveal it, and then he will handle it for us."

Beverly said, "I trust all of you men. Now I realize that greed is a powerful force, a force that Satan can use against us. Realize that if worse comes to worst, you may have to put a guard on the hole and patrol the whole area to stop someone from digging another hole."

The man looked at each other and then looked at Beverly with new admiration. Joe said, "I would like a day at least to think about this and work up the right words to present before the men. Did you ask the men who went down in the hole not to talk to the other men?" He was looking at Jacob.

Jacob said, "I told these men that you were going to make things right with all of the men and not to say anything about it."

Ed said, "I heard some of the men talking about it in the bunkhouse last night, so yes, they have been talking about it."

Joe asked them, "Have any of the men left the ranch since you have gone down in the hole?"

Ed said, "No, but some of the men will go into town tonight, and I am afraid they will talk about it."

Joe said, "Gather the men together if there are men out on the range. Find work for the ones that are here and send someone out on the range and bring all of the men in, and I will talk with them at lunch. That way, maybe we can contain the information."

Ed came to Joe about lunchtime and told him that all of the men were in the bunkhouse, and the cook had them something to eat. Joe said, "I will be there in a few moments." And he told Beverly what he was going to do."

Beverly said, "I will pray for you while you are talking to the men, and he will give you the right words to say."

Joe went into the bunkhouse and spoke to each man individually as they sat around the dinner table. Joe went to the end of the table opposite of Ed and sat down. The cook asked Joe if he was going to eat with the men, and Joe said that he would be honored to eat with the men that he had rode with and fought with. They were served and ate their lunch; then Joe started his proposal to the men, and he had to stop a few times because the men were so happy that they all started talking at the same time. Joe would just wait until they finished and looked at him again. Joe finished up by telling the men that if word got out about the gold, there would be more men coming here just like the ones they had fought before. "And maybe none of us will survive this time." All of the men looked at one another like they were wondering if the one across the table or beside them would be the one to let the word out. Just like it was when they were taking the herd to the railroad for shipping. Joe said, "We must trust one another. We know each other now. If we work together, you one day may have your own ranch, some of you may want to move to other parts of the country, some of you may want to go into other types of business. If we work together, you will be able to do it. I do not know how much gold we will get out of here maybe not enough to get what we want, but I believe that we can. I want to help this country grow with more water, maybe your spread can grow from it. I will do my best to help each one of you to do what you want. But I will not pay you off in gold and not one of you can show another person a golden nugget, nor mention it to a living soul. Is that perfectly clear?"

Each man shook his head yes he understood; Ed raised hand, and every one of the men looked at him, and Ed said, "Guys, you are hardworking men, and you believe that every man is just as honest as you are. But remember my brother and how he turned out. He would kill anyone who stood in his way from what he wanted. He never worked an honest day in his life."

Jacob stood up and said, "You did not know my brother, but he would have shot any one of you out of the saddle if he was told to do it. So do not tell anyone what we are doing here."

Joe said, "Remember, you are hardworking cowboys, and you can only afford what money that you get on payday each month. What money that is put back for you is yours but only if you be quiet and say nothing. When the time comes, you will have your share however much."

One of the men raised his hand and asked a question, "If the gold cannot be shown, how are you going to get rid of it without anyone knowing about it?"

Joe said, "I will box it up and send it to the capital as metal parts or horse shoes or something different every time and send it to my friend and lawyer who will take it to the Federal Reserve and deposit it as an inherited fortune. Then he will deposit the money into the account that I own, but it is not in my name, and it cannot be traced to me. I will send it often enough that it will not tempt even him, and he will send me back the deposit slip for each shipment. I own the land for miles around the hole, and nobody should even be there. But people wander all over this country, and when we get started we will set up a cabin at the sight and watch over it. If a person comes along, we will be friendly and treat them friendly and even feed them if necessary and let them go on their way. If they ask what you are doing there, tell them you are on patrol against unwanted animals because of the cattle ranch."

One of the men said, "Joe, is that a lie that we would be telling them?"

Joe said, "What is a man, a bird or a fish? No man is an animal, and we are guarding unwanted animals, and who do you work for, isn't it a cattle ranch?"

The men all agreed in what he said; they were not necessarily smart or dumb men; they were just not knowledgeable men. They knew cows and any work that they normally did. In their trade, they were experts. Joe asked the men who among you would be willing to go underground and work? I want you to know that none of you have to. I would like some of you to volunteer, but I will not be mad at you if you do not go.

About half of the men said, "I will try it and see if I can do it, but I do not know for sure."

Five of the men said, "I will go and work. I have done work like this before."

Joe said, "I am proud of every one of you. We need men to go down. We need men to guard the hole, and we certainly need men to work the ranch, and you will be working shorthanded. We will also rotate the jobs the best that we can. Do any of you have any questions about anything that we are doing?"

The men looked at each other, then looked at Ed and Jacob, then they looked at Joe. There were no comments. Joe thanked them and told them that Ed would continue to run the ranch; Jacob would run the underground. "If you have problems, come to me at any time." Joe left the bunkhouse and went back to his bookwork.

Joe sat down and wrote his lawyer a letter and explained he had found a little gold and he would like to send it to him and have him deposit it for him in the Federal Reserve. It probably would not be very much, but he did not want someone to think that there was a gold strike anywhere on his property. So what would be the best disguise to send it to him? A few days later, he received a letter from his lawyer, and the lawyer told Joe that he would be glad to help him. He thought that sending him for the first few packages sealed and oversized box and put the gold in the center of the box and pack sacks around it and put on the box "caution: books." He said, "I have bought some books that nobody knows about, and I will let them think that these boxes are the books. Then send me some metal ornaments wording labels on the outside of the box and the gold on the inside."

Joe said, "I might as well see how this is going to work for the railroad."

He had one of the men prepare a wooden box of medium size, and he placed some burlap feed sacks in the box and the bag of gold nuggets in the center of the box and lifted it, and it seemed that the weight was normal for a box of metal parts. The next day, Ed had men taking tools, and they built a small log cabin on the upstream side of the hole. They had plenty of close water; they had a great view of the hole. The cabin was far enough away so that the average person coming to the area would see the log cabin first. Ed also had a crew of men who dragged dead trees and limbs into the area so anyone riding in the area would just normally not want to get off a horse and move the trees out of the way but ride around them without giving it a thought. With someone riding in that area, they were either hunting game and would avoid that area, or they were looking over the land and would still avoid trying to climb over the dead trees and piled every which way limbs. It looked like there was a hard windstorm at one time and left a mess there. The hole could not be seen without traveling over the downed timber. But if someone came from the upriver side, they would come to the log cabin, and a corral was between them and the hole that they wanted to not be seen. There was no guarantee that someone would not see the very large hole in the earth, but there would be men in the cabin who would tell them whose property they were traveling on. If they were lost and looking for a way out of the country, the men who worked for Joe would mount up and show them the way either to the town of Bender or the town of Jameson. They were not to order anyone off the land or be rude to anyone but to protect the operation that was going on down in the hole. There was also a signal to the men down in the hole so they would know that there was a stranger in the area, and that way, they could be quiet and not be heard or seen. The work down in the hole was going along fine, and the men were going along the river and panning out the gold; they started at the hole and were working away from the hole in both directions. Soon, they were well away from the hole; the men upstream from the hole were finding much more than the men downstream. Jacob talked to Joe, and they decided to put all of the men upstream from the hole, and they found much more gold. The men above ground were to also keep an eye on the weather, and if there were storm clouds upstream from the hole, they were to get word to Jacob. He would pull his men out of the hole and watch the level of water and see if a storm upstream would make the water rise and see how much that it would rise. Joe decided that he would take a little trip; the weather was getting warm, and he and Beverly wanted to ride some. They took the map that Jacob had made of the underground river and took two men with them and started across country; they took packhorses with them and plenty of supplies. They travel up the dry streambed and wound through dry canyons, or in some places the streams came off the mountains and would pool up some, but the water was sinking in the ground. Joe told Beverly that he had seen things like this, but he had never thought of where the water went; it seemed to just sink into the ground, and maybe in many places—that is just what happened. They traveled for four days and camped in the forest at night and saw some beautiful property. Joe took the time to make maps as he traveled; they came to a community and stopped and visited and inquired about water in the area. In a store they bought provisions for the trip, and Joe met a farmer in the area and asked how the water in the area was. The farmer said, "I have enough to irrigate my farm, but most of the land is too dry to farm." Joe said, "Could a man run a herd of cattle on this land?"

The farmer said no. He irrigated his farm from a stream that came off the mountain and sank in the ground.

Joe looked at him kind of strange and said, "Is it desert the reason that the water sinks into the ground."

The farmer said, "No, it is not a desert. It is green grass, but below it where it used to run it is going to brush and is no good for anything."

Joe asked, "Are there not any rivers in this country at all? Are there no streams that flow down the valleys?"

The farmer shook his head and said, "This is a strange country. Where I came from, there were rivers that flowed in the valleys and were fed by streams coming down off the mountains."

Joe asked the farmer if he knew how far it was in the easterly direction before a man would run into a river.

The farmer said he came into this country about five years ago, and he has never heard of a river anywhere in this country.

Joe thanked the farmer and the storekeeper, and they loaded their supplies and moved on heading east following the slight valley that they were traveling in. The land was almost flat where they were now, but according to what Jacob indicated, they were heading correct, but of course they were farther than Jacob had ever been underground. But with the farmers stream going underground then they probably on the right trail. They traveled for another two days and found nothing they were getting clear out of the country. They later came to a large town and still found no river, but they did find the railroad tracks, and Joe said, "I believe that we have traveled enough for this visit, and if I want to go farther, I can catch a train up to this town and go by horse from there, but I do not see any need to travel farther. Do you, Beverly?"

Beverly said, "I have seen some wonderful country, but country that is not worth much without water. But, Joe, with the knowledge you could use the land and make it worthwhile."

Joe looked at the two men that were with him and said, "So couldn't these men if they wanted the land could put down a well into that river and pump the water up with a windmill and support a good herd of cattle."

The faces of the men lit up, and one of them said, "Joe, I would have never thought of that, but you are right."

He turned to his friend and said, "Robert, would you like to go into partners with me, and when the time comes, we will buy some of this property and start a ranch."

Robert had a smile on his face, and he said, "I have always liked you, but I never thought of going into the ranching business with you, but yes I would like that very much."

The men shook hands from one saddle to the other, and a partnership was started. Joe felt good about what happened; he realized that he was going to lose his men eventually, but wasn't that what it was all about? Joe and his party went to the train station, and Joe bought tickets to Jameson and when the train came, they loaded their horses in a car and left them saddled because it was going to be a short trip home. When they came to Jameson, they unloaded and took a short ride to the ranch. Ed was surprised when they came in from the road that went to town. But they were glad to be home, and Joe talked with Ed about how things were going. And how the ranch was growing, it seemed that the cattle were thriving in the grass at

Joe's ranch. They had been pretty bad shape when Joe had bought them from Ed's father. Joe was asking about the amount of gold that had been taken out of the hole. It seemed that they had cleaned the gold out of the gravel in the underground river for a long way up the river. It was getting hard for the men to breathe; they were so far away from the oxygen of the outside air, so they were going to have to quit pretty soon or open another hole to the outside air. Joe did not want to do this. Joe had shipped a lot of gold to his lawyer and had received the receipts from the bank. Joe was figuring the amount of money that each man had coming to him. It was a tidy sum more than they could earn in ten years of working as a cowboy. Joe was glad that he had done this for his men. He or the ranch had enough money to buy a drill and start drilling holes down to the river, and he had priced some windmills to pump the water to the surface, and then he was going to build some water dams so he could hold the water for times when the wind would not be blowing. Joe talked to Jacob and told him to quit the work in the hole tomorrow, because they were just too far from the hole. Tomorrow, take the ladder out of the hole, and they would do something to close the hole so none of the animals would fall into the hole. Also that would keep people out of the hole also. The ladders would be taken apart or brought to the ranch to keep anyone else from looking around down there. Joe told the men in the cabin to leave wood in the cabin, leave food in the cabin, and keep it in case someone would get stranded in the area in the winter storms. Put a sign up: "This belongs to Joe Manning ranch" and use it freely but leave it so someone else can use it also. Joe considered the gold project at an end.

The next afternoon Jacob came into Joe's office and said, "Joe, you made a wise decision to stop the working of the gold; we were getting ready to pull the ladder out of the hole, and I heard a roar down in the hole. I stayed on top and took a rope and let a lantern down into the hole, and I saw flood water coming down through the tunnel. It rose six to eight feet deeper than what it was before. If we had been in the tunnel, we would have been swept away and drowned. I guess God stayed the water until we brought our men out of the tunnel."

Joe said, "I am so glad that we stopped. All of the gold in the world is not worth taking a man's life."

Joe told Jacob to take four men back there and haul some logs and put clear around the opening and help keep anyone from coming near the opening, and maybe nobody will venture near it and fall in. "We will send a man out that way from time to time and make sure that area is kept clear of people. Maybe some of our men would like to buy the land that borders my property, and we can keep anyone from being trapped in there and being washed away."

Joe contacted a company he knows about a drilling rig that they can purchase; it has a steam-driven engine on it, and Joe can get enough wood from his ranch to put down many holes into the river. From time to time, he will have to be the one to go back down into the underground river and check on the place to drill the next hole. He will not send a man down there and risk his life; Joe will risk his life instead. It took about two months for the drill to be delivered to the ranch, with the drill two men came with the machine. Joe thanked the men for bringing it to him, and he started to turn away and one of the men said, "We thought that you might need a helper and an operator to run this machine."

Joe stopped and looked at the man and said, "Is the machine that complicated to run? I have been around steam engines before, and I can handle them."

The operator said, "What would you do if you got the drill steel stuck in the ground. How would you get it free."

Joe said, "I never thought of that. Does it happen very often?"

The driller whose name was Tony said, "It happens when you go through a seam of stone that for some reason is cracked or broken up, and sometimes you will hit a place where there is a cavern and you will lose your steel if you are not really careful."

Joe said, "I guess I can use the both of you if you want the job and welcome to our ranch."

Joe also said, "I will have wagons here in a few moments to pick up the drill and all of the piping that goes along with it."

Joe got the drill rig moved to the first valley that he wanted to water and marked the place that he wanted a well; he has a crew of men already building a dam to hold the water and men digging a ditch to pipe the water to the area of the dam. The driller said, "Sir, I do not believe that I would go to all of this trouble to put water until we first drill the well and hit the water, because there might not be any water here."

Joe said, "Do not worry, there will be water here but after you drill for a ways you will probably hit an opening before you hit the actual water. Just trust me, sir, I think that I am right."

The driller, Tony, said, "All right, sir, it is your money, but in my experience this is not the best place to put down a well to drill. Here we might have to go very deep but over on the other side of the valley we probably could hit a shallow well."

Joe said, "Tony, just call me Joe. That is what everyone calls me. I am not trying to tell you your job, but I have advance notice of an underground river running through here, and I believe that it is right under us."

Tony looked at Joe with a lot of doubt in his face; he turned to his helper and said, "My helper's name is Randy, and, Joe, we will drill wherever you say and as deep as you say. This business is hard to predict, and I have been wrong many times, and I have seen strange things that lead some people to hit water the very first time."

Joe gave Tony, wranglers to help him set his machine up, and wood was brought to him in a wagon cut to the length that Tony wanted; he had everything that he needed to drill the well then the men went back to preparing the valley to hold the water once it was pumped out of the ground.

Joe did not know how long it would take to drill the hole and put everything in place to bring water to the top of the ground, but he had his first windmill due to arrive the next day; he would have a wagon and some men waiting on the train to receive it and bring it to the ranch. There was a little problem—the people of Jameson were wondering where Joe was getting all of his money to buy this equipment. A couple of the men came to Joe and said, "The bartender said the folks were wondering where Joe was coming up with all of his money to do all of this work."

The cowboy looked at Joe and grinned and said, "I dunno maybe he had a rich uncle that died. He took a trip some place a while back."

The bartender said, "Oh, tell Joe I am so sorry about his rich uncle, and tell him I hope that the rest of his family is doing well."

The cowboy said, "I told the bartender that I will tell him what you said, and I know he will be glad that you are thinking of him. Now, Joe, I did not lie to him. I just let him think what he really wanted to think."

Joe said, "I understand and you did the right thing just as long as we do not lie to people, then we have not done anything wrong. I guess if we just let them think what they are going to think anyway, then we have not done them any wrong."

After a week, Ed brought Tony to Joe and he said, "I have hit what looks like a lot of water and from the sound coming up through the pipe it is a large river. How can this be? You said that there was a river down there. How in the world could you have known?"

Joe said, "There are no rivers in this area, and there should be, don't you think? With all of this land, shouldn't God have put a river here someplace?"

Tony just looked at Joe like he was stupid, and he nodded his head and said, "How would I know what God would do? I had better get back to the rig and tear it down. Where do you want to find another river?"

Joe said, "I have been thinking about that."

He glanced at Ed who could hardly keep from laughing, and Joe pointed his hands together and was thinking very hard and he said, "I know where the other river is. I will show Ed, and we will drive a stake. Now don't miss the stake because it might be a narrow river."

Tony looked like he was ready to run out of there because he thought that Joe was some kind of crazy person. Joe looked at Tony and said, "Tony, I was just kidding you about the size of the river. I think that you will find about the same thing that you found in the last well, at least I hope so."

Tony looked kind of relieved after Joe said what he did, but he still wondered how Joe knows so much about where the water is running. Ed talked Tony back to his drill rig, and they started making preparations for the move to the next location. As they left the first well, the windmill was unloaded from the wagon and Joe's men under the guiding hand of Ed who had been briefed by Joe. At the end of the day, they had the base set in the ground and anchored to the ground where strong winds would not tip it over. Joe told Ed that he wanted it anchored good enough that the strongest winds would not damage it or turn it over. Joe met Ed and Jacob that evening and got a report on the jobs that they had going on. Joe asked if any of the employees have made any plans to leave the ranch and move on to their chosen land, ranches, or businesses. Jacob said, "The men have been talking and wondering if the high water that came down the underground river had carried any more gold down to be trapped in the sand."

Joe said, "I have been wondering that myself, but I do not want to put any men in that hole after seeing what the water could do if it caught them too far away from the hole."

Jacob said, "We could hear the water a long time before it came roaring through, if we do not work too far from the hole, we should be plenty safe."

Joe said, "What if you are wrong? Now I am not saying you are wrong, but what if you are."

Jacob said, "Joe, if we explain to the men what the dangers are and they decide to go ahead and work it, would you go along with it." Joe said, "I will go along with working the gold if you do not let them get out of sight of the hole. Would they go along with that? If they cannot get enough gold to do what they need, then they will have to wait until there is another flood."

Jacob said, "Let me tell the men what you said and see what they say after that would that be all right with you."

Joe said, "I hope this gold business is not getting out of hand. I do not want to lose any man to the floodwater. I do not mind them losing me to go to their own business but not to death."

Jacob left Joe's office and talked with the men and returned a short time later and told Joe that every man said, "They would want to go back down and see if they could get more gold out of the hole. They felt that the noise of the water would give them plenty of warning to get out of the hole."

Joe was pacing in his office, and he stopped in front of Jacob and said, "I guess if the men are aware of the danger, then I will go along with them. I have no right in denying them this opportunity to a better life."

Jacob said, "One man did have a suggestion, and that was to make two other ladders and that would let more men come out of the hole at a time."

Joe looked pleased at the thought of more ladders, and he said, "Have the men to make three more ladders and give the men all the chance that they can to get out of the hole."

Jacob turned to leave, and he said, "I will have those ladders make right now, and we will be ready to get back in there by tomorrow morning."

He left Joe's office, and he met Ed in the doorway; they exchanged greetings, and Ed came into Joe's office and greeted Joe. Ed said, "We are ready to start up the first windmill, and I thought maybe you and Beverly might like to be there to see it."

Joe said, "Yes, I or we would have my horse saddle and brought around would you."

Jacob was smiling at Joe, and he said, "Your horse is tied to the hitch rail in front of the house right now."

Joe looked at him and smiled at his good friend. Beverly was walking by the office, and she stuck her head in and said, "Did I hear my name mentioned?" Joe said, "They are ready to start the windmill, and Ed wanted to know if we wanted to see it."

Beverly turned around and yelled over her shoulder, "Ed, have my horse saddle and brought around, would you?"

Her voice was trailing off as she was hurrying away, and Ed did not bother to answer her; he and Joe just looked at each other and smiled. In just minutes they were at the windmill, and Joe sat on his horse with Beverly waiting for Ed to throw off the brake and allow the wind to take the blades and make them turn. He threw the lever and the blades started to turn, and it was pretty smooth; there was a little noise; one of the men put some oil on the packing on the pump shaft, and they waited and nothing happened; the wind was rather strong but no water. Beverly said, "What is wrong with it?" Joe said, "Nothing, right now, it will take a bit to draw the water to the surface. Ed, did you prime the pump good?"

Ed said, "I thought I did. Maybe I can prime it again."

He reached for the lever to stop the windmill and they could hear sputtering and in a moment there started some water coming, there would be water and then air and final there was a steady flow of water. They all sat around for a while and watched the water flow like they had never seen water before. But this was not just water; this was the life flow of the ranch. They sat on their horses and watched the water flow out of the pipe and start filling the tank that the cattle and horses would drink out of. When the tank would fill up, the overflow would carry the water down to the dam that would make a small lake that they could use as a reserve and would water the ground from the tank to the lake and would help the grass all along the way. Joe sat there and thought of how they had found the river underground and how after all the problems they had. God really blessed them in finding the gold, and in return it was going to help so many lives. He was thinking how we are going to explain all of this to the neighbors. Where did all of this money come from? He would tell them the truth God provided by his blessings. Jacob came galloping up the windmill, and he said, "Joe, we have trouble. There are some people who are planning on homesteading on your property close to the hole. I have some men there, and they are keeping the people away from the hole."

Joe said, "Ed, cut out about one hundred cows from the east pasture and move them over to the valley just east of the hole. Jacob, pull all of your men back away from the hole."

Joe thought for a minute and said, "Beverly, you and I will take a ride over there and talk to these folks. We need to figure on a place that would be good for them to farm away from our property."

Beverly said, "I do not believe that they will travel very far from where they settled unless we can talk them into believing we own this land."

Joe and Beverly rode toward the valley where the hole is, and they talked as they rode. They came to the hole and kept riding as though it was not there. They went past the cabin where the two men were and went on up the small stream, and there was a wagon and a tent put up. They slowed up and walked their horses up close to the tent; a man and woman was standing there; the man had a rifle in his hand, and he raised it as they came closer. Joe raised his hands and said, "We are not going to harm you. We want to help you." The man said, "This is my land, and I want you off it."

CHAPTER 20

Joe asked the man if he and his wife could get down and talk to them. The man said, "No, you cannot get down."

His wife said, "Henry, what has happened to you? These folks have come to visit, and you act like a villain. Folks, get down and sit a spell."

Joe said, "Folks, there has been a terrible mistake. This is my ranch, and right now I have some cattle coming to put on this meadow. I bought this land all of it, and I would like to show you some better land than this for farming."

Henry said, "I came through here a few years ago, and there was nobody even in this area. I saw this little valley, and I wanted it for a farm, and now you tell me that you own it. I am sorry, I do not believe you. Why are you trying to get rid of me?"

Joe said, "Henry, which way did you come into this land?"

Henry said, "We came across the mountain from the south, and here we are going to stay." And Henry said, "We are also going to buy the next valley to our north, and you cannot stop us."

Joe said, "Would you like to take a little ride with me and let me show you something."

Henry said, "Where are we going?"

Joe said, "Over across the hill to the next little valley. I want to show you that the valley over there is also bought up and being used. Henry, this land is being bought up pretty fast."

Drucilla said, "Henry, calm down and at least ride over the hill with this man and see what is going on."

Henry and Joe mounted up and went over the hill to Thad's place, and they went down the hill a little and saw the house that Joe and Thad had built and the cattle and horses that were grazing there, and Henry realized that things had changed.

Henry said, "Mister, I guess that I jumped to conclusions about all of this, and I am sorry."

Joe said, "My name is Joe Manning, and I am pleased that you are here in this country. I believe that I know of a place that would be perfect for you and your wife, if you would care to look at it. It is on the other side of my ranch, and it is closer to town and could be made into a great farm.

Henry said, "Why didn't you take that also? It seems that you have taken a lot of land."

Joe said, "Well, I guess that with all of the years that I have been here I have taken a lot of land, but cattle require a lot of land. If you want a lot of land, then you have come to the right territory because there is a lot of land still available."

Henry and Joe went back to where their camp was, and Henry told his wife that they had to move to another place. Joe went over to the little cabin at the hole and told one of the men to come over to the camp and help the folks load up and get ready to move out. The man came over to the camp, and as Henry turned around he looked at the man who worked for Joe and said, "Don't I know you? You look like someone that I know."

Joe's worker said, "No, sir, I don't believe that we have ever met." The worker told Henry that he had come from Alabama about twenty years ago.

Henry said, "That is where I came from, and I knew a family that sure looks like you. They lived beside a river at a little crossroads and had a fair farm down by the river."

Edwards who worked for Joe said, "My pappy had a farm that sounds like the place that you are talking about, but I have not seen it for so long. I could not tell you what it looks like now."

Henry said, "That man did me a good turn back about ten years ago. I was hurt in an accident, and they took me in and doctored me up and fed me until I was well enough to go on my trip, and I have never forgotten it."

As they were loading up Henry's things, he asked Edwards, "What kind of a man is Joe Manning?"

Edwards said, "I came to work for Joe after we had some real hard trouble, and I saw him put some outlaws down in the dirt, but man they deserved every bit of it. And I can tell you that Joe is a fair man to deal with, and the best man that I have ever seen in my life."

Henry said, "Joe said he owns this land that I stopped on, but he will take me to a better place for me to buy as a farm."

Edwards said, "Henry, you do not want this place. It is pretty but the soil is only inches deep and below that is solid rock you could not grow anything but grass on this place."

Henry looked around and took the heel of his boot and started kicking the sod and sure enough he went down just a couple of inches and he hit rock. He looked at Edwards and said, "I am glad you guys stopped me before I built a cabin here and filed on this land."

Edwards said, "I believe that you can trust Joe and Beverly. They would have no reason to steer you wrong; he has done right by all of the men here."

After they had the wagon loaded and everything was ready to leave, Joe and Beverly started out down the country past the hole, and they went through the woods and out of the valley; they came out into the main pastures. Joe told Beverly if she wanted to go on back to the house and do her things and that he would take the folks out to the valley toward the ranch of Ken Lincoln where the bottom land is rich and will grow about everything. That way, they can farm on rich soil and make something of their place. He said, "We need new neighbors at least good ones." He told Henry about this valley as they rode through the pasture fields, and he could see some of his cattle in the distance. He told them to look way off to their right, and they could see his new windmill that they just got it started yesterday. He said, "This valley is pretty dry, and we had to drill down and get water to keep this part of the land from drying up and blowing away."

Henry said, "How did you get enough money to afford that? You must be a very rich fellow."

Joe said, "God has blessed us we had a war against some very evil people not too long ago, but God brought us through it, and we are doing great now."

Henry wanted to know how the cattle market is doing right now.

Joe said, "I sold a herd of cattle not too long ago, and I came out pretty good on them." Henry said, "I wish I was a rancher instead of a farmer."

Joe said, "It takes both of us to make the land worth working, we all need beef, and we all need vegetables so it takes all of us to do the job. I used to plow up some land and set out the garden for my family to eat during the year, even while my cattle were getting bigger so I could sell them. But the farm product was what we lived on. Now that we have a real farmer, then maybe I will not have to do so much farming."

Henry said, "Maybe I can put out a big enough crop to furnish your ranch and other ranchers' in the area.

Joe said, "Also the town of Jameson is pretty close to you, that would also be a source of people to sell to, you probably could do pretty good in this area if you are satisfied in this area of the country."

They came around the end of the ridge; Joe showed the valley to Henry and his wife. Joe told them that they were standing on the end of his property, and from here to the other end of the valley it was open to buy. There is also a stream that is running about halfway down this valley, and then it goes into the ground. You may want to put up a dam and hold back some of the water for the dry spells. That is what we are doing over in my valley.

Joe said, "Figure out what you want to do if you do not like this land there is other land closer to the town. I am not trying to sell you anything. I have no claim on any of this I will be honest with you. I was planning to buy this property as soon as I could come up with the money. But if you want it, then that would be final with me."

Joe was sitting beside the driver's seat of the wagon, and he shook hands with Henry and turned his horse and rode away toward his ranch house. Henry and his wife, Drucilla, were watching Joe ride away, then Henry said, "This land is so much better than what I had wanted back in the back country. I am so glad that we have met Joe and his pretty wife, but I really like the looks of this land. We will go on up there and look it over and decide what we want to do. I think that we would have nice neighbors here, and if we moved on we would not know for sure who we would have as neighbors."

They drove up into the valley farther and came to the stream of water and saw where it went into the ground. Henry sat on the wagon for a long time and looked at it and turned around on the wagon seat and looked back along the valley and said, "If that stream could be made to travel on down the valley, then this place could be really something." Drucilla looked at him and said, "But it does not go farther down the valley."

Henry smiled at her and said, "No, dear, right now it does not."

Then he spoke to the team of horses, and they continued farther up the valley; they came to a little alcove in the mountain which was a little higher ground. He stopped and turned to her and took her hand and said, "Dear, look at that place over here and see if you can picture a house there and all of the other buildings. But look at all of those shade trees, and the wind that is moving the tree limbs it looks like home to me."

She looked at the place that he was looking at she saw the beautiful mountain behind it. Then she looked across the valley at the mountain which rose into the sky and the giant trees that were growing there. In her mind she could see the trees in the fall turning to every color of leaves that the mind could imagine. Then she looked straight ahead at the valley and she could see the great fields of corn, beans, cabbage, and so many other crops. She said, "Henry, I think that area would be the most beautiful place on the earth. We have just found out new home." Her mind would hold these pictures until they would become a reality. Henry's mind just saw the house and how it was going to look sitting back there in the shade of the trees.

Joe rode up to the ranch house, and Beverly came out on the porch and met him and asked, "How do you thing they like the valley that you showed them?"

Joe said, "Who in his or her right mind would not like that valley I almost built there myself and then I came on over here and fell in love with this place."

Ed moved the cattle into the little valley and as he passed the valley below the hole he was looking at the waste of the valley that had no water to feed it. It was just briars and scrub bushes in places the valley was a half mile wide and could be just as pretty a place as any on earth, but there was just no water. He sat on his horse and was looking up the valley, and then he would look back down the valley; he sat there and looked; he let the men and the herd move on up the valley until they were almost out of sight. One of his men cane back to where he was sitting, and Ed was not even aware of him being there; he was so engrossed in his thoughts. The drover cleared his throat, and Ed looked around; the drover said, "Boss, are you all right?"

Ed said, "Well, yes, I am all right. Why do you ask?"

The drover said, "You have been sitting there and looking at nothing for about a half an hour and I was just checking to see if you was all right."

Ed looked around him and saw that they were alone, and he said where did you put the cattle? "They had better be where I told you to put them."

The drover smiled and said, "What were you doing daydreaming about that girl you saw last week in town?"

Ed just smiled and said, "You and that horse that you are sitting on has better get to work or both of you will be walking back to the bunkhouse now get out of here and leave me alone."

The drover smiled because he caught the boss daydreaming and he said, "Yes, boss, er, should I say dreamer boss." He laughed and rode away.

Ed said to himself, "I am certain that it will work. I will run it by Joe and see what he thinks. It would be less expensive than drilling a hole and installing a windmill." He rode on up to where the cattle were grazing on the grass and he sent the men back to the ranch. He dismounted and walked the ground upstream from the hole and was thinking the men who were staying in the cabin came out and was watching Ed as he was checking the ground. He would look up on the hill on both sided and then he would walk back and forth on the ground again. He left his horse where the ground hitched him. Meaning he just got off the horse and left the reins lying on the ground and walked away, the horse knew that Ed wanted him to stay right there. The horse was eating grass but if he walked forward he would raise his head up so he would not step on the reins, this was the way that Joe and his men had taught every horse on the ranch. After a while Ed went over to the men and asked them if they needed anything before he left. "By the way, I want you guys to gather all of the dead limbs up all around this area from the tree line down to the water level and haul them into the cabin and cut them up for fire wood. Winter will be coming on one of these days, and we would not want you poor hard working men to get cold, now would we?" He went to his horse and picked up the reins and mounted up and rode on down the valley. He did not ride back the way that he had come he went back down the other valley. Right below the hole the ridge ends and two valleys begin and they are both are dry both are worthless as far as grass is concerned and Ed wanted to look at the other valley and see what it looks like. He believed that he had an idea that will benefit the ranch greatly, but he wanted to get all of his facts together before he talks to Joe about it. The next day Ed came into Joe's office, and he sat down and said, "Joe, can I talk to you about something that may be crazy, but I believe that it will work and save you a bunch of money." Joe said, "Go ahead."

And he put everything aside and gave Ed his full attention. Ed wanted to burn off the valleys that are cluttered with worthless scrub brush and plant grass seed. He wanted to build a dam across the creek above the hole and divert the water down both of the valleys. And turn them into pasture fields for the cattle, and if they can hold the water on the surface, he wanted to build spreader dams along both valleys to retain water at places in the valleys. Joe sat there and looked at Ed until he got a little uncomfortable about Joe looking at him. Joe said, "How dumb I am? That is an idea that I have never thought about, and it is a little risky because we might not be able to hold the water in those valleys; it might sink. But I do not think so, Ed. That is a fabulous idea! Before we fire one of the valley, we need to have water available like a wagon with a tank on it. If we can find one or make one."

Ed said, "We have a man that works for you who can make a large tank for you. We will have to cut a few white oak trees."

"What are you thinking of an earth dam in the valley?" Ed said, "Yes, I thought that we could put a large pipe in the bottom of the dam to drain the water while we were making the dam. I will have to see if there is a good dirt bank close by because there is not dirt on the valley floor. We will have to dug it down to rock and take the rock down to the solid stone to get rid of all the cracks. Then we can start building back with dirt."

Joe said, "How are you planning to carry the water over the hole?"

Ed said, "I thought as wide as the valley is around the hole. We can make a creek bed on either side of the hole and let the water run back in its natural course before the upheaving of the earth made the hole."

Joe said, "If we cannot get the right elevation, we can always put large pipes in the dam and flow the water over the edges of the hole."

Ed said, "That is a better idea than I had, but we need to get the valleys fired and the ground ready for the seed before we complete the dam and turn the water down through the valley. Now tell me what you think about that, right or wrong?"

Joe said, "Yes, I agree with that, but, Ed, let me also say the valley that Thad has I bet the same thing could be done to that valley. Maybe that is what happened to the water there."

Joe sat there and thought about it for a little bit and said, "Before long, I want to take a ride over the hill and look at Thad's creek and maybe we can talk to him about his problem."

Joe leaned back in his chair and was looking out the window and a smile on his face, and Ed said, "I would like to know what you are thinking on about now, boss."

Joe turned around to his desk and said, "You know, God has been so good to us he gives us everything that we could possible want or need. There is no problem that he has not given us a solution for. We carry our guns sometimes, and we do not need them. We have small problems, and the solutions just happen to come along. We have about everything that we need. Except for one thing that I can think of at the moment."

Ed said, "What is this problem that you think that we need at the moment?"

Joe smiled and said, "I was thinking that at the moment you and Jacob each need a wife to take care of you. How about that problem?"

Ed's face turned a little red and he said, "I have also been thinking about that and maybe I have a solution to part of that problem. I have been seeing a young lady in town every now and again."

Joe laughed and clapped his hands and said, "Well, now I am very happy about that good news. Maybe one problem is about to be solved, but what about the other problem?" Beverly was walking to the office with some coffee and three cups; she came through the door and said, "What problems do we have today, gentleman? Anything that I can help with."

Joe said, "You know what, honey, there just might be something that you can do to help with the problem."

Beverly said, "What would you like for me to do, Joe?"

Joe said, "I believe it is time for us to have a party here and show off our new house and have good dance and invite some young ladies so we can have a dance for the men."

Beverly said, "I believe that I can handle that problem. Joe, if you will just give me a few days to work out the details."

Joe said to Beverly, "I leave it up to you, and I will not interfere with whatever you plan.

It was a few weeks later, Ed came to Joe and told him that they had two large tanks made out of wood, and he was ready to fire the valleys that they had talked about. Joe went over to the valley with Ed, and the whole crew was there; they had shovels, rakes, and buckets with them, and they had already made a fire break between the forest and the valley. Since there were no leaves on the trees at this time, it was a greater danger of fire going to the woods, but they felt that they could contain the fire. All they wanted was to fire the brush and the shrubs in the valley and kill them out so they could plant grass and start growing something of value in the valley. They started at one end of the valley and fired it from the edge of the grass land and along both sides of the woods. The fire started easily enough, and the men kept it under control and watched it burn from time to time; they would start a back fire and let it burn back to itself and that way hold the fire to a small burn and not let it get out of control. Joe was very satisfied that the men knew what they were doing; they burnt the valley, and as they let the fire move up the valley, they kept a couple of men behind the fire to make sure that it did not start up again. The smoke rose high in the sky and sometimes blotted out the sun. All of their attention was kept on the fire, and nobody noticed that there was a group of men that was coming up the valley behind them. Joe finally noticed the wagons and saddle horses coming at a fast pace toward them, and he went to meet them. Joe was thinking that there was an emergency some other place he never thought that the smoke would be seen in Jameson. But here came the town out to help him; they thought that his house or something else was on fire. Joe stopped them and told them what the men were doing. Joe apologized to the men for dragging them away from their homes and businesses. Sam said, "I have not been out here, Joe, since the day that you were shot, and personally I believe that it has been too long."

The town men and Joe stood out on the burnt ground, and Joe explained that Ed came up with a great idea of damming up a creek that went underground, and they think that they have come up with a way of piping the water over the broken up land and bringing it on down the valley. And this would be giving the ranch a few hundred acres of more grass land. One of the men said, that he had a piece of land that had a nice stream of water that just drops out of sight and maybe he could do something like this to reclaim his property. It would give him many acres of land that he certainly use.

Joe said, "We will work on this idea and make sure that it will work; there may be more than one broken up area that we do not know about, but the idea is sound, and I believe that Ed is a smart enough man to come up with whatever solution that will solve the problem."

There were many comments about Ed and how smart that he is. One of the men made a comment that maybe he would like to change jobs and work for someone else. Joe said, "All I can say is you will have to ask Ed. He is a big boy, and he is smart enough to make up his own mind."

The answer came back to Joe. "You must be pretty sure of yourself that he will not leave you or you would not say that."

Joe said, "Ed is my friend as well as my foreman, and I would only want to do what is best for him."

The men visited with Joe until the men working the fire were getting clear out of sight. Joe said, "Gentlemen, I really appreciate that you came over here to help me and I would do the same thing if I saw a lot of smoke coming up around the area of the town. And I am sorry that I did not let you know that we would be doing this controlled burn. But I need to get back with my men. We wanted to shut down the fire before it get to the big timber at the head of the valley. I know that you will excuse me so I can get back to my business before my men fire me and send me home."

He said his goodbyes to the men from town and headed back up the valley to the fire, and he saw that the men were already shutting down the fire, and they were almost to the big hole in the ground. He did not want to burn so close to the hold that it would stand out and be seen by everyone. There was brush and trees growing in the broken up ground at the bottom of the hole, but he wanted to keep everyone out of there. He wanted the gold that was at the bottom of the hole in the banks of the river, but he also wanted to keep anyone from drowning because of the floodwater that they had seen come down the underground river. He still wondered where the river went underground, and he wondered where the seam of gold was that was washing down the river. He guessed that God would be the only one who would ever know. Maybe someday technology would get so advanced that men would be able to go down in the ground and find and mine the gold. But he did not want to risk any of his men on this venture anymore; he felt that it was not worth it. Jacob came to Joe and said, "Joe, this idea is fabulous, and it can be applied to a lot of other areas around here where the ground has given away. Joe, would you mind if I bought a track of land which is close to bordering your property on the north side. When we first came back on the train and was going back in the wilderness to hide from the outlaws. I saw the land one day while I was on guard duty and I fell in love with it."

Joe said, "Jacob, I would hate to lose you as a worker, but I would love to have you as a neighbor, and you will always be my friend. Are you planning to make this move any time soon?"

Jacob said, "No, I do not have enough money yet to buy the property that I want, but when I do I wanted to make sure that it did not interfere with any of your plans."

Joe said, "I do not know for sure where you are talking about the only place that I thought about buying was for Thad and that land which joined his valley. If we could help him expand his holdings, it would greatly help him. Is that the place that you are talking about?"

Jacob said, "No, that valley is not the place. It is one more valley over to the north, but it is similar to that place, come to think of it the two places looks kind of alike to each other."

Joe said, "Jacob, I will do whatever I can to help you when the time comes, and that is a promise."

Joe started to wonder how many men he would lose when they had collected all of their money and moved out and started their own life. He could not blame them if all of them left him and started their own spread or store or hotel, whatever they wanted to do with the rest of their life. Joe went out on the front porch and was checking the weather when he saw a buggy coming down the road. If his eyes were not betraying him, he was seeing the Lincolns coming. He had not seen them for a long time. He went back into the house and called to Beverly and told her that her uncle and aunt were coming down the road. He went back out on the porch and waited until they were close, and then he went down to the road and waited to greet them. By the time they arrived, Beverly was on the road beside Joe, and they greeted the two lovely people warmly. They stood beside the buggy and talked for a while, and Beverly said, "Let us go into the house, and I will finish up the pot of coffee that I just put on." They went into the house arm and arm like the old friends that they were.

Ken said, "I went to town yesterday to pick up a few things, and they told me about the track of land that you burnt off and is it right that you are going to dam up a creek and pipe the water over a sink place and water the whole valley with this creek."

Joe said, "Ken, Ed, our foreman, came up with the idea, and we talked it over. I like his idea, so we burnt off the scrub brush and the briars and brambles so we can plant grass seed just before we turn the water loose to water this valley.

Ken said, "Where is this sink that you are talking about?"

Joe said, "Do you remember the big hole that we almost fell into the night that we were running from the outlaws. Over nest to the valley that Thad owns."

Ken said, "Yes, I remember that hole, now that was an ugly piece of property, but if you could get grass growing there, you could extend your ranch to handle a few hundred more cattle."

Joe said, "You remember the hole, but there is a river running under the ground through the hole, we have been both directions up and down the river, and it seems that it never surfaces. I drilled a hole in the west pasture where the water is so scarce, and I put up a windmill plus we built a large tank for the cattle to drink out of, and we built a dam to hold back a small lake during the times that the wind does not blow."

Ken said, "Do you have any idea where the river travels to? It should surface someplace, but I have never heard of a river that comes out of the ground."

Joe said, "Let me get a couple of horses saddled, and we can ride out there, and I will show you what we are doing. I believe that once we get a few dams in place and conserve the water that we can get hold of that we can handle a lot more good stock and a lot less problems."

Joe went out to the corral and told the handler to saddle two horses and to bring them around to the front of the house. He talked to Jacob while he was there and asked him how he was coming along with his project. Jacob said he had put a ladder down in the hole, and he went down and looked around; it was really low and the gold was more plentiful than it was the first time they went down. He said he was having a couple of shaker tables made to put down there, and they could screen the gold in about one/third of the time than they could by panning it. They should have the shaker tables made today. They are making them out in the barn."

Joe told him that sounded like a great idea but be careful today. Joe said, "Mr. Lincoln, is here, and they are going to be riding up to the hole and I do not want to be looking at any ladders in the hole. Because he will be asking questions about it, and I will not lie to him so please do not let him see anything here or there."

Jacob went over to two of the men working on the shakers he talked to them for a moment and they grabbed all of the parts and the completed one and took them away from the barn so they would be out of sight. Jacob also sent a rider out to the hole to tell the men there to pull the ladders out and take them a safe distance away from the hole until he told them to bring the ladders back. Joe went back into the house and talked with everyone until they brought the horses to the front of the house. He told Beverly that he was going to show Ken around the ranch and their new windmill and their burnt valleys and show him the new improvements, and they would be back in a few hours. He kissed her, and she held his hand while he was walking away until they had to release each other. Mrs. Lincoln watched them and smiled to herself about these young lovers. Ken and Joe rode slowly over the ranch and talked about cattle, grass, weather, and other things that they had in common. Ken looked over at Joe while they had stopped and was watching the windmill pump out water, and he said, "It seems so long ago that the outlaws were trying to kill us, and it seems that we have been so much happier since then than we ever was before. Joe, does it seem like that to you, like life is so much more precious now than it was before."

Joe looked down at the ground, and then he looked at Ken and said, "I have thought a lot about that Ken, and I agree with you there for a while I thought that I had lost everything that was worthwhile. But now after it is over with, I feel that I have just now found the life that is worth living for the first time in my life. I had to trust God, and I knew that there was nothing that I could do to make things better, and God was the only help that there was, and maybe since that trust in him it has changed me forever for a long time after the outlaws were killed and captured I felt empty. I was relieved but not right but after a while something happened to me, and maybe the love of Beverly overcome me. But I am happier than I have ever been in my life. I believe that God gave me time to heal from the trouble that came upon us, but I am well and happy now."

Ken said, "Yes, that is just about what I feel. It is just harder for me to find the right words to explain it. I not only want our life to be nice, but I want the life of every man that works for me to be nicer also."

Joe said, "I have also been feeling the same thing about my men. I want them to be able to strike out on their own and make something of themselves. we are not just a bunch of people who came together. It is like we are all family, and a close family at that."

The two men rode along enjoying the weather, their own company, and the family-like conversation that they so enjoyed between them. Ken was really interested in all of the improvements that Joe had done on the ranch especially the spreader dams that scattered the water all over the bottom lands. Not just allowing the water to just travel down the lowest places but put water all over the valley and the grass grew better and healthier and faster which means more feed for the cattle to eat. And as Joe said that is the way that it is. After their ride they came back to the ranch house, and there were two horses tied to the hitch rack in front of the house. They dismounted and went up the steps and started in to the house. A man came out of the house; he was tall and broad of the shoulders and a good-looking young man with dark brown hair and a big smile on his face. Joe yelled, "Thad, how are you, man? I hardly knew who you were. You have spread out in the shoulders and grown up all of a sudden."

Thad said, "Joe, Mr. Lincoln, how are the both of you? It is so good to see you. Malinda and I decided that we should come over and see you guys. We saw some real heavy smoke over this way, but I could tell that it was a forest fire, and then it was gone so I knew that it was under control. I was afraid for a while that it might cross over the mountain and I would have my hands full. I saw this morning as we came over what you were doing and stopped and talked to your men at the hole. I saw that cabin a couple of months ago while I was getting us deer. I thought that some hunter had moved into that area I didn't stop maybe I am still a little jumpy about the outlaws I don't know."

Joe said, "Don't worry about it. There was not any harm done. The men did not even know that you were around. I guess that you are still silent in the woods as you used to be."

"I will keep a couple of men up there from time to time if you ever need me for anything just get word to one of them, and they can come after me, and I will be right there. If I am not available, then Ed or Jacob will get to you as soon as possible."

Thad looked at Joe, and he wanted to tell Joe how much that he really loved him but that is something that one man does not tell another man, so he just said, "Thanks, Joe, I will remember that."

Thad did not know it, but Joe felt about the same way about him. When you stay with someone the way that these two men stayed with each other and fought the outlaws and helped each other stay alive, you really care about each other. Finally, Malinda came out to where the two men were talking, and she walked up to Joe and threw her arms around his neck and hugged him and said, "Thanks for helping my man stay alive before I had a chance to meet him."

Joe had his arms around her and said, "Thanks for the hug, but I don't know which one of us saved the other one. The most it was kind of a tossup if you ask me."

She looked at Thad and said, "Now I have not heard about him ever saving anyone, it was always you saving him from someone or the other."

CHAPTER 21

Joe said, "Maybe we ought to go outside and walk around and I can tell you a few things about that guy that I do not think that you have ever heard."

He looked over a Thad who was standing there with his head down and his face very red, and he was shuffling one foot on the porch floor. Joe punched Malinda and pointed to Thad, and she just cackled and went over and threw her arms around his neck and kissed him on the mouth and his face turned even redder than before. Thad said, "Don't do that in front of everyone, what will they think?"

She said, "Honey, they will think that we do that all the time, isn't it what we do all the time?"

Thad said, "Yes, it is, but do we have to tell them about it?"

Malinda said, "I will behave in front of everyone, but you just wait until I get you home or at least into the woods, and then I will teach you a thing or two about kissing. Or are you going to get all red on me again?"

Thad put his arm around the waist of Malinda and silently thanked God that he had given Thad a wife that would help him get over his shyness around other people. She was so open and honest that he just wondered at her sometimes. She was the exact opposite of him; he was a loner; he was comfortable by himself and with her but not around other people. She was open with anyone, and she loved other people, and everyone loved her. Thad went to Beverly and thanked her for having them for the visit, and Beverly hugged him and kissed him on the cheek and said, "Thad, as far as I am concerned you two are family, and you are more welcome in this house anytime that you want to be here than anyone that I know of. And, Thad, I think that you have picked the perfect wife. She is a dream girl."

That lowered his head and said, "I fully agree with you on that. She is so kind, gentle, and loving. I am a very lucky man to have her. I thank God for her every day."

Beverly said, "Thad, if you ever need anything please let us know. God has been very good to us, and like I said you and Malinda are family. More family than anyone we have in this world."

Thad and Malinda hugged the both of them mounting up, they rode off in the afternoon sun going back to their valley home. Since Joe had the valley burnt, and they could ride their horses up through the valley at a faster pace, it did not seem so long before they came to their valley and was home. Thad was happy in this valley; his herd was growing; he had many new calves; and he had to either sell off some of the cattle or think about expanding his land. What Joe had done to the valley that he had burnt gave Thad some ideas about the valley just out through the narrow opening of the valley that he lived in. Tomorrow he would go out in that valley and look it over and see what the possibilities were there.

Ken Lincoln was driving along, and he looked at his wife and said, "Martha, that Joe is one smart man. He is taking worthless land and getting ready to turn it into wonderful pasture land. He and Beverly are going to have the richest ranch in the whole state pretty soon. I am really glad for them, but he has given me some great ideas that I am going to put to work on our ranch. Can't let these kids have all the great ideas now, can we?"

Martha just looked at Ken and smiled and said, "Ken, I am certainly glad that God has given us Joe as a member of our family. He really makes me proud to know him. You just go ahead and have all the ideas that you want to, just so long as you clear them with our Lord before you start them."

Sunday morning, Joe and Beverly are getting ready for church, and just as they come out of the house, most of the men led by Ed and Jacob ride around the house and fall in behind the buckboard and Joe looked at them smiling and nodded his head. Without saying anything, they all know that he and Beverly are tickled that they are going to church with them. They arrive in Jameson and ride right up to the church and Ken and Martha come right behind them with some of their hands. When they get in the church they just about filled up the church, and when the pastor stood up and he looked at the full church, he is just beaming with pleasure. They sang a couple of songs; the pastor led them in a prayer for peace and understanding of God and his works in their life. He started his message which is on brotherly love; he delivered a wonderful message, and then they sang another song, had prayed, and he let church out. Outside the church as is the custom of this church, everyone stood around for a few minutes, and they all visit with their neighbors, and Beverly announced that there is going to be a party and a dance at the ranch in two weeks on Saturday afternoon and evening, and everyone is welcome. "Come ready to have a good time." Most of the ladies gathered around Beverly and asked, "What do you want me to bring?" They talked about that for a long time and as usual everyone brought what they do every time anyway, so the question is really just a lead in to what everyone already knows as the answer. "Honey, you bring whatever you feel like bringing, and it will be just great."

After church, the crew went home, and as they came to the house and Joe and Beverly was getting out to go into the house, one of the men said, "Joe, after we eat we will be playing horse shoes out behind the blacksmith shop." He was smiling when he said it. "That is if you don't mind getting beaten." And he rides on.

Joe yelled at him, "I will be there, and we will find out see you."

As they go up on the porch, Beverly said, "Do you think that you can beat him?"

Joe looked at her and said, "I seriously doubt it, but sometimes they just need to beat the boss at something. We will see just how the day turns out. It does not matter to me who wins. I just need to go out at times and spend some time with them. Do you want to see your husband take a licking?"

Beverly said, "I used to be good at playing horse shoe, but that was a lot of years ago, and I would like to watch if you don't think that it would bother you for me to see you beaten."

After they had eaten their lunch, Joe helped Beverly clean away the table, and they both went out to the blacksmith shop, and the games were already under way. The different teams were playing, and Joe and Beverly sat down on a log and watched the game. The men were rooting for the favorite player of theirs and always someone was rooting for a different player to get a ringer or get the closest shoe. There was a good time had by all, and it was a serious game but not one that left hard feelings because they were all good players, and at any given time any player could win over another previous winner. Finally, it came the time for Joe to play with the last winner; they gave Joe time to get used to the shoes and the way the pegs were put into the ground by throwing a few shoes before the game started. Before the game started, they knew that Joe was not as good as some of them, but that did not matter to the men. They were just glad that Joe had come out and spent time with them doing one of the things that they liked to do. Joe was a man that they admired so much; it did not matter whether he could play horse shoe or not. When the game started, they were all rooting for Joe to beat the other guy. He beat Joe pretty bad; fact is Joe did not score a point. At the end of the game, Joe shook the hand of the man who beat him; while shaking his hand, Joe said, "I know how I can beat you with these shoes." The man looked kind of puzzled and Joe said, "I will have the blacksmith put my shoes on the fastest horse on the ranch, and I will horse race you—that would be the only time that I could beat you at horse shoes."

The men went wild with laughter and so did the man who beat him. Maybe not Joe. One of the men said, "What if I put the horse shoes on that rabbit that you found out in the country when we were taking the cattle to the railroad. Just maybe that rabbit could beat your horse." And again everybody laughed. Joe said, "I forgot about that rabbit, maybe I had better get it so I could be sure and beat this guy. He put one hand on the shoulder of the man and said, "When I get time out working on those blasted ledgers maybe I should come out here and throw some shoes. And maybe I could give you guys a little competition, but I doubt it." He looked at his opponent and said, "Good game. Now let me get out of here and take my seat again and watch some real horse shoe players."

While they were talking, Beverly picked up a shores shoe that had rolled close to her and walked over to the closest peg and threw the horse shoe at the other peg and made a ringer. The men let out a cheer that could be heard for half a mile, and they grabbed a set of shoes and said, "Here throw these and see if you can do it again."

They were certain that she could not even come close, but they were having fun and wanted her to be a part of the fun. Joe encouraged her to throw a few shoes, and she said, "Why not throw a few and show these men what a real horse shoe pitcher can do?" She seriously doubted that she could do any good, but she threw another shoe which went around the peg and then came off. The men howled again cheering her on. The next shoe was another ringer; the next one came down beside the peg; she threw a few more but did not do as good as when she first started and she said, "Beginner's luck, guys," and she walked over and sat down with Joe. But the men cheered her like she had just won the grand prize because according to the men she had done more than just won anything; she had won their hearts all over again. Joe and Beverly had done much more than just spend time with the men. They had made the men feel that they were more important than just employees; they were special to Joe and Beverly. Most of these men did not have any family or at least not any family who they would ever see again. Joe and Beverly they felt were their family, and today proved that to them because they included themselves into the lives of the employee, and these men would never forget this day. The men of the times were fiercely loyal to the brand or another way to put it—they were loyal to their employer. But these men would go a long way further, and since Joe and Beverly showed how much they really cared about these men, the men would forever show how much they cared about them. Finally, it started to get dark, and Ed stepped up and said, "We have had a great day, but we have chores to do, and we need to get ready for tomorrow which is a workday. I am glad that we had a fun day today, and thank you, Joe and Beverly, for spending your day with us."

Joe and Beverly stood up and Joe said, "Guys, let me say that I had a lot of fun being with you guys, and I want you to know that each and every one of you are important to Beverly and me. You do not know how much all of you mean to me, including the men who could not be with us today because of their duties. I hope the next time we can include them."

Joe took Beverly's hand, and they went back into the house and left the men looking at them with a great big smile on their faces. Some of the men patted Joe on the shoulder as he passed by them, and all of the men felt like they were a part of a family here. Monday morning, the whole ranch started their duties, and each person went to work with a purpose and that purpose was to make the ranch a little better than it was yesterday. The men worked for people they really cared about, and they knew that they mattered to the boss.

Jacob had men to put the ladders down in the hole; they put the lanterns in the hole; the water level was low; they put the shakers in the hole, and the men went down the ladders. Before lunch, the men had worked out more gold with the two shakers than eight men could with pans in three days. At quitting time, they had worked out enough for Joe to make up another box and send it off to the lawyer in the capital. Joe made up an address sign and put it on the box that had already been made up for this shipment. The box was put into the buggy, and Joe took it to the depot and made out the shipping papers to send to the lawyer at the capital. The station man was looking at the address and said, "Joe, you send more things to the capital than a governor would." Joe said to the station ticket agent, "The lawyer is a friend of mine, and he likes some of the things we have around here. He collects metal things that we wear out and get ready to throw away. He will wind up getting rid of it someday also."

The agent said, "Some people save the darkest things."

Joe said, "Each to his own."

Joe asked the agent, "Have I gotten a telegram from this man in the last few weeks."

The telegraph agent said, "No, Joe, you have not received any telegrams at all."

Joe said, "I just remembered I have to make a trip to the capital, and I clearly forgot it. I have to go home and pack a few things, and I will be right back. Do not send that box or wire to him that it is coming. I want to surprise him with a visit."

Joe headed home and called Beverly and said, "I have not heard any confirmation from the lawyer about the previous shipments of gold. Something is wrong. I want to go check on what is happening on that end."

Beverly wanted to know if Joe wanted her to come with him to keep him company and Joe said, "No, I am going to go alone, and I want to keep an eye on this box and find out what is going on. I trust Jeremy, but something is happening to the gold, and I want to find out what. Joe got on the train and told the telegraph operator to send another telegram that another box is coming on this train and give him time to meet the train. Joe asked the conductor where the box would be normally kept on a schedule like this, and he said, "Right where it is lying would be okay. It is out of the way and is easy to unload when we get there."

Joe leaned back in his seat and dozed along as he was sitting in plain view of the box. When the train pulled into the station, the box was taken off and set on the platform in plain sight. Joe's sitting on a bench a little away from it and reading a newspaper when a man came out of the station and looked at the label on the box and picked it up and took it into the station. Joe got up and went to the window so he could see back into the station. Joe could see the man back in the baggage area, and he was prying the top off the box. Joe walked through the station and told the man to stop. The man looked around at him and said, "You are not allowed in here. You are going to have to leave."

Joe said, "Why are you taking the lid off that box?"

The man looked at Joe, and holding a hammer in his hand, he started toward Joe; he raised the hammer into the air, and the station manager yelled at him to stop. The manager came up to the man and said, "What are you trying to do? Why are you threatening a customer of the railroad?"

The man said, "He came back here threatening me, and I was just defending myself."

The manager turned around and looked at Joe and said, "What was he threatening you? With his newspaper? Because he does not have anything else."

Joe said, "Can I say something? This is the third box that I have sent to Jeremy, and he has not received any of them, so I thought that I would send the usual telegram, and when I put the box on the train, I got on the train with it. The box was left on the station platform, and this guy came out and picked it up and brought it back here and started to open it up. And I came back here and just asked him what was he trying to do, and he grabbed the hammer and that is when you came back. I believe that he stole the last two boxes and the content of the boxes, and I would like to have them back."

The station manager said, "What is in the box, Mr. Manning?"

Joe said, "Like the label says, 'metal parts.' I wanted to know where the other boxes have gone to so we just put metal in the box."

The station manager said to the warehouse man, "What have you done to the other boxes and where is the content of the other two boxes? Unless you want to go to jail you had better tell me and tell me now."

The man looked at Joe and said, "Can we make a deal? Can I talk to you in private?"

Joe said, "We can talk, but I will make no promises to you, but we can talk."

Joe looked at the manager and said, "Can you give us a few moments to talk? He will not hurt me, and I will not hurt him."

The manager walked away, and the man moved closer to Joe and said, "The other two shipments of gold are hidden safe. I will give them back to you if you will not prosecute me with the law. I promise I will never do anything like this again. I have it all here. I did not know what to do with it, and I have been scared to death that someone would find out."

Joe looked at the man and asked, "How did you know that it was gold in the box?"

The man said, "The box slipped out of my hand and fell. It busted open, and I saw what was in the box. Could I ask where it came from, and I promise I will not tell anyone anything about it."

Joe said, "It was just a lucky find in a river way up country, and now it is over. There will be no more of these type of boxes coming through here. Now do you have the other boxes here and is the gold here? This belongs to a lot of different people, not to me alone."

The man said, "Yes, it is still here, and I put it back into the original boxes."

Joe said, "How do I know that you are telling me the truth about what is in the boxes? How can I trust you after what you have done?"

The man said, "Sir, I have been terrified that something like this would happen, and it did. I want no more of this kind of thing. I do not want to go to jail like my daddy did, and I want to stay out and take home a paycheck for my mommy. She is ailing, and if something would happen to me she would not have anybody to look after her."

Joe said, "You put that lid back on and make it solid. You get those other boxes, and you had better make them just like I shipped them. And if you say anything to any person about the gold, I will know of it, and I will have you arrested and put into prison. I will talk to the manager. What about the telegram that I sent for this person to pick up the boxes?"

"I still have the telegram, and I will deliver it just as soon as I get these boxes on the platform, and I will look after them personally."

Joe stood back and watched as the baggage man put the boxes on the platform, and he headed down the street to deliver the telegram. Joe went into the station manager's office and sat down with the man and tried to explain what had happened and asked the manager to give the fellow another chance. But Joe added I believe that he will do you a good job, but I believe that I would watch him for a while."

The manager looked at Joe and said, "Aren't you the Joe Manning that helped out a good friend of ours? The cattle buyer."

Joe smiled and leaned back in his chair and said, "How is he anyway out chasing cows?"

The station manager laughed. "Yep, you are the one all right." And he reached across the desk and said, "I want to shake your hand. We started out about the same time, and he was just a lot smarter than I was. But he gave me a second chance, and I guess I could give this guy a second chance also."

Joe thanked him and walked out of his office; he was sitting on the bench on the platform when Jeremy came driving up in his carriage. He was overwhelmed when he saw Joe standing on the platform. He jumped out of the carriage and grabbed Joe and shook his hand. He said, "I wish that I had known that you were coming. I would have been here to meet you. Why didn't you let me know that you were coming?"

Joe said, "I had not heard from you when I sent the first two boxes, so I knew that something was wrong, so when I put the third box on the train, I came along with it. I found that the baggage man had intercepted the first two boxes and took the third box into the back and started to open it, and I stopped him. We had a long talk, and I am going to let it slide if he does not do anything like that again. I do not want to get involved with the police or anything like that because I do not want to draw attention to the gold. Will there be any problem putting this gold into the treasury or into the system of where it goes?"

Jeremy said, "I have talked to them, and they are glad to get the gold, and they do not care where it comes from so long as I certify that it has been obtained from a legal source. I gave them all the paperwork, and they are satisfied with the papers that I gave them." They took the boxes into Jeremy's office and stacked them into a corner. Joe asked when he was going to be able to put the gold into the exchange. He told Joe that he could take one of the bags over to the exchange right now. They opened one of the boxes and Joe handed him the bag of gold and asked him, "How are you going to carry this? You cannot just walk the street with a bag of gold." "I have a briefcase that will hold about all of this, and I can carry that from my carriage to the exchange when I am inside, then I am under their protection." Joe said, "I will be your driver, and I will carry my pistol under my jacket, and I will be between you and anything that might happen."

They pulled the carriage into the carriage house, and Jeremy went into his house and brought out his briefcase. While he was doing that, Joe emptied the boxes and put them against the wall and was ready for him to load up the brief case. The gold seemed a little heavy for the briefcase, and Joe asked Jeremy if he would like to make two trips or could Joe carry one of the bags for him into the exchange.

Jeremy said, "It would be a little unusual for that to happen, but I did not see anything wrong with it, just do not go any farther than the guard at the door. You are not allowed to carry a gun into the exchange, but under the circumstances I think that it would be all right for you to go that far."

Joe drove the carriage to the exchange and got out of the driver's seat and opened the door on the carriage and handed Jeremy the briefcase. Then he picked up the other item and carried the other item to the door of the exchange. The guard stepped in front of Joe and said, "I am sorry, sir, this is as far as you can go. The other gentleman can go alone from here."

Joe said, "Is it all right if I hang out here with you until the boss gets back?"

The guard said, "Sure you can hang out with me. I guess I could use the company. It seems that nobody wants to talk to a guard. They are too busy doing their business."

Joe said, "Is it all right for me to leave the carriage sitting there while I am waiting for him to finish up his business?"

Joe and the guard were sitting there and talking. Joe was watching some men out along the street; they were talking among themselves, and Joe saw one of the men open his coat, and he saw a sawed-off shotgun under his coat. The guard looked around and saw what was about to happen, and he pushed an alarm button on the wall. Bells started going off, and he yelled for Joe to grab that metal grate like door and close it on the main opening. Joe saw what he was talking about and grabbed the door; it slid on some kind of rollers and slid shut and closed the opening where there were only glass doors. He saw one of the men bringing his shotgun out from under his coat, and Joe grabbed the guard and pulled him away from the glass door. They now were standing behind the wall protected from the guns outside of the exchange. The robbers shot the glass out, and Joe pulled his pistol and shot the man that was getting ready and aiming at the door to shoot the shotgun at them again. The man fell on the steps and grabbed his chest; he was not dead, but he would not be doing anything for a while. Another man who was also a robber had made it to the steel bar gate, and he reached through with his pistol and yelled for them to open the gate, or he would kill someone. Joe shot his gun hand since he was just a few feet away; this was an easy shot for Joe. The man dropped the pistol, and screaming, he grabbed his hand and ran back down the steps; blood was flowing from his arm where the artery was severed. He was sitting on the cement walk, trying to stop the flow of blood. All of this happened in just seconds; the guard still had not pulled his gun and had not realized what was going on or was just too rattled to act. The other men started shooting through the opening; the people had gotten out of the way, but if the men could get up the steps, they could shoot at anyone who was in the room. Joe would look around the corner from time to time, and he would draw fire from them. He looked once and saw two men coming up the steps; he fired at them, hitting them but was forced back with gunfire from the outlaws. Joe thought, *Why is this happening all over again like it did years ago back in the town of Jameson?* He prayed to God for help and guidance because he did not want to kill any more people. All this time, he was watching as he kept looking from time to time and keeping them back. He heard other noises from the street, and he heard, "This is the police. Drop your weapons, and we will hold out fire." Joe looked around the edge of the wall and saw four policemen who were standing in the street without any cover, and the robbers raised their guns, and the police opened fire on them with pistols and one shotgun. The men were mowed down like they were weeds in a field, and the police had a mowing scythe. Soon, it was all over, and the street was quiet again. Joe looked out, and there were bodies all over the sidewalk and on the steps coming up to the door of the exchange. There was a sergeant from the police department coming up the steps and calling out to anyone from the inside. Joe stepped out; he had already put his pistol up, and he said, "Thank you, Sergeant, for getting us out of trouble." The sergeant said, "Thank you for keeping the people in there safe. I watched it for a bit, but I needed a few more guns in order to stop them here. That way, they will not be doing anything like this again."

Joe stood there and waited for Jeremy to come back out; by the time he came out, Joe was made out to be a hero, and he did not want to put into the public eye. He told the sergeant that he did not want to be singled out; he wanted the police to get all of the credit. The sergeant would not have it any other way until Joe took him aside and said to him, "Do you think that I want all of the relatives and the friends of those guys coming to look me up for killing their friends or relatives? I do not want my name used if at all possible. Is that all right with you?"

The sergeant said, "I understand. We stand in the gap and get paid for it. You are a private citizen, and you do not want to be bothered with it."

Joe said, "Now you have the problem that I want to avoid. Will you leave me out of it please?"

The sergeant said, "You have done us and this city a great service today, and for that and the fact that nobody else would even put out any effort at all, I will do that for you. But, Joe Manning, I really feel bad taking the credit for doing what you did. You took the chance at getting a bullet in the head all for nothing."

Jeremy came out and said that he heard what Joe had done to keep the rest of them safe, and he really appreciated it. "The bank president wanted to know who the man was who kept us safe, and I told him who you were. He said he would hire you for a bank guard, and I told him that I could not get along without you, so he said he would not say anything."

They left the bank, and Joe drove Jeremy to the train station, and Joe took the receipts for the gold and said goodbye to Jeremy and waited for the train home which was not long in coming. Joe sat in his seat and went over the figures as to the amounts of gold that each man would get and how much the ranch would get. The figures came out to a tidy sum for all of them. Joe felt good for his men and for the blessings that God has given him and his family. Joe came home, and Beverly was so glad to see him that she just kept hugging him and kissing him, and Joe said, "Honey, what is the matter? You would think that I have been gone for a year not just a few days."

Beverly said, "Joe, you will never know the dreams and the thoughts that I have had about you while you were gone. I imagined that you had been shot during a bank holdup, now I know that was dumb, but it seemed so real that I woke up bathed in sweat. And the next day, I just could not get it out of my mind."

Joe sat there and thought, *should I tell her the truth?* And he did not know what to do. She asked him did anything happen on this trip. Joe opened his mouth and then closed it; he said, "Beverly, sit down, and I will tell you all about my trip to the capital."

He told her about the man who had found the gold and took it and what happened to the third box and how he had gotten it back. About the trip to the exchange and the holdup attempt and what he had done, and he said, "I was not in any danger at any time, so you had all of that worry for nothing."

Ed came into the office to see Joe, and he came around the corner where they were talking, and Beverly proceeded to tell him what they had just been talking about. He listened to her for a while, and he looked at Joe, and he shook his head and said, "Wow, Joe, can't we let you off the place without you getting into trouble?"

Joe said, "You know I was standing in the bank, and I was kind of thinking the same thing. It seemed that something happens around every corner sometimes."

Joe asked, "Ed, how is Jacob and his guys doing down in the hole? Is the water staying down? Have they had any trouble?"

Ed said, "They are doing fine, Joe. They are very careful, and there is a man who is staying upstream from them, and he is far enough away, so there is not any other noises. His only job is to listen to the water, so I believe they will be okay.

"The drillers have put down two more wells, and they have hit the river every time. They are having trouble understanding how we know exactly where the river is every time, but they are doing a good job.

"The grass is eaten away in the valley above the hole, and I moved the herd down out of the valley yesterday. I hope that is all right with you." Joe said, "You know that is all right with me, Ed. You are out there, and you see what needs to be done so go ahead and make the decision."

Joe asked, "Ed, are any of the men asking about their money?"

Ed looked at him and shrugged his shoulders. Joe said, "How much money they have in their account?"

Ed said, "Yes, they are wondering, but they know that you will let them know when you find out, so they will just wait and see."

"Let them know that I received the figures today, and I will have their totals in a day or two."

Ed said, "I will tell them tonight or maybe tomorrow. If I tell them tonight, they will not get anything done tomorrow, and I do not want the men down in the hole to be thinking about that tomorrow. I would rather wait and let them keep their minds on their jobs tomorrow."

The next morning, Joe took his papers out to the bunkhouse and caught the men before they left the bunkhouse before breakfast and told them he would meet with them when they came in to eat. "There will not be any work in the hole today. We will work on the dam today instead." The men looked at each other and shrugged their shoulders and went on about their getting ready. When the men came into the dining area, their meal was put on the long picnic type table with benches on either side. There were seats at either end of the table for Ed and Jacob. Joe stood off to the side. The men sat down and were watching Joe. Ed walked over to Joe and motioned to the chair he usually sits in and said, "Joe, why don't you sit down here, and I will scoot over on the side."

Joe said, "You go ahead and sit in your usual place, and I will stand beside you and talk to the men. I really do not want to sit down anyway."

After the men had started dishing up their food, Joe knew that there would not be much if any talking anyway, so he could talk without bothering the men. He stood beside Ed and addressed the men; he said, "I know that you are not very interested in how much money you are going to make from the gold that we have gotten out so far, but I am going to tell you anyway."

The heads of all of the men came up looking at Joe; most of the men were forgetting to chew their food. Joe looked at them and smiled; he said, "Go ahead and chew your food before you get choked on it. I want you alive to spend your money once you get it." He gave the men the amount of money that they have earned so far.

All of the men were to get the same amount. Only he, Ed, and Jacob knew that they were going to get a bonus because they were the ones that were making it happen.

Joe said, "I want to press the importance upon you that you do not go on a spending spree. You can blow your monthly salary, but this money will be held in reserve for you until you decide what you are going to do with it. I know how cowboys are with money. You spend it as soon as you get it. I want this money to help you set yourself up for the rest of your life. Ed, Jacob, and I will help you talk about it. We will help you plan it, and when the time comes, I will help you get it done."

Joe gave them the amount, and he told them that it was enough to buy some land to farm. There would be enough money to start a ranch and buy some cattle. There would be enough to start a store of some kind and stock it. Then he gave them the amount that they would get. The men were silent for a long time and not looking at anyone; they just looked down at their plates. Joe knew that they were thinking about something that they had planned for their whole life while they were riding somewhere and doing something.

Cowboys have always planned while they were riding; it was just the way that it was. The cowboy did his best thinking while he was in the saddle, which is where he was at home.

Joe said, "I did not want you to go down in the hole today, like Jacob said he wanted you to have clear heads while you were down there. I want you to also be safe and take care of yourself because now you are owners of your dream, and it will come to pass if you keep a cool head. But remember if there is talk, that will start a stampede of people in here, and we will have the same kind of people in here that we had before, and I know that you do not want that."

Joe said, "Is there any question you want to ask me?"

One man raised his hand and said, "Joe, can I talk to you after we quit eating?"

He looked at Ed, and he knew that he should have asked Ed before he asked Joe. Ed just looked at him and nodded his head yes. Joe caught the play, and he told the man to come to his office as soon as he finished eating. Joe said, "Listen to me, guys, we still have work to do, but if any one of you want to talk to me, check it out with Ed or Jacob, and if it is all right with them, come and see me anytime that I am available."

Joe turned and left the men to talk among themselves, and as soon as he was out the door there was excited talk like everyone was trying to talk at the same time. Joe smiled to himself and thought how much this means to these men, and he realized that he's going to lose most of his men, maybe all of them, but that is all right. Joe remembered when he was the only one on the ranch, and he got by, but now he would need some men because the ranch was much larger. And was going to get larger all the time if all of this is the Lord's will for his life, and Joe believed that it was the Lord's will because the Lord gave all of this to him, Beverly, and these men. Change was again coming to the ranch, and Joe could not look into the future and see what it was naturally. God was going to have to take care of the changes as they happened. Joe was going to try to pray enough to get the guidance to make the proper decisions to keep God's grace in his life. Joe realized that he belonged to God for all eternity. And he realized that he could never be lost again. This was not a worry, and it was not a concern, but Joe had to always keep in mind that his daily walk must be with the will and the pleasure of God in order to stay in the good graces of God. And he certainly did not want to go off on some tangent and forget God for a moment after God has done so much in his life.

Joe's worker came into Joe's office and removed his hat and stood in front of Joe's desk with his head down shuffling his feet. Joe knew that the man was wanting to quit and move on. Joe looked at him and said, "When will you be leaving me?"

The man looked up with a surprised face, and he started turning red, and he said, "Joe, I do not want to leave you. I feel like this is the only home that I have ever had. I will leave if you want me to, but I would rather stay right here if you will let me."

Joe was shocked and said, "I would love it if you would stay with me. But what about the money that you have? What do you want to do with it?"

Jorry, the ranch hand, said, "My mom and my dad who live in New York, they said that I would never amount to anything. I would like to go visit them and give them some of the gold money to let them know that I have amounted to something, and then I would like to come back. What I will do with the rest of the money? I do not know yet. Is that all right with you, Joe?"

Joe said, "Jorry, figure out how much you want to give them and remember you do not know what they need yet. And you can always give them more later. And while you are traveling, stop a few times and look around, and when you are ready come on back home."

Jorry felt relieved that Joe understood, and he thanked Joe and went back outside, and as he was going out the door, he put his big cowboy hat back on his head. Joe did some more work on the money that the ranch shared in and the money would help improve the ranch in a lot of ways, but the men were the important thing in his eyes. Joe had to go into Jameson to pick up a few things for the ranch; he went to the house and asked Beverly if she would like to go into town with him; they could even stop at the diner and eat their evening meal. Beverly jumped at the chance to go with Joe. In a few minutes, she was ready. Joe went out and had a man hitch up the buckboard so they could go to town. On the way to town, Joe told Beverly about Jorry wanting some time off to go to New York and check on his family. He wants to give them some money to show them that he has amounted to something in life. Plus Joe said, "He wanted to come back and stay with us. He said this is the only place that he has ever felt at home."

They pulled into Jameson and went over to the mercantile store and walked in and spoke to Sam and exchanged greetings with his wife. Joe looked at a couple of figures in the back of the store and walked back a little closer, and it was Henry and Drucilla, and Joe walked up to them and greeted Henry and asked how they were getting along. Henry said that they had gotten a crop in the ground. Henry stated that the top soil was so rich that he should be able to grow just about anything."

Joe said, "I am very pleased to hear that. I was hoping that the valley would be a great farm for you."

Joe asked him to excuse him; he needed to order some seed himself. Henry said, "What crop are you going to put out, Joe?"

Joe said, "The only crop that will do me any good. I am going to plant grass. That valley below where we first met up with you is where I am going to try to grow grass."

Henry said, "Joe, you will never get grass to grow where all of that brush is growing, besides that where are you going to get water to grow the grass."

Joe said, "Ed, my foreman, came up with the idea of damming up that little creek and piping it around that big hole and push it down the valley. We are not sure that we can do it. It may be that the floor of the whole valley is broken up and it is useless, but it is worth the try since I own it anyhow."

Joe also told him that they burnt off the brush and hopefully burnt the roots so it will not grow back. Henry said, "You may come up with a good valley after all. That is a lot of land if you can get grass to grow in it."

Joe was walking back to the front of the store, and he turned and smiled at Henry and said, "I hope that I can get something to grow there. If not, I have thrown a lot of money down a hole. Henry, it is good to see both of you again please don't be strangers."

He talked to Sam a bit and then asked Sam. "Do you have grass seed? I believe that I am going to need about six hundred pounds of it."

Sam said, "I do not have anything close to that. I could let you have about two hundred pounds right now. I could get some in from the train in two days, how would that be?"

Joe said, "I will send a wagon into town in a couple of days to pick it up. Beverly, do you need anything while we are here?" Beverly said, "Just the things that I have piled on the counter and the things that have already been put in the buggy."

Joe laughed and said, "Maybe I should not visit so long while I have you with me."

He settled up with Sam, and they left and went to the diner to the evening meal and visit with old friends. Joe thought about all of the friends that they have and about his men who work for him and his love for them. Joe knew that he is going to lose most of his men to their own enterprising ventures, but that is a part of life. He looked at Beverly, his wife, and he thanked God for giving her to him. His life, it seemed, could not be better, but he has a sad memory that another time not too long ago he thought the same thing and his life came apart, and he lost everyone that was important to him. Will it happen again? He sat where he is in the diner, and he prayed silently to God to keep his friends and Beverly safe. After their meal is finished, they go out into the street and decide to go on home and see if they can get the buggy home before dark. Joe went to the buggy and checked his supplies and made sure that everything is secured and will not be lost on the way home. Joe started back up on the sidewalk to get Beverly who is still inside the diner. He heard something and turned back to the street; he saw a horse and a rider coming down the street; he turned back to the diner, and he heard the rider say, "Joe Manning, I am going to kill you because you killed my brother."

Joe turned back to the rider wondering about his thoughts at dinner and wondered if he had prior notice that he was going to die this day. But he looked at the rider and said, "I do not know who you are, and I do not remember killing your brother."

The stranger said, "I see that you do not have a gun unless you have a hideout. Well, that does not make any difference to me, and I am going to kill you anyway. Was my brother so small in your eyes that you do not even remember killing him?"

Joe asked the man, "Where was this supposed to happen that I killed your brother, and how do you know my name?"

The stranger said, "Walk back away from the door of that diner, do it now."

He pulled his gun, and Joe did as he was told; he did not want a bullet to go into the diner and one of his friends or hit Beverly.

The man watched Joe back down the sidewalk until he was at the corner of the building, then the man said, "Get out into the street. I do not want a coward like you try to duck around the corner, and if you make me mad, I will just kill someone else, then I will come after you, and then I will kill you anyway."

Joe was easing over behind the buckboard and out in the street. The stranger then dismounted the horse leaving the horse in the middle of the street. He walked a few steps toward Joe and holstered his gun; he looked at Joe and said,

"On the count of three, I am going to draw, and you can pull your hideout gun and try to shoot me."

Joe said, "You know I do not have a gun, but who was your brother, or are you just paid to kill me, at least tell me that before you kill me."

The stranger said, "What difference does it make?"

Joe said, "At least I will know which rattlesnake I can thank for the likes of you, and how do you know that it was me who shot your brother? One thing that I am sure of, he did not tell you who killed him if anyone did."

The man looked at Joe, and an evil smile came over his face, and he said, "When the gang came into this town to rob it years ago, my friend, who was at the end of the street and heard you yell at them to surrender just before you killed all of them? That is how I know."

Joe said, "When they came into town, they asked for what they got. Now I know you will not ride out of town alive because there are good men in this town who will shoot you down like a dog that you are. You had better surrender now before it is too late, or the same thing will happen to you as it happened to the robbers before you. Will you lay down your gun and surrender, or will you die right here in the street?"

The stranger said, "One, two . . ." And he drew his pistol and started raising it and pointing it at Joe and started to form his mouth to say "three." A rifle shot came from the diner, and blood flew from the side of his head, where the bullet passed through his skull, and he never got the sound of "three" from his mouth. His finger squeezed the trigger, and the bullet hit the ground just in front of Joe's left foot. The door burst open, and Beverly came out into the sidewalk, still pointing the rifle at the stranger. She was sure that he was dead, and she turned to Joe, and he came running to her and took her into his arms and said, "Honey, are you all right? Don't worry about him. You did the right thing. He was an outlaw wanted by the law, I am sure."

Beverly looked at Joe and handed the rifle off to Abby and said, "Abby, here is your rifle back. I do think that I will need it anymore. Joe is safe and sound."

She turned to Joe and said, "Honey, I am fine. I am trained to save lives, and I saw that guy was going to try to take your life, and I figured I would do what I was trained to do."

She threw her arms around her man and kissed him on the lips long and hard. Then she looked him in the eyes and said, "To answer your question, I am just fine as long as I have the man that God has given me, no more and no less."

Joe turned to the people who were gathered around and said, "In case you do not know what this is about that man, he was a brother of one of the robbers that tried to rob the bank years ago. He was told that I killed his brother who was in the robbery, and he came to get even."

There was a stranger in the crowd, and he said, "Could I ask who it was who killed this man?"

Joe said, "That man killed himself. He just came into this town and killed himself. You can see the bullet hole in his head. I was standing in front of him, but when he came in here, he just killed himself."

The stranger said, "Now that is very strange, strange indeed. He would travel all of this way to shoot himself."

Joe looked at the stranger who had a pistol on his side, and it seemed that it had seen a lot of use. Joe took a step forward and to the side until he was next to a cowboy, and when he got close to the cowboy who wore two guns, he put a hand on the shoulder of the cowboy and slid down his arm and slipped the throng off the pistol. The cowboy moved his arm a little to the front of the gun, and Joe slipped the gun out of the holster and put the gun into his waistband. He stepped back away from the cowboy and moved to face the stranger, and he said, "Look here, stranger."

The man turned to face Joe, and he saw the gun in Joe's waistband, and he took a step backward and turned a little pale. Joe said, "A moment ago, you said that man rode a long way just to shoot himself. Now you tell me just how you know that unless you were riding with him."

The man acted like he was going to draw on Joe, but Sam spoke to the stranger, saying, "If you are thinking about drawing your gun on Joe, let me tell you that would be a very bad mistake. But if you happened to outdraw Joe, look at all of the other guns around you, and you know that you would surely die. Maybe you should just tell Joe what he wanted to know. If you are not a wanted man, you can get on your horse and ride out of here and live."

The stranger said, "I am not with that bunch, and I am not an outlaw, but he was a cousin to me. I am not going to draw on anyone. I am just angry that we came here and that he was so stupid. I would like to take his body back to Eastern Virginia, if that is all right with you."

Joe said, "Who was the two men who was at each end of town when the robbery attempt took place?" The stranger said, "I do not know for sure, but I think they were two cousins of his, and if I am right, they are both dead, shot down in some small town. They are all dead, and there is nobody who wants any more revenge."

Joe looked around him, and from the look on everyone's face, it looked like everyone was just like him. Joe walked over to the stranger and said, "Take his body and go back to your home and your family and please do not come to this town again. We will fight if we have to. We will defend each other to the last man. But we want peace. We just want peace."

About the Author

I was a coal miner in West Virginia. I went into the coal mines because, first of all, there were basically no other jobs. I wanted to learn a lot about electricity and the mines were better than college, which I could not afford. I spent eighteen years in the coal industry and then the major coal firm shut down all operations. I discussed with my wife the options and decided, since I loved to design things, that I needed an education in Drafting. I contacted a local collage and found I had to enroll in a full semester and the classes included English. I survived the first part of English and the grammar, the second half of the semester was writing short stories. The professor would give us a title and we would write a short story. She loved the first one I wrote. She read it to the class and they seemed to like it. After about fifteen different stories, my grade point average came up because I received an A+ on all of my stories. The professor told me that I should think seriously about writing books, that I had the talent for it. After a few years doing nothing about writing, my wife became very ill. I was in the house most of the time taking care of her. I finally sat down at the computer with an idea. I found that it was really fun. I love to watch a story emerge that anyone could read and hopefully enjoy. I want some literature that my thirteen-year-old granddaughter could read and feel good about.